Praise for Jackie Ashenden's
Having Her

"Let me repeat that author Jackie Ashenden is a superb writer; her stories are emotionally gripping, they make you think and feel, and they are not pretty. [...] These books aren't for people who want the fairy tale; these books are for people who know sometimes you've got to crawl through the trenches to come out on the other side alive, whole, and happy."

~ *Guilty Pleasures Book Reviews*

"I find books with a dom that is commanding without resorting to punishment to be incredibly enthralling. Vin fits into the role perfectly. Ms. Ashenden's storytelling talents continue to keep me on the edge of my seat, only wanting more when the book ends. If you are in the mood for a well-written erotic romance, read this book."

~ *Harlequin Junkie*

"When I say this *Having Her* was an emotional read for me, I mean it was all cheering, laughing, yelling, swooning, and crying in large amounts. Jackie Ashenden knows how to make you feel for her characters in a way that pulls at your heart without piling on the drama in outrageous ways or unbelievable amounts."

~ *The Romance Evangelist*

Look for these titles by
Jackie Ashenden

Now Available:

Falling for Finn
Black Knight, White Queen
Living in Shadow
Living in Sin
Living in Secret

Lies We Tell
Taking Him
Having Her

Having Her

Jackie Ashenden

SAMHAIN
PUBLISHING

Samhain Publishing, Ltd.
11821 Mason Montgomery Road, 4B
Cincinnati, OH 45249
www.samhainpublishing.com

Editing by Christa Soule
Cover by Lyn Taylor

First Samhain Publishing, Ltd. electronic publication: February 2014
First Samhain Publishing, Ltd. print publication: February 2015

Dedication

To Christa, best editor ever. For encouraging me and pushing the writing even to the really difficult places. I've learned so much.

Chapter One

Kara strode out of the run-down apartment block, heavy biker boots resounding on the cracked lino floor then scraping harsh concrete as she stepped out the front door.

Don't cry. Don't fucking cry.

She blinked furiously. No, she wouldn't. Third time in as many months she'd chickened out of a one-night stand, but she'd damn well never cried about it before. She never cried about anything. Despite the shitty things the guy had thrown at her as she'd escaped out of his apartment.

Tease. Slut. Bitch.

At least he hadn't called her a scared little virgin. She didn't mind being a tease or a bitch or a slut. But she couldn't handle being called a scared virgin.

Mainly because that's exactly what she was.

She came to a stop on the footpath outside the building and took a couple of deep breaths. Closed her eyes and put a hand over them.

God, what was she doing? She'd picked up the guy— Wayne. And he'd been semi-okay. Looked normal at least, so that was a start. Could string words together and had no piercings that she could see. No tattoos. Standard white bread dude. Her polar opposite which made him perfect. And yet...

When the time had come to get her clothes off, she couldn't seem to go through with it. He'd sat on his couch, lasciviousness written all over his moderately handsome face. Waiting. And she knew he was waiting for her to do something and probably something naughty. Dirty. Except she couldn't. A thousand things had run through her head—she was a virgin but she wasn't ignorant—yet she really hadn't wanted to do any of them. Something about the guy's passivity had made her doubt herself.

Jesus, sex was way more difficult than she'd ever imagined it would be. She'd thought she'd be overcome with a wave of lust and getting down to business would be easy. But it hadn't been. She'd just stood there feeling cold and vulnerable and awkward. And definitely not sexy.

Kara's hand dropped. Would it be this way all the time? Shit, it was just bodies meeting, no big deal. So what was it about sex that made her want to run and hide?

Man, if she couldn't get over this she was going to remain a virgin her entire bloody life, and she was already a big enough freak without still being a virgin at twenty-five.

Sometimes she liked being a freak. And sometimes all she wanted was normal.

Digging around in the cavernous interior of her messenger bag, she brought out her phone. Checked the time. Eleven p.m. Not late enough for Ellie to be asleep, please God, and perhaps not late enough to beg a lift home. She couldn't face the bus and she didn't have the money for a cab.

Dialing, she waited for her best friend to answer.

"Kara?" The voice was not Ellie. The voice was deep, male, and with that familiar rough edge to it that always had the ability to make her shiver.

It was Ellie's brother. Vin.

Oh. Great. She'd never got on with him. The guy was a complete control-freak, arrogant, and the most patronizing bastard she'd ever had the misfortune to come across.

He was also possibly the most beautiful man she'd ever met. A fact that never ceased to annoy the shit out of her.

10

"Vincent," she said, using his full name to irritate him. "You're answering Ellie's phone now? Why not put her in a room, lock the door, throw away the key and be done with it?"

"If I could, I would, believe me."

Yeah, that she had no trouble believing. "You're a jerk, you know that?"

"Of course I know that."

Kara nudged a cigarette butt on the pavement with the toe of her boot. "So where's Ellie and why are you answering her phone?"

"At home presumably. She left her phone here in the office." Down the other end of the line a chair squeaked, the sound of him moving.

"You're still at work? At this time of night?"

"Someone has to be." The rough edge in his voice had deepened. He sounded tired.

"Oh...well..." She stopped, not really sure what else to say.

"Did you need something, Kara?"

"No. I just rang Ellie to see if she could give me a lift home but it's okay, I'll get a cab or something." Goddammit, it would have to be the bus.

"Why? Where are you?"

"In the city. Fort Street."

"Stay there. I'll come and get you."

Oh man. That was Vin. Always with the instructions. She was sure he must have been a dictator in another life. "Don't be stupid," she said, irritated. "I can find my own way home."

"If you could do that, then why were you phoning Ellie to come and get you?"

"Because I wanted a girly chat, okay?" She paused. "But y'know, if you wanted to put on a dress and—"

"Stop wasting time and tell me exactly where you are."

Kara rolled her eyes. "No way, dude. If you're going to be a grumpy bastard about it, I'll take the bloody bus."

At that point a car full of guys cruised down the road, the bass from the stereo thumping like the pulse of some giant beast. One of them spotted her on the sidewalk and leaned out the window. "Hey, how much?" he shouted, the rest of his mates laughing.

Kara pushed her glasses determinedly up her nose then gave him the finger. More laughter, the car moving on up ahead.

Then it stopped. Began to turn around again.

Shit. That was the last thing she needed. Being harassed by a group of dickheads.

"Kara?" The sharp sound of Vin's voice made her blink. "What's happening?"

The car was definitely turning, coming back down her way. A chill slowly settled in the pit of her stomach. It was late, dark, and there was no one else around. Just a car full of drunken louts.

She should have thought this through instead of running blindly from the apartment. She should have had some back-up plan. God, what an idiot.

"Nothing," she snapped, looking back over her shoulder to the apartment building. Perhaps she could wait in there until they'd gone? "Just some guys being pricks."

"Where are you?" There was no tiredness now in his tone, just his usual note of command, the one that always had her grinding her teeth with irritation.

But for once she didn't argue. Having to suffer Vin picking her up and no doubt his normal third degree about what she was doing out here so late by herself, was way better than risking possible sexual assault.

"You know the tacky red apartment building where all the Uni students hang out? I'm there."

"Yeah, I know it. Go wait inside the foyer. I'll be five minutes."

She was already inside by the time he hung up. As much as she hated doing anything Vincent Fox told her to do, it was common sense. Especially with that car full of idiots still cruising up and down the street outside.

Kara glared at them through the windows of the foyer. Really, this was the perfect ending to an extremely shitty evening. All she needed now was Wayne from upstairs to come down and find her still lurking around.

Outside, the car full of drunks had pulled up to the curb. Fear twisted low down inside her as a couple of them got out. Clearly they'd seen her go into the building and were now in the process of coming to find her.

Kara's jaw set. She had no self-defense skills whatsoever, but she could be pretty mean and sarcastic when she wanted to be. Perhaps that would work?

As the guys approached the building, laughing and catcalling, another car pulled up. A cherry red vintage Corvette Stingray.

The twist of fear became relief. Jesus, she'd never been so glad to see Vin's pretentious car in all her life.

The Corvette's door opened and Vin got out, striding toward the building. The men in the other car made some sort of comment, but Vin ignored them as if they didn't exist.

Bloody hell, some days the confidence of the guy made even God look like he had self-esteem issues.

Kara let out a breath, put back her shoulders and went out of the apartment building for the second time that evening.

Vin stopped as she approached, dark winged brows pulled down, and her heart sped up like it always did whenever he was around. Man, she hated how hot he was and how she responded to it like every other chick.

He had the most perfect bone-structure of anyone she knew, his looks saved from prettiness by the hard, uncompromising cast of his jaw and a pair of dark blue-gray eyes that somehow reminded her of the color of the clouds before a particularly vicious thunderstorm.

Whenever she saw him she wanted to reach for her pencil, aching to draw another panel of the superhero comic she'd been drawing since forever. Make him the villain.

The sexy, hot, fascinating villain.

"Jesus, Kara, are you seriously looking for trouble?" he demanded before she'd even had a chance to speak. "Because you're going to find it wearing that."

She glanced down at the skin-tight black dress she wore. "What's wrong with it?" It had been perfect for her purposes. It had got the guy and nearly got her laid.

Vin opened his mouth to respond only to be interrupted by the drunk guys who'd been looking for her.

"Yo dude. We were here first!" one of them said in a stupid attempt to sound tough and gangster.

Vin turned his head and stared the guy down. "Fuck off," he said in a low, cold voice.

The other man took a couple of aggressive steps toward him only to be grabbed by his friend who murmured something in his ear. Both men, obviously seeing something mean in Vin's gaze, shrugged and moved off, hurling abuse as they did so.

Vin didn't bother looking at them as they got into their car and drove away; his dark, stormy blue eyes were firmly focused on her.

"What the hell were you thinking being out here by yourself at this time of night?"

"Chill with the judgmental attitude." She pushed her glasses back up her nose, scowling at him. "You really don't want to know what I was thinking."

"Try me."

"Look, Vincent, I'm not Ellie. I don't have to explain myself to you. So you can take your testosterone elsewhere, okay?"

Blue eyes gave her a cold sweep up and down. "You didn't seem to mind it just now."

"Well, duh, obviously not. I'm not stupid."

"Your dress would beg to differ."

Kara shut her mouth before something really dumb came out of it. If there was one thing she hated it was male judgment about her clothing choices and Vin was nothing if not judgmental. It was all part of his "protective", AKA oppressive, shtick.

"Are you going to give me a lift home or are you going to stand around making stupid comments about my dress? Because if it's the second option, I think I'll take the bus."

Vin didn't reply. Just stared at her. She stared back, feeling a little like a rebellious teenager being told off by her father.

Was this what Ellie had to deal with every day? No wonder the poor girl was desperate to take up the new job she'd just scored with a fantastic computer game design studio in Tokyo. So would Kara if she had to deal with Vin on a daily basis.

After a moment, the line of Vin's impressive jaw hardened. "Don't play games with me tonight, Kara. I'm not in the mood."

Yeah, she had to say, he didn't look in the mood. Then again, when was he ever in the mood? Back when she and Ellie had first met, in their first year of high school, Vin had been a remote, stern figure, seeming far older than his twenty years.

15

She'd supposed he'd had to be, what with having to look after a much younger sister and a seriously mentally ill mother. Not much to smile about there.

Still. Would it kill him to be pleasant for a change?

She wanted to tell him where to stick his stupid lift but given that the chance of drunken lunatics appearing again was fairly high, she wasn't *that* much of an idiot.

Kara gave him what she hoped was a sarcastic smile. "Play games? With you, Vincent? Wouldn't dream of it."

She walked past him to where the Corvette was parked, pulling open the door and getting in.

Yeah, pretentious as hell this car, but actually she liked it. Liked the curvy shape, the smell of the leather seats Vin must have spent serious cash in restoring, the mirror-like red paintwork.

Not that she'd ever let him know that.

Inside, Kara debated putting her feet on the dash then decided against it. With Vin in this mood, there was no telling what he'd do. She settled for the vocal equivalent instead. "So," she said as he got in and pulled on his seatbelt, "you really want to know what I was thinking tonight? I was thinking I wanted to get laid."

"How? By standing on the side of the road like a hooker?" Vin pulled the car into the traffic. "I wouldn't have thought you'd be that stupid."

A small kernel of anger hardened inside her. "Well *obviously* not," she replied, not holding back on the sarcasm. "I picked up a guy in a bar."

"How is that any more intelligent?"

"And I suppose you've never picked up a woman in a bar?"

"No." He said the word so flatly she had no doubt it was the truth.

"Oh. Uh. So *you'd* stand on the side of the road then?"

He gave her a cold, sweeping glance, once again making her feel two inches tall. "What are you doing picking up men in bars, Kara?"

She leaned back in her seat, folding her arms. "I thought I was clear as to why. Perhaps I should spell it out?"

He did not, unfortunately, rise to the bait. "And you're doing this by yourself?"

Kara bit her lip, glancing out the window. "I wasn't by myself." At least not after Wayne had showed up.

"So that would be a yes then?"

Abruptly tired of his questions and sick of his attitude, Kara snapped, "Okay, fine. Yeah, I was by myself. And no, I know it's not the most intelligent thing I've ever done but hey, what would you do if you were twenty-five and a virgin?"

She had to be joking. Though sometimes with Kara it was difficult to tell.

Vin glanced at her and met her gaze staring back belligerently at him. Purple eyes, long blue hair, square, black-framed glasses, a skin-tight short black dress and biker boots. A ring through one eyebrow and a blue stud in her nose. By rights she should be scaring people away looking like that— perhaps she even meant to. But of course nothing about her weird appearance masked the fact that Kara Sinclair was beautiful.

Twenty-five and virgin? Yeah, she had to be joking.

"Didn't I tell you I wasn't in the mood to play games?" he said, not bothering to hide his irritation.

"I'm not playing games."

"You can't seriously be telling me you're a virgin?"

Kara's pale eyebrows, the only sign of her true hair color,

pulled down. "You think I'd say something like that as a joke?"

"I have no idea. It's sometimes difficult to tell with you whether it's the truth or just another sarcastic remark."

Her thickly mascaraed eyelashes—blue mascara, of course—veiled her gaze. "Jesus. Forget I said anything, okay?" she muttered, turning her head to look out the window.

Vin frowned. She really could be the most irritating woman on the planet when she put her mind to it. Always ready with a quick comeback or a snarky statement. And she'd always made it very obvious she didn't much like him. Not that he cared what she thought of him, he had far too much on his plate already to deal with his little sister's annoying best friend.

Yet the innate protectiveness that was part and parcel of his makeup, that had forced him into the car to come and get her tonight, couldn't help noting that there was something a little off about her. A little bit quiet. Normally she wouldn't have been able to shut up, but now she'd gone silent, her shoulders hunched. With her long blue hair over one shoulder, the pale, vulnerable skin of her neck was revealed and just beneath her ear, he saw a bruise.

A love bite.

Shit. What had happened to her tonight?

Long years of being the one who had to make all the decisions, the one in control, made him want to demand an explanation. Because although he may not like her much, she was still vulnerable. And since she was Ellie's best friend, she automatically came under his protection whether she wanted to be or not, though mostly it was not.

But demands didn't work with Kara. His best friend Hunter was better at doing the good cop stuff, while he was always the bad cop.

"What happened tonight?" he asked, trying to find some of Hunter's good cop tone.

Kara didn't look at him. "It's a little late for Mr. Nice Guy, isn't it?"

"You've got a bruise on your neck."

Her shoulders tensed and she raised a hand, touching her skin lightly. "Oh," she mumbled. "Bugger."

Christ. His hands clenched on the wheel. She wasn't his sister but still, he'd known her for over ten years, ever since she'd befriended Ellie at high school, and by default she'd become part of the family he had to look out for. Especially once he'd found out that the reason she came round to visit so often wasn't just because she was friends with Ellie. Her foster family clearly had a policy of benign neglect.

"Tell me what happened, Kara," he said curtly, ditching all attempts at moderating himself. If something had happened to her he needed to know and he needed to know now.

"Nothing." She shrugged. "Wayne got a little over eager, that's all."

"Wayne?"

"The guy I picked up." She gave him an annoyed look. "And before you start getting all Neanderthal, it was nothing like that."

"Nothing like what?"

"I bit him first."

"Jesus, Kara."

"What? Look, I was telling you the truth, okay? I'm a twenty-five-year-old virgin and I'm fucking sick of it." She crossed one booted foot over her knee. "Man, I never thought it would be so difficult to get laid in this stupid town."

Vin found himself staring at the way her black dress had ridden up her legs, revealing what looked like the top of a stocking. Shit. Was that lace? And suspenders? On Kara?

He jerked his gaze back to the road as a feeling

uncomfortably similar to lust shot straight to his groin.

For fuck's sake that was all he needed. Kara had always been in the realm of the untouchable, too many associations with his sister for anything like attraction. So why he should be getting a hard-on for her now was anyone's guess. Maybe he was just tired. He'd been working like a dog for the past week, and God knew it had been months since he'd taken any time for himself, too consumed by the needs of his business in a difficult economic climate. Not to mention making sure his mother was secure in hospital.

Clearly he needed to go let off some steam somewhere.

"So that's what you're doing?" he asked. "Going around picking up men just to get rid of your virginity? I take it back, clearly you *are* that stupid." He'd never been one to sugarcoat the truth. He didn't have time for that shit. Except for the kind of truth that affected his sister. And that he'd do anything to keep from her.

"You prick. Thanks so much, Mr. Sensitive."

"Well what do you expect me to say? You've got a bruise on your neck and you're standing out on the road at eleven p.m. at night. I did think you had some sense."

Her head was turned resolutely toward the window, her shoulders stiff with tension. "It's not like I planned for the evening to end this way."

"Then how did you plan it?"

She had her arms crossed over her breasts, her fingers white where they lay against her upper arms. "I thought I'd stay over at Wayne's place."

"You thought you'd stay overnight at your hook-up's place? Are you really that naïve?"

"Hello? Virgin here."

She still had her head turned away but he heard something

in her voice. A small tremor.

"Fuck, did he hurt you?" Vin demanded, a sudden ice-cold anger going through him. "Because if he did—"

"No, he didn't," Kara said flatly. "I left."

For some reason that didn't make him feel any better. "Why? What did he do?"

"Nothing. He didn't do anything." She fell silent for a long moment. "And that was kind of the problem. I think he was expecting me to do something."

"What?"

"I don't think I want to be discussing this with you right now."

He didn't really want to be discussing it either if he was honest. But he didn't like the idea of Kara picking up strange men in bars just because she wanted to lose her virginity.

"Jesus, Kara. What's the rush?" he asked, when she didn't break the silence. "Surely you don't have to resort to bar hook-ups?"

She let out a short breath. "The rush? I'm twenty-five for God's sake. Hardly normal, is it?"

He didn't want to point out the obvious but someone had to. "Normal? You?"

"Yeah, yeah, hysterical, I know. So shoot me if I want a little bit of normality in my life."

"If you want normality in your life, then dressing like that isn't the way to go about getting it."

Kara turned her head, giving him a hard stare. Then, pointedly, she pushed her black-framed glasses up her nose with her middle finger. "I'll dress any way I damn well please, thank you very much."

Christ almighty, the woman was asking for trouble with that kind of attitude. "I hate to be the one to point this out to you, Kara, but if that's the way you treat all your hook-ups, no wonder you're a virgin."

"You're an asshole, you know that?"

Yeah, he kind of did. But shit, he wasn't going to apologize for pointing out the truth. "All I'm saying is—"

"All you're saying is that I can't get laid because I'm an evil bitch," she interrupted, shifting her leg which only pulled up her dress more. "Well, maybe you're right. But I'm not looking for a relationship or someone special. I just want to get this stupid virginity thing out of the way before I get a complex about it."

Vin dragged his gaze away from the tantalizing glimpse of black lace and suspenders showing beneath the hem of her dress. He couldn't think why he wanted to look. He was driving for fuck's sake. And this was Kara.

"Sounds to me as if you already have a complex about it," he said, staring out into the darkness beyond the front window. They weren't far from Kara's apartment now. Thank Christ.

Kara waved a hand. "Hence the bar hook-ups."

"Why?"

"Well, bars are full of guys looking for sex. I thought it would be easy to find someone who wasn't too hideous and who wanted a bit of fun."

Vin couldn't help flashing her a glance. "Someone who wasn't too hideous? You're really selling yourself very high there."

A stain of color crept over her cheeks. She looked out of the window again. "As you say, I dress weird. I have an attitude problem. Beggars can't be choosers, can they?"

He didn't know what to say to that. Didn't she know she was gorgeous? That she could have any guy she pleased? Or at least she could if she didn't dye her hair stupid colors or wear contacts that made her look like an alien.

"That's what you want?" he said. "To lose your virginity to some random stranger who isn't too hideous?"

"Yeah, so?"

"You can do better than that, Kara. Shit, you *should* do better than that."

"What do you care?"

Kara's apartment building loomed out of the darkness and he pulled the car over outside it.

"Because you're Ellie's friend. You're like my own goddamned sister. And I don't like the idea of you trolling bars for sex just to lose your virginity. It's not only wrong, it's dangerous."

An odd expression crossed her face, one he couldn't interpret. Then it was gone, her usual sarcastic exterior firmly in place. "I don't give a shit what you think. You're not my brother or my father and even if I had either of those, I wouldn't let them dictate to me what I did with my time or my body."

He ignored that. "But surely you can see what a stupid idea it is, right?"

She put her hand on the door handle, preparing to get out. Her eyes were the deep purple of violets, an unnatural color. "How else am I supposed to do it? Sell my virginity on eBay?"

"Find a guy you like. Tell me about him. I'll investigate—"

"Oh my God, you've got to be kidding." Her gaze went wide. "You'll vet my potential sex partners? Do you have any idea how ridiculous that sounds?"

Vin tightened his grip on the steering wheel. Yeah, okay, he was kind of over the top with stuff like that. But someone had to look out for those who didn't have anyone else to look out for them. He didn't know much about Kara's birth family—she was notoriously private about them and not even Ellie knew much—

but he did know that her mother lived down south and her father wasn't in the picture. That her foster family was long gone and she had no one here in Auckland. Which for Vin automatically meant it was his job.

"I don't care how ridiculous that sounds. I don't want you ending up raped or murdered because you chose the wrong guy."

Kara rolled her eyes. "Jesus, Vincent. Give the bloody protective crap a rest, okay? I'm not your damn sister, I don't need it."

But Vin had never backed down over what he saw as his responsibilities and he wasn't going to start now. "What you need, Kara, is for someone to show you all about sex in a safe environment, not some fucking bar."

"A safe environment? My God, if you could only hear yourself. And I suppose next you're going to offer to find a nice man who'd do that for me?"

"I think that's the first sensible thing I've heard come out of your mouth all night."

Kara stared at him for a second, as if she couldn't believe what he said. Then she turned abruptly, pulling on the door handle and opening the car door. "As much as the offer of you choosing my sexual partners for me fills me with joy, I'm going to have to decline. Then perhaps I'll burn an effigy of you in the back garden." She slid out of the car, her dress sliding up over the tops of her stockings and shit, yes, they were actual stockings. With suspenders.

Vin tried not to look.

She turned, leaned in, one hand on the car door, clearly wanting to have the last word. "Unless you're offering yourself of course."

It took a moment for her words to make sense. And then when they did, the surge of lust that accompanied them took him by surprise. No. That was not happening. No fucking way.

"I'm not sleeping with you, Kara," he said curtly.

She lifted a shoulder. "Then keep your nose out of my sex life."

And she slammed the door in his face.

Chapter Two

"I got my costume!" Ellie leaned over the counter, gray eyes alight with excitement, as Kara put the finishing touches on the lattes she was making.

Kara pushed the coffees toward a couple of people waiting at the other end of the counter, then turned back to her best friend. "Oh crap, already?"

"Of course already. NZ Con's next week, Kar."

Yeah, so it was. She and Ellie had been waiting for it for months, the last big deal before Ellie left for Tokyo. A couple of days of hanging out with the gaming/manga crowd and, Kara was hoping, making a few more contacts in the comic industry. Always useful when you owned a business dealing in manga, gaming and the Internet.

Ellie, with typical Ellie enthusiasm, had been getting her costume custom-made. Unlike Kara, who hadn't been able to afford it. All her spare cash went back into Manga Café Extreme, the manga/Internet café she owned, and every cent had to since the rents in central Auckland were exorbitant.

"What about you?" Ellie asked as Kara started preparing Ellie's usual latte. "Have you got one yet?"

"Uh...no." She'd done a trawl through various costume shops and had come up with nothing. Or at least nothing she wanted to wear. There had been the slave costume, the one that Princes Leia had worn in *Return of the Jedi*, but every bloody Con she'd been to there'd been at least a half dozen slave Leias. It wasn't like the costume was original or anything.

And then there was the fact that the costume exposed a lot

of flesh. Kara wasn't skinny like Ellie. She had curves. Lots of them. Far too many for a metal bikini and bit of fabric to be the only thing between her and total humiliation.

"No?" Ellie frowned at her. "But you're looking, right?"

"Yeah, I'm looking."

Elle's frown deepened. "Hey, anything up?"

A small stab of guilt went through Kara. She'd totally meant to tell her friend all about her hideous evening with Wayne and yet every time she went to talk about it, all she could see was Vin's perfect face and the anger in it. And the hot, liquid rush of humiliation that had swept over her.

I'm not sleeping with you, Kara.

She couldn't think why she'd even suggested it in the first place, only that she'd been so pissed off with his arrogance. With his patronizing insistence on looking out for her. She'd been looking out for herself since she'd left her foster home at seventeen, and she didn't need him assuming he had some sort of responsibility because of her association with Ellie. She was twenty-five, for Christ's sake.

So yeah, she'd said it to get a reaction. But the look on his face had hurt some part of her she wasn't quite prepared to acknowledge yet.

As if she'd ever want to sleep with an arrogant son of a bitch like him anyway.

"No," Kara said, shoving the nozzle into the milk jug and pulling the switch to turn on the steam. The noise effectively cancelled out any further comments her friend wanted to make. At least for the meantime. But Kara could feel Ellie's puzzled gaze on her, probably wondering what the story was.

Your brother's being a prick. He won't sleep with me and I kind of want him to.

What? No, she did *not* want him to. Not in any way, shape

or form.

"Kara," Ellie said as the noise from the espresso machine died away. "Come on. What's got you so pissed off?"

"Go sit down and I'll bring you your coffee."

"Kara—"

"And then I'll tell you, okay?"

Perhaps it would be good to tell Ellie. Not the stuff about sleeping with her brother because that would be weird, but maybe about Wayne. And maybe she could ask her why Vin was always such a grumpy, mean bastard.

Not that she cared of course, but still...

The rest of the customers in the café were either all busy in the Internet part of it or sitting around various tables talking or reading, so Kara skirted around the counter with Ellie's coffee, coming over to their usual table which consisted of a couple of ragged sofas that gave off a student-flat kind of vibe.

Ellie folded her arms as Kara approached, platform boots on the low table in front of her, a stern look on her face. The resemblance between her and her brother was slight and yet sometimes Kara caught echoes of Vin in her friend's delicate features. Especially when Ellie was giving her a *tell me everything you know* look.

Kara put the latte on the table beside Ellie's feet then sat on the couch. "Yeah, okay," she said. "Something's up."

"Huh. No kidding." Ellie reached for the coffee. "So? Spill."

"A couple of nights ago, I picked up this guy in a bar."

Ellie's eyebrows lifted. "A one-night stand, Kar?"

"That was the idea. Except..." She stopped, that strange sense of vulnerability and humiliation washing over her again.

"Kar?" her friend murmured. "What happened?"

"Nothing bad." She met Ellie's worried look. "I couldn't go through with it. I just got... I dunno. We went back to his place

28

and he just sat there, looking at me, waiting for me to do something and I couldn't think of what to do and..." She hesitated. "I felt like an idiot. So I left."

Ellie leaned forward, put her coffee down, then put an awkward hand over Kara's where they were clasped in her lap. "Aw, Kar."

The sympathetic expression in her friend's eyes and the comforting hand over her own made Kara uneasy. She could give out plenty of sympathy and comfort herself, but she didn't like being on the receiving end.

Gently she eased her hands away from Ellie's. "It's okay. I was fine. I tried to ring you but you'd left your phone at Vin's office."

"Oh, yeah, I did. Sorry. He gave it back to me yesterday."

"Actually, he ended up picking me up from the guy's place and taking me home."

"Of course he did. I hope he wasn't a prick about it."

"He kind of was."

Ellie rolled her eyes. "I'd apologize for his prickishness, except you know what he's like."

Kara sighed. "I do. He was meaner about it than normal though." Way meaner. If she'd been a weaker kind of woman, the comments about her appearance and attitude would have hurt.

Luckily she wasn't that kind of woman.

Yeah? Then why did you get so angry with him?

Well, she'd tried not to. Had done her best to let it go. Because what did she care what he thought of her? She didn't, that's what.

"Don't tell me," Ellie said. "He complained about your clothes."

"Yeah."

"God, did he give you the third degree about what you were doing out at night by yourself?"

"That too."

"Oh, Kar—"

"It's fine. I told him he was an asshole."

Ellie let out a sigh. "Look, I know he's difficult sometimes, but he means well."

"Yeah but he doesn't need to do that by being all judgmental and crap." Kara smoothed down the stretchy blue miniskirt she wore. "Or telling me that my attitude is the reason why I'm still a virgin."

Her friend's red brows rose into her hairline. "Oh my God, you told him about that?"

"I did." And she'd been rather pleased with the look of surprise that had crossed his handsome face. Pleasure that had swiftly turned into regret when he'd gone into *must protect the virgin* mode. Not a huge shock knowing Vincent Fox as she did.

Ellie sat back on the sofa. "Why?"

"He was pissing me off with his attitude. And I guess I wanted to shock him."

"I can imagine how that went down."

Kara fiddled with the hem of her miniskirt again. "Yeah, not good. He seems to think I can't look after myself."

"Welcome to my world," Ellie said dryly. Then she sighed again. "Look, if it helps, he's kind of been looking out for me my whole life, and I think that just naturally extends to anyone associated with me. It's just the way he is."

"It's annoying." She wouldn't mention Vin's offer of vetting her potential sexual partners. Man, maybe Ellie had gone through the same thing. Maybe Vin had even vetted Cam, Ellie's ex. God, if he had, Kara didn't want to know.

"Tell me about it." Ellie picked up her coffee again and took another sip. "He's just trying to make sure everyone's safe, I guess."

Safe. Yeah, well, she couldn't deny that she did feel safe with Vin. Especially when he'd turned up that night and those guys had gone running. But for another part of her, safe was the last thing she'd felt. Such as when those storm-blue eyes of his had glanced down at her legs in the car as she'd crossed them. Where the hem of her dress had ridden up. His gaze had lingered and she'd felt a shiver go through her. A delicious shiver.

"Kar?"

Crap. Please don't say she was mooning around about Vin. He was hot, oh God was he hot. But it's not as if she wanted to lose her virginity with him. Because in addition to being hot, he was also the most take-charge son of a bitch she'd ever met.

Y'know, in certain situations, that could be quite good. Especially in situations where you don't know what you're doing...

Kara's mouth went dry and she was conscious of a sudden, deep ache between her thighs. Vin, telling her what to do. Exactly what to do. And when. And where...

"Kara?"

Kara blinked. "Yeah, what?" Her voice had gone a little husky.

Ellie frowned at her. "Are you okay? You're blushing."

Holy shit, she probably was. "I'm fine." Kara pushed herself off the couch and turned toward the counter. There were no customers but surely something needed cleaning. Anything so she didn't have to confess that she was having illicit thoughts about her best friend's older brother.

"Hey, where are you going?" Ellie said. "I wanted to talk about your costume."

Kara stopped. "I'll probably go with slave Leia." Really, why the hell not? And hey, if she was lucky, she might pick up someone from the Con. He probably wouldn't be quite the kind of normal she wanted, but who knew?

Ellie gave her a skeptical look. "Really?"

"Yes, really. Nothing says I want to get laid like a metal bikini." Thing was, for some reason she couldn't stop thinking of Vin seeing her in it. Man, if he'd thought her black dress was way too much, the slave Leia costume would give him a heart attack.

"You're smiling," Ellie observed. "You have a plan?"

Kara grinned. "Maybe."

One was certainly coming to her. A way to goad the hell out of Vincent Fox. Pay him back for all the crap he'd said to her in the car. All the humiliation.

Oh yeah. He wasn't going to know what hit him.

Vin narrowed his gaze at the two apprentices playing silly buggers with one of the nail guns not far from where he and Hunter were putting in some roof beams.

"Hey," he said. "What the fuck are you two doing?" He didn't raise his voice—he never had to. The apprentices soon got the message that he didn't stand for any idiocy on his building sites. Not ever.

The two guys shot him guilty looks and instantly stopped waving the nail gun around, getting back to work.

"Got a problem?" Hunter asked, standing away from the ladder as Vin came down it.

The midday sun was hot, shining through the ribs of the roof beams, scattering barred light over the dusty floor of the half-built house. Once on the ground, Vin dragged off his T-shirt, wiping away the sweat on his forehead with the warm cotton.

"No. No problem," he muttered. A complete lie of course. He'd been a foul mood for the past couple of days and couldn't seem to work out why.

Of course you know why.

Yeah, dammit, he did. Kara Sinclair.

He hadn't been able to get the bloody woman out of his head. That tantalizing glimpse of her stocking as she'd gotten out of the car, black lace against skin the color of pale honey.

"Unless you're offering yourself of course..."

Vin cursed, passing the T-shirt over his forehead again before throwing it over one shoulder.

He didn't want to be thinking of her like that.

She thought she projected this tough image, but he knew she wasn't as tough as she seemed. He'd sensed the vulnerability beneath. He didn't know what she was protecting herself from, but he knew it was there nonetheless. A warning enough for him to keep away from her because smart aleck, snarky, vulnerable women weren't anyone he'd touch with a barge-pole. Oh no. He liked his women strong and able to take care of themselves. Mainly so he didn't have to.

"Yeah there is." Hunter folded his arms. "You've been in a shitty mood for the past couple of days. What's up? Don't like Ellie going?"

Well, no, of course he didn't like Ellie going. His sister would be leaving for Tokyo to take up a new job in a month and while a part of him didn't like she was going away, another felt relieved. For the first time in years she'd actually be where Lillian couldn't reach her.

"I can handle Ellie going."

"So what is it?" Hunter frowned. Then, as if he'd read Vin's mind, "Lillian?"

Vin was tempted to say yes, it was Lillian. Because most of the time that's what it was. The whole of his early life had been formed around his mother's schizophrenia and the departure of the prick who'd called himself his father. And whenever there was a problem, it was usually due to Lillian having another episode. And Vin having to take care of it.

But today Lillian was having another stint in hospital and Vin was relatively free from the constant worry that always dogged him when his mother was living in the community again.

"No, not Lillian." Vin had never thought of his mother as Mum. Or even Mother. Because she'd never been a mother to him. She'd only ever and always been Lillian. "It's nothing. Work." He didn't want to get into a discussion with Hunter about Kara, not when he was having difficulty with it himself.

But his friend's dark eyes missed nothing. "A woman?"

Vin gave him a narrow stare. "Don't you have something better to do? I'm still chasing a couple of council consents, for example."

"So yeah, it's a woman."

"Oh for Christ's sake." Vin turned and went over to where a water bottle had been balanced on a sawhorse. He picked it up, suddenly desperately thirsty, taking a long drink.

"Hey, I don't give a shit what your problem is," Hunter said levelly. "But sort it out, okay? The attitude isn't helping maintain a good on-site atmosphere."

"Since when have you been interested in a good on-site atmosphere?"

Hunter let out a breath. "Since you did that site management course last year and wouldn't shut up about it."

Shit. He had no comeback to that since his friend was

right. On both counts. Yeah, he was being a prick and yeah, it didn't make for a good working environment. He liked to feel he was in control and on the ball most of the time and hated when he wasn't.

Maybe that was the source of his foul mood. The fact that Kara Sinclair had made him feel a little less in control than he normally was.

At that moment a silence fell on the site. An unnatural one.

Vin knew what it meant. Wolf-whistling wasn't done these days, but when a hot woman walked by, all the guys fell silent watching her.

He turned and sure enough, a woman was making her way down the front path toward the building site.

Jesus Christ. It was Kara.

Today she wore what looked like a skirt from a school uniform, black plaid that came barely to mid-thigh, along with a tight black button down shirt. Her blue hair was in a high ponytail, a neat plain black Alice band holding it back from her face. Making the ring in her eyebrow and her silver nose-stud more noticeable. But what really made him stare was the fact that she was wearing suspenders and stockings again. Blue suspenders and black fishnets, and lots of golden skin.

He couldn't seem to stop looking. She looked bloody weird. And also hot. Too fucking hot. The way his body responded to her made his foul mood even fouler.

Striding toward the front of the house and through the gap that was the front doorway, Vin planted himself on the front step, stopping her before she could enter the site proper. "Where the hell do you think you're going?" he growled. "This is a hard-hat area."

Kara rocked back on the heels of her lace up platform boots and folded her arms. Today her eyes were bright blue to match her hair. "Well hello, Vincent." She gave him a smile. "Nice to see you too."

Her mouth was wide, generous, glossy with some kind of candy pink lipstick that reminded him of sugar. He shouldn't be looking at it but somehow he couldn't help himself. "What do you want?" he demanded, unaccountably annoyed.

Kara lifted her chin. "I was after you actually. Your receptionist told me where to find you. But since you seem to be in as shitty a mood as you were a couple of nights ago, I think I've changed my mind."

"Hey, Kara," Hunter said from behind him. "What's up?"

"Hi, Hunt. And nothing in particular. I've just got to go get a costume for NZ Con and need a guy opinion."

"A guy opinion?" Vin didn't really want to know. He didn't. And yet something made him ask all the same.

"Yeah." Kara's smile widened. "I want to get something hot."

"Something hot?" Again the question came out more as a demand.

Her gaze met his. "What are you? A parrot? Okay, so you know that little mission I'm on? The one we talked about when you picked me up a couple of nights ago? Well, I'm still on it."

Oh Christ. So she hadn't listened to a word he'd said, had she?

"What mission?" Hunter asked.

"I'll handle this, Hunt," Vin said tightly before Kara could respond.

Behind him, he could almost feel his friend's surprise. But Vin didn't turn. Kept his gaze firmly on Kara's. She was still smiling, looking exceptionally pleased with herself for some reason.

"Be my guest." Hunter's voice was mild. "Say hi to Ellie for me, Kar."

"Will do." She cocked her head to one side as Hunter's

footstep faded and the sound of a circular saw started up. "You look annoyed, Vincent. Was it something I said?"

His irritation kicked up a notch but he didn't let it show. He'd be damned if he let her get to him any more than she was already. Leaning one shoulder casually against the doorframe, he folded his arms. "So you're still looking for a quick fuck, Kara?"

A stain of red tinged her cheekbones but she didn't look away from him. "Must you be so crude? I prefer the term shag."

"Fuck. Shag. Same thing, isn't it?"

"True. So will you come with me then?"

"Why?"

"Like I said, I want a guy opinion. And since you've made it clear you'd like to vet my sexual partners, I thought you might want a say in the kind of costume I'm wearing in order to attract said sexual partners. I wouldn't want to wear anything you might not approve of."

She was playing with him, no doubt about that. And he didn't appreciate it. Not one bit. "I don't give a shit what kind of costume you're wearing."

"Really? You don't? Oh, well then. There's this one I'm thinking of getting. It's nothing but a metal bikini. It's going to be great. I'm sure I can—"

"Metal bikini?" He didn't like the sound of that. At all.

Kara's mouth curved in a smile that made something clench tight inside him. "Well, you know, if I want my mission to be successful, I have to look the part."

"Like a hooker, you mean?"

"Sex worker, please, Vincent."

"Kara."

She blinked at him. "What?"

"You think I told you all that stuff for fun?"

"The stuff about pre-approving my one-night stands? Oh no, I think you told me all that because you're a controlling a-hole."

Vin pushed himself away from doorframe, the lid he normally kept on his anger starting to slip. "I don't give a shit what you think. I'm just trying to keep you safe. I've already got enough to worry about with Ellie, let alone you as well."

"I didn't ask for you to worry about me."

"Too late for that, baby."

Kara's mouth went flat with annoyance. "Don't call me baby, asshole."

Oh, so finally something had gotten to her. He stared at her. "I'll call you whatever the hell I please."

For a second neither of them moved, and he knew the tension between them shouldn't be there. And that all he had to do was turn away and it would vanish.

But he couldn't seem to bring himself to do so.

It had been a long time since a woman had got under his skin like Kara bloody Sinclair had, and no matter how many times he told himself it was wrong, he couldn't deny that he liked it.

Kara felt hot. Extremely hot. And it didn't have anything whatsoever to do with the sun.

Vin stood on the top step of the of the half-built house and she couldn't drag her gaze away from him. He wore a pair of denim cut-offs, a tool-belt slung around his lean hips, a hardhat and nothing else. And, God, he was beautiful. His torso was all sharply defined pectorals and abs, tanned and sheened with sweat. Over one brown shoulder was what looked like a T-shirt, and she badly wanted him to put it on because him half-naked was making it difficult to remember just what she was here to do.

You're wanting to annoy him, remember?

Oh yeah, that was right. And from the expression on his face and the flame that burned in his eyes, it looked like she'd managed to do that, at least a little. Which would have satisfied her if she hadn't then gone and lost ground by betraying her own annoyance over the baby thing, if she didn't feel like she was burning up and couldn't think of a single thing to say.

The costume, idiot.

"Fine," she finally said in what she hoped was a level voice. "You call me baby, I'll call you asshole and we'll be even." She gripped the strap of her bag. "So are you going to come and approve my metal bikini or not?"

Vin's gaze didn't waver. "You don't want my approval, Kara. You just want to play games with me. And like I told you the other night, I don't play games."

Dammit. She didn't want to lose this one, not after she'd spent all morning tracking him down and planning all the ridiculously porny outfits she was going to try on to really irritate the crap out of him. "You saw *Return of the Jedi*, right?" she said. "You remember Princess Leia at Jabba the Hutt's castle? Wearing that tiny metal bikini?"

Vin shifted on his feet. "Yeah."

"That's what I'll be wearing." She put one foot on the front step and looked up at him. "That's *all* I'll be wearing."

He glanced down and she saw him take in the hem-line of her little plaid skirt and how her stance had made it slide back, revealing more of her thigh. His gaze lingered there and she was conscious of a little burst of satisfaction. And excitement.

You like him looking at you.

Maybe she did. Maybe she liked it very much. And maybe she liked taunting him even better.

"So?" he said, the husky edge in his voice pronounced.

"Did I mention the slave collar I'll be wearing around my neck?" she went on, letting her own voice get a little lower. "With a chain?"

Vin's gaze flicked up to hers again and Kara felt her breath catch at the look in his eyes. "Do you have any idea what you're doing, baby girl?" he murmured. "Because I'm not sure that you do."

Baby girl. Patronizing bastard. And yet her mouth had gone dry, her heartbeat suddenly a hell of a lot faster than it had been before. "I'm not doing anything. I'm just telling you what kind of costume I'll be wearing." She licked her lips. Deliberately. Watched his gaze zero in on her mouth. "Or," she added, "with any luck, the costume I won't be wearing once I've found the lucky guy who can take it off me."

Vin had gone very still. And for one single moment, Kara felt sure he was going to come down the steps and...and she didn't know what really, but given the amount of adrenaline currently firing around her body, probably something pretty intense. And very exciting.

But when he moved it was only to pull his T-shirt around the back of his neck, gripping the ends of it in his fists. The hot look in his eyes had faded, the expression on his face becoming detached. Dismissive even.

"If you want me to keep my nose out of your sex life," he said in a flat tone, "you'd probably better stop giving me updates. Now is there anything else you want? I've got a roof to get on by the end of the day."

Kara had the sudden, strong urge to stick her tongue out at him. Or flip him the bird at the very least.

So much for her grand plan. If he wasn't going to play ball she could hardly make him. And what did she care anyway? It wasn't like she *really* wanted him to see her in that costume.

Especially when she didn't know if she was going to get the costume anyway.

Are you kidding? After that? Of course you're going to get the bloody costume.

Kara stared at him. At the cold look in his blue eyes. At the implacable set of his impressive jaw.

Yeah, she was going to get the stupid costume. And she'd send him photos of herself in it. She wasn't going to let him win this. No freaking way.

Kara lifted a shoulder. "Suit yourself," she said, as if she didn't give a damn.

Then she turned on her heel and went back up the path.

Chapter Three

Vin's phone vibrated silently in the pocket of his suit jacket. The meeting he was having with the bank was important—he was trying to negotiate some extra finances for the Fox Chase business expansion he had in mind—but he was also expecting a call from the hospital psychiatrist about Lillian. And that too was important. There had been talk of releasing her early and he wasn't happy about it.

Luckily the manger handling the Fox Chase account was female, which was very handy since most women could be charmed into granting him his way.

He gave her a smile. "Sorry, do you mind if I answer a call? It's important."

The woman, predictably enough, melted. "Certainly, Mr. Fox. I'll give you some privacy."

As soon as she'd left the meeting room, Vin stopped smiling and whipped out his phone.

It wasn't a call. It was yet another text from Kara, with yet another NZ-Con photo attached.

She'd been sending him photos all bloody day and no amount of ignoring them or curt responses telling her to cease and desist had gotten her to stop. Mostly they seemed to be of various different men, or her actually standing with various different men. Men in all sorts of different costumes, looking stupid or weird or sometimes just downright dangerous.

Seemed like all she'd done at the Con was take pictures of men and/or herself.

Vin leaned back in his chair, holding his phone. He wasn't going to look. No, he wasn't.

You are. You can't stop yourself.

And sure enough he found himself going through all the pictures to the one she'd sent him a couple of days ago. The one that had come after she'd flounced off his building site in a huff.

The one of her in a tiny metal bikini. With a slave collar and chain around her neck.

He'd always preferred tough women. Women with hard bodies and harder personalities. Who weren't vulnerable either physically or emotionally. Women who could take care of themselves.

So he had no idea why the sight of Kara in her slave costume should cause him to catch his breath. Make his cock hard. Because she wasn't tough in any way, shape or form.

She was soft. All over. Generous breasts barely contained by the metal cups of her bikini. Wide hips. Gently curved stomach. Rounded thighs. And all of it on show.

She'd had to have someone take the photograph because she stood far enough away from the camera to have gotten a really good shot of her whole body. In one hand she held the chain that attached to the collar, the other hand on one hip. The look on her face was a masterpiece of challenge and sexy submission all rolled into one, and even though the glasses she still wore should have blown the whole outfit, they didn't.

They made her look vulnerable and sweet, and yet strong at the same time.

Jesus, why could he *not* stop looking at that picture?

Irritated with himself, he swiped at the screen, scrolling back to the one she'd just sent him. Her on her knees, her arms wrapped around Darth Vader's legs while he held her chain. He didn't know much about the *Star Wars* canon but he did know that Darth Vader should not be looking at his daughter in that way. The whole image was disturbing on so many levels.

The text said, *What about him? He's an accountant called Darren. You approve?*

Shit no. He did not approve. But replying to the text would only enter into the game she was playing and he wasn't going to do that.

His phone vibrated again. Yet another text.

You don't like Darren? BTW, my virginal hymen is still intact. In case you were worried.

Vin cursed and put down the phone. He had better things to be doing than reading stupid texts from Kara. This meeting with the bank for one. Talking to the psychiatrist about his mother for another.

Since when have you done something for yourself?

The thought came out of nowhere, making him scowl. How was that in any way relevant? Doing this stuff for his business and making sure his mother was looked after *were* things he did for himself. His business, because this was what he'd been working toward for just about ever and making sure Lillian was okay, so he didn't have to worry about Ellie.

And anyway, what did Kara have to do with doing something for himself?

Vin turned off the screen without replying to Kara's text and put his phone back in his pocket.

He'd just ignore her. With any luck she'd give up and go away.

However, a few hours later, his meeting with the bank over and after yet more assurances from the hospital that they were going to keep Lillian in, he got another text from Kara.

Clearly giving up was not something the damn woman was capable of.

He didn't want to look and spent a good half hour

determined not to, busying himself with taking his temper out on some subcontractors who hadn't done their job properly. And yet as early evening began to set in, he couldn't help himself. Something just made him reach into the pocket of his trousers and grab the phone.

This time the photo was of her with a number of other Princess Leias, all in slave costumes. *Look*, the accompanying text read, *I'm not alone. We're all out to get laid.*

Kara was lying on the ground in front of a crowd of Leias, right in the center, her blue hair and glasses making her stand out from the rest of the women. That and her body. She wasn't lean or long like some of them, but there was something indescribably sensual about the way she lay there, head propped on one elbow, her soft breasts pressing against the cups of the bikini.

Oh she was beautiful. She really was.

"Hey, Vin?"

Vin turned the screen off and just about threw the thing on his desk. "What?"

Hunter was at his office door. "I'm taking a couple of the boys out for drinks. You want to come?"

"No." He leaned back in his chair, shoving one hand through his hair. Tried to ignore the tight feeling in his groin. "I'm not in the mood."

Hunter shrugged. "Okay. You heard from Ellie?"

Vin schooled his expression. "Yeah. She said she and Kara were going to have drinks at the convention center tonight."

A shadow crossed Hunter's face. "All right. Let me know if they need a lift home or anything."

"I'll give them a lift if they need it." He'd be in town anyway since he'd now started building his new house out at Piha, one of Auckland's surf beaches. To save money he'd decided to sleep at the office since it was far cheaper than renting anywhere.

Hunter paused, his hand on the door. "Yeah, well, let me know if you change your mind. I'll be in town till late."

As Vin nodded, his phone vibrated again. He cursed, reaching for it as Hunter left.

Bloody Kara again. This time she had a drink in one hand, her arm around the waist of some weirdo with odd hair and some seriously strange looking armor. *What about him?*

Jesus, she was pushing it. Seriously pushing it.

He tossed the phone back down on the desk and tried to busy himself with some more work. When that palled, he found himself pulling out the application forms for the architecture degree he'd spent the better part of fourteen years having to put off.

Yeah, that was something for himself too, wasn't it? Pursuing the dream he'd had ever since his father had told him to draw him a house when he was seven years old. A house their family could live in together.

Before the prick had decided having a mad woman for a wife was too hard. Before he'd fucked off leaving fifteen-year-old Vin in charge of an eight-year-old girl and a mother who thought her own daughter was the devil's child and had to die.

No one knew about Lillian's voices. The ones that told her Ellie had to be killed. Not Hunter. And most especially not Ellie herself. No one except Vin and her psychiatrist. No one else needed to know.

Vin stared at the forms. Yeah, he'd been putting it off because he simply didn't have the time or the mental energy to be able to focus on study. But once Ellie had left the country, was safely in Tokyo and out of the way of their mother's madness, then perhaps he could manage.

His phone buzzed yet again and he wanted to throw it at the wall but he didn't, picking it up instead and checking the screen.

A picture of some guy dressed up like Spock from *Star Trek*, complete with rubber-looking ears. The man was tall and grinning down at the camera. Or no, not the camera. His gaze went below the camera, to about where Kara's breasts would be.

What about Spock? I'm definitely thinking Spock.

Vin bit off a curse. He was sick and tired of this game. Obviously she wasn't going to give up and if he left off replying to her maybe she'd even start sending him pictures of her and her suitor in compromising positions.

That thought made him angry. Very bloody angry.

The woman was insane. And irritating. And had no sense at all.

And the hard-on in his trousers whenever he thought of her in that wretched costume wasn't going to go away any time soon either.

Vin cursed again and typed out a short and sweet text.

Stop it.

She replied almost instantly. *You don't approve?*

No. I don't.

Why? Got someone else in mind?

He bared his teeth at the screen. *Yeah. I do. Meet me at the pool bar near the convention center and I'll tell you who.*

There was a small pause. *When?*

Fifteen minutes.

He didn't know quite what he was going to do with her once he got to the bar. Tell her to quit texting him pictures, to quit wearing that revealing costume, to stop picking weirdos for her first time, to stop being so damn, sexy for a start.

You do know what you want to do with her.

Vin ignored his libido.

No. He was quite definitely *not* going to do that.

Kara dodged the crowds as she left the convention center's bar, feeling bad about leaving Ellie alone. She felt bad about leaving full stop, but knowing Hunter was coming to get her friend helped.

Hiding the fact she was going to meet Vin didn't.

Then again explaining to Ellie that she'd been sending the pictures Ellie had been taking of her, including the ones containing various potential suitors, to Vin all night, for reasons she couldn't have explained even to herself, would also have been a little difficult. Ellie probably wouldn't have cared but Kara felt awkward about it all the same.

Plenty of time to tell her friend later though. When whatever was going to happen with Vin had happened.

A small burst of excitement went through her as she went down the main set of stairs and out through the entrance into the brightly lit city beyond. An excitement she couldn't pretend she didn't feel.

I'll tell you who...

God, did he truly have someone in mind for her or was he teasing her in return for the whole day she'd spent teasing him? Perhaps she'd get to the bar to find no one there.

Kara pulled the long duster-style black coat she wore tighter around her as she stepped out onto the pavement, concealing her costume.

No, that wasn't Vin's style. He was a straight-up kind of guy not a game-player. He was probably meeting her so he could give her another lecture, then he'd take her home. Like a child.

Kara began walking in the direction of the pool bar. Man, if all he was going to do was give her a talking to then she'd be forced to take more serious action. Like drop the coat and do a sexy dance in the middle of the bar. Not that she knew any sexy dances, but she was sure she could improvise. That would probably embarrass the crap out of him.

The pool bar itself was dimly lit, a bit shabby and full of the usual Saturday late-night crowds, an odd cross-section of people ranging from students and business types to a group of old guys and what looked like a hen party.

As Kara scanned around the pool tables looking for Vin, she soon discovered why the hen party was making rather a lot of noise. There was a tall guy playing the table next to theirs, causing them do a lot of whispering, pointing and giggling.

No wonder. It was Vin. And his tall, lean figure in low-slung jeans and a black T-shirt was enough to make anyone stare.

Kara wound her way slowly through the tables, unable to take her eyes off him as he lined up a shot, one muscled, tanned arm out, his cue held firmly between long fingers. The severe beauty of his features was shadowed by the overhead lighting as he focused on the ball, but the light picked up the sheen of copper in his dark hair, the only other similarity he had with Ellie.

The sheer physical magnetism he possessed held her and the entire hen party at the next table absolutely hypnotized as he drew back his arm to take the shot. The white hit a green ball which then bounced off the side of the table and hit a red with unerring accuracy. The red shot straight into one of the pockets.

The hen party clapped but Vin didn't look at them. He lifted his gaze from the table and looked at her instead.

Electricity whispered over her skin as she met his dark, stormy blue eyes, and she had to take a deep breath, trying to slow her racing heartbeat.

God, this was insane. Where had all this sudden sexual tension come from?

Telling herself to move, she approached the table, her coat still pulled tight around her. He straightened, holding his cue by his side, looking her up and down.

"I'm still wearing the costume," she murmured, wanting to push him in some way. Get him back for the way he made her feel so off-balance. "Wanna see it?"

His gaze didn't move from hers. "Show me."

Kara caught her breath. She hadn't expected him to want to. She'd thought to flash him and catch him off guard. Shock him and maybe embarrass him a little. Part of her had even been looking forward to it. But now, perversely, she wanted to refuse. Deny him just to taunt him.

She lifted a brow. "My, Vincent. So demanding. Say please and I might."

"No please." His voice held a note of command she'd never thought she'd ever want to obey. "Show me. Now."

But she did want to obey. Because another, secret part of her wanted him to see her.

So she let the two halves of her coat open, giving him a glimpse of the slave collar and chain, the metal bikini top and exposed length of her torso and thighs.

Vin didn't move but the way his gaze swept from her head to her feet made her whole body prickle with heat. She felt like she'd been licked with fire, scorched. A voice inside her head screeched at her to cover herself, that she'd made herself vulnerable, but she resisted the urge. She wanted a reaction from him first. Some evidence that she hadn't shown herself to him for nothing.

Because somehow it felt important.

Slowly Vin lifted his gaze from her body to meet her eyes. The look on his face was hungry, skin drawn tight over the classical bone structure beneath it. His eyes glittered. The intensity of him held her motionless, made it difficult to breathe.

He liked what he saw, that much was obvious. And the fact that he did made her ache. Made her want.

"Stop, Kara," he said after what felt like an age, that edge of command still in his husky voice. "Stop sending me texts. Stop sending me pictures. And stop pushing me. Because you may not like the consequences."

Slowly she leaned her hip against the side of the pool table and folded the coat around herself again. Breath, long denied, filled her lungs. "Why? You don't like?"

"I don't like you messing with me, no."

"Sure you do. In fact, I think you love it." She eased away from the table and came closer to him. He watched her approach, unmoving. "I think you want me to mess with you more."

She didn't know quite why she felt the urge to keep pushing at him. Or what reaction she wanted from him.

Sure you don't.

Kara inhaled. Yeah, she knew. And perhaps it was time to stop denying her own feelings. Her own needs. Perhaps it was time to admit to herself what she wanted and why she could not leave him alone.

She hadn't wanted any of those guys at the Con. The guy she really wanted was Vin.

For a long moment neither of them said anything, the space between them full of tension and unspoken desires.

Then he said, "What do you want, Kara?"

"You said you were going to offer me an alternative to all

the guys I've been sending you." She turned, leaned back against the pool table, her hands gripping the sides. "So here I am. What's your alternative?" Somehow telling him exactly what she wanted felt too hard. Made her too vulnerable. She'd been rejected too many times before to leave herself open to the possibility of it happening again.

His gaze had dropped to where the coat had opened a little, giving him a glimpse of her bare leg. Good. Let him look. Let him see what he could have if he wanted. He just had to say it. Just had to tell her.

"An alternative?" he murmured. "You really want to know?"

"Yeah." Her voice wasn't as steady as she would have liked it to be.

Vin didn't move, but his gaze lifted from the gap in her coat back to her face again. "Me."

The word gripped her. Held her fast. He'd said it. He really had.

Losing her virginity to Vincent Fox. God. The thought made her mouth go dry with a strange combination of intense desire and absolute terror.

Kara looked down at the floor, suddenly unable to meet his eyes. "You? Well, that's something I didn't see coming."

"Bullshit. Isn't that why you've been playing games with me for the past couple of days?"

She tried to force a sarcastic laugh but it came out sounding strange. "Don't be stupid. I'm not some silly teenage girl."

There was a silence and she knew he'd moved, could feel that he'd closed the gap between them. He was right next to her, the heat from his body near her arm, making a shiver creep across her skin. He smelled good. Like a forest in summer, spicy and warm, with the faintest edge of musk. It made her want to turn her head into his neck and inhale him.

But she didn't. She kept her eyes on the floor because she knew if he looked into her face he'd see her desire. See it written there as obvious as spilled red wine on white velvet. And the thought of being so obvious was too much for her.

But a finger caught her beneath the chin, tipping her head back so her eyes met his whether she wanted it or not. And although she tried to school her expression she knew he'd seen through her. Knew he'd seen everything.

"Ah," he said softly, his intense gaze burning into hers. "I was right. You do want me."

Kara's jaw went tight with the urge to jerk away from him. His finger underneath her chin made her tremble for some reason, but she tried to hide it, not wanting to give him the satisfaction of knowing he affected her.

"Okay, so you're right." She lifted an eyebrow, going for bold and uncaring. "Did you mean it?"

His gaze flicked to her mouth then back again. "What? Offering myself as alternative? Yeah, I meant it."

"Why?" She felt suddenly angry with him for the way he'd made her so vulnerable. And the way he'd forced her to reveal it. "Would it be like a pity screw? Show the poor virgin what she's missing?"

Vin didn't release her, just stared down at her. "No. I don't pity screw anyone."

No, of course he wouldn't. Vin wasn't that type of guy and she knew it. But still, part of her wanted more than just "I meant it".

"Then why? You've never shown any interest in me before. Or perhaps it's because you just haven't had it in a while?" Great. And now she sounded overly defensive.

"You want me to want you, Kara?"

She didn't know how he managed to see through her all the

time. See what she barely understood herself. "Yes." She forced the words out because they were so damn difficult to say. "Yes, that's what I want."

His thumb brushed along her jaw and she froze, the touch making everything inside her go quiet and still. "I wouldn't have offered if I didn't want you."

She let out a breath she hadn't even realized she'd been holding. "And what exactly are you offering?"

"You know what I'm offering, baby girl. You want to lose your virginity? Then it needs to be with someone who'll keep you safe. With someone who knows what they're doing and who'll make it good for you. Who won't take advantage of you."

Her mouth was dry, the movement of his thumb on her skin sending little shockwaves through her. "Well that sounds kind of boring," she said, the bravado undermined by the way her voice shook.

Vin didn't smile and she knew he could see beneath all her defensive sarcasm, the snarky comebacks she used to protect herself. And she'd never felt so exposed in all her life.

"Don't be scared," he said. "I won't hurt you."

"I'm not scared," Kara lied and pulled away from him. "Come on then. If you're going to fuck me then let's get it over with."

But Vin's fingers were holding her chin in a grip she couldn't break, turning her head back to face him. And then his mouth covered hers.

For a minute, Kara was too shocked to do anything but stand there. Then, like the sun slowly melting a fall of snow, the shock began to seep away, becoming a deep, liquid heat that crept through her body. Making her tremble. Burn.

His mouth was so hot, coaxing her lips apart, deepening the kiss into something gentle and yet so demanding she could do nothing else but respond to it, leaning into him, her hands reaching for him.

Until he pulled away, blue eyes glittering. "I'm not going to fuck you, Kara," he said distinctly. "I'm going to do something else entirely."

Then he took her hand and led her wordlessly through the pool bar and into the night.

Chapter Four

"Where are we going?" Kara asked, breaking the unbearable silence as she got into the Corvette, jamming her hands into her armpits so he wouldn't see them shake.

"Your place." Vin pulled the car out into the stream of traffic, his attention firmly on the road.

Shit. She closed her eyes a second. Thought of her tiny apartment full of mismatched furniture and an eclectic mix of brightly colored throws and cushions that kind of clashed if she was honest. Then thought of Vin, standing tall and dark and stern in the middle of all the clutter and mess. About to have sex with her.

Double shit.

She hunched her shoulders. "Can't we go to yours?"

"I'm living at the office at the moment so no."

"The office? Why?"

"I started work on my house out at Piha and I need to save cash. The office has a kitchen and bathroom." He lifted one shoulder. "And a couch I can crash on."

"Oh but—"

"I'm not having you on my office couch, Kara," he interrupted with some finality. "It's not going to happen."

Having her. A shiver crept over her skin. She could still feel his kiss burning her mouth, an ache deep down inside her. Tension began to grip her. No, she didn't want that feeling, that awful feeling of pressure, of exposure, of vulnerability. Not now. Not with Vin.

"Okay," she said, hoping her voice didn't sound as shaky as she suspected it did. "But you're going to have to deal with unwashed coffee mugs and clothes, and—"

"Stop talking now, baby."

Kara closed her mouth with a snap, the words of protest about the *baby* dying unsaid. Arrogant son of a bitch. But quite honestly it felt good not to have put up the snarky front. To obey the command in his voice and do as she was told. She had too many other things to worry about right now, Vin's high-handedness being the least of it.

The silence in the car grew, along with the tension.

Her breathing had become faster the closer they got to her apartment, and she tried so hard to keep it contained, to not let him hear how that tension was getting to her.

She didn't want to be scared. Or nervous. Or any of the things she'd been with all those other guys. Because she'd never wanted any of them the way she wanted Vin and, Jesus, she didn't want to ruin this.

It didn't take them long to get to her apartment, but by the end she was desperate to get out of the car and away from the silence and her own conflicted feelings.

On the walk to her front door she was achingly conscious of Vin following behind her, not saying anything. He moved so silently for such a tall guy it was kind of unnerving.

Her fingers trembled as she tried fitting the key into the lock, cursing when it wouldn't go.

Then Vin put his hand on the back of her neck, his palm warm against the top her spine, long fingers brushing the bottom of the slave collar. And the breath froze in her chest.

The warmth of his touch washed over her, rooting her to the spot.

"You're nervous," he said quietly. "If you don't want to do

this all you have to say is no and I'll stop. At any time."

Beneath the fear and desire, a small spark of anger glowed. Yeah, she was nervous but she wasn't a bloody coward. She *wanted* this. She really, truly did.

"I'm not going to say no," she said thickly and jammed her key into the lock.

His hand slipped away as the door opened and as soon as it had gone, she wanted it back. But she didn't know how to ask, didn't know how to get the words out without her voice shaking, without revealing herself even more, so she said nothing, stepping inside and heading automatically down the hallway toward the lounge.

Except that when she got there, she didn't know what to do. Crap, why had she come here? If they were going to have sex then maybe going into her bedroom would have been better? And man, look at this stupid place. Empty coffee cups, books and comics scattered everywhere. Her art stuff on the dining table because she didn't have a proper desk to draw on. Some cushions on the floor that she hadn't picked up.

Kara went to the coffee table and collected the coffee cups, turning toward the kitchen area. Only to come to a halt when she almost crashed into Vin standing right in front of her.

"Where are you going?" he asked.

"Oh...uh...I need to put these in the kitchen."

He didn't look at the cups. He looked at her.

Goddammit. She didn't want him to look at her. Didn't want him to see the fear that was probably written all over her face. Because if he did he might change his mind and more than anything in the world, she didn't want him to change his mind.

Wordlessly, Vin reached out and took the cups from her hands, putting them down on the dining table. Then he looked at her again and she found she couldn't move. Couldn't seem to speak.

"Here's how we're going to do this," he said with absolute authority. "You're wearing a slave costume which makes you a slave girl. *My* slave girl."

She didn't miss the emphasis. Oh Jesus. Her mouth felt dry as a desert in summer, her heartbeat thundering in her ears with shock at the implications. At the weirdness of the whole situation. Uptight Vincent Fox? Into a bit of kink? And slave kink at that.

"You don't have to do anything," Vin went on, still quiet, still in charge. "All you have to do is follow my orders. Because you're here for my pleasure and my pleasure alone. Do you understand?"

His pleasure alone? Shit. She should be protesting, shouldn't she? Telling him where to stick his sexist bullshit? Yet the words stuck in her throat.

Because this is what you want. This is exactly what you want.

Kara struggled to take a breath. Yeah, God, it was what she'd fantasized about. Someone telling her what to do. Taking away the burden of her inexperience so she didn't have to worry about it. And even more important than that, he was giving her a role to play. A mask to wear. Some extra armor to protect herself in a situation where she felt unprotected. A way to feel less vulnerable.

She didn't have to be Kara, the freaky-ass chick with the weird hair who dressed funny. The girl nobody, not even her family, wanted. She could just be a slave girl.

Vin's slave girl.

"I understand," she heard herself say hoarsely.

The blue of his eyes darkened, a storm gathering. "I'll keep you safe, Kara. If there's anything you don't want to do, say stop and I'll stop."

She couldn't look away from him. The hunger in his face, the glitter of desire in his eyes. "Okay," she croaked.

A seemingly endless silence fell.

"Take off your costume," Vin said at last. "Everything except the collar. I want my slave naked."

Kara swallowed. Undress in front of him? This was where she'd always failed in the past. As if taking off her clothes meant not just physical nakedness but emotional nakedness as well. Her soul exposed along with her body because she'd never been able to divorce the two.

"Don't think." Vin studied her, as if he knew exactly what was going on in her head. "And don't speak. You're my slave so do as I say."

You're my slave...

Yes, that's what she was. Not Kara. And by undressing she wasn't exposing anything but her slave's body.

She slipped off the coat and let it drop. Then her hands began to move toward the fastenings of her costume, unsure at first as she undid the bikini top. As the material came away, she looked down at the floor, not wanting to meet his gaze, trying to lessen the feeling of exposure.

"Yes," he murmured, "that's good. Look at the ground, slave. Looking at me is a privilege you have to earn."

How he understood what she needed without having to ask she didn't know. But the fact that he'd somehow managed to incorporate her need to protect herself within the game they were playing made warmth bloom inside her. Made her realize there was another reason it was Vin she'd chosen to bring here and not anyone else.

Because she knew him. And as much as he annoyed her, she trusted him.

The thought gave her enough confidence not to fumble

when it came to getting the rest of the costume off. Yet when she finally stood there, naked but for the slave collar and chain, all her nervousness and vulnerability came rushing back, threatening to choke her. She kept her eyes glued to the floor but it didn't seem to make any difference.

She was naked, her less than slender curves on show. While he was still fully clothed.

It was all she could do not to run and hide.

Vin moved, coming close and she couldn't seem to breathe. This whole situation was so screwed up. She felt ridiculous standing there with nothing on, goose bumps rising all over her skin, letting him stare at her. Dear God, she just wanted to—

He took the end of the chain that dangled from her collar in his fist. Then wrapped the chain around his wrist, pulling the thing tight.

"Breathe. I don't want you passing out on me before I have a chance to explore you."

Kara closed her eyes and tried to take a calm, measured breath. Failed pitifully.

Vin pulled on the chain, tugging her closer. He was so warm and he smelled so good. Shit, why couldn't she get some control here? Why couldn't she act cool and calm and with-it? Why the hell did she have to shake like the scared little virgin she was?

"I don't want you to hold back," he said in her ear, his breath warm on her skin. "I want to know what you feel. How you feel it. You're here for my pleasure, don't forget. And my pleasure involves getting you off. Making you scream. Understand?" He tugged her even closer, so they were almost touching, her senses filled with the heat of his body, the spicy scent of his skin. "You're a slave, remember that, baby. Your entire function is to please me."

A slave. That's what she was. In this moment that's *all* she was.

For some reason the fear and the worry began to seep away, a deep sense of calm spreading through her. The tension in her muscles eased, the tightness in her chest vanishing.

She was a slave. Here for him. She could *so* do that.

"How?" she asked thickly. "I don't know anything. And I don't want to disappoint you."

"You won't disappoint me. You can't. I wouldn't blame a saw for not cutting the wood properly. I'd blame myself for not sharpening it when I had the chance." He leaned closer, so agonizingly close. "If I'm disappointed, baby, it'll be my own fault for not instructing you well enough."

And something inside Kara fell away at that. The last shred of resistance. The last protest.

"Tell me what to do," she whispered.

"Tell me what to do what?"

She only hesitated a second. Then she stepped into the role he'd given her and drew it around herself like a blanket. "Tell me what to do, master."

The chain tightened again. "Come here."

Slowly he began to back toward the couch, drawing her with him. Then he sat, still holding the chain in one hand, patting one thigh with the other. "Sit."

On him? Naked? Didn't ask for much, did he?

Kara started to turn around only to be drawn up short by the chain. "No," he ordered. "Facing me."

Oh God. Facing him. Naked.

You're a slave. Do it.

Yeah. What had he told her? Don't think. Just do it.

Kara somehow eased herself forward and into his lap without making an awkward mess of it, her thighs spread, her knees resting on the couch cushions on either side of his thighs.

But once she was there, once the rough denim of his jeans rubbed against her bare skin, the heat of his body burning like a furnace beneath her, nervousness threatened again. With her thighs spread, her naked body on show, she felt open. Exposed.

"Look at me," Vin said.

She didn't want to. So didn't want to. But the urge to obey him was too strong to deny. And when she did, everything drew tight inside her because his eyes were almost black with desire, hunger etched in every perfect line of his face.

He leaned back against the sofa, his gaze hooded. Watching her. The dim light in the room picked out aristocratic cheekbones and the full curve of his lower lip.

"You see?" he said softly. "See how you please me? I'm showing you and you want to know why?" He pulled the chain, tugging her forward a little, that hungry gaze sweeping down her body then back up again. Burning into hers. "Because you're mine. You're my property, slave. I can do whatever I want with you."

His property. She should have hated the arrogance of him. The possession implicit in his tone. But she didn't. She'd never been anyone's before. Had never belonged to anyone. Had never been claimed with such certainty. So there could be no argument.

It was sexiest thing she'd ever heard.

She shivered, the heat of him stopping the breath in her throat. Against her thigh she could feel the hard length of his erection and it made her shiver again. To know that she was doing that to him. Just by sitting on him, she was making him hard.

"Yeah," he murmured, "that's right. You're a good slave, baby. All you have to do is show your beautiful body to me and

I'm hard." His gaze moved down again and this time he lifted a hand, cupping her breast, his thumb gently circling her achingly hard nipple.

Instinctively she tried to stifle the gasp his touch brought from her, catching her lip between her teeth and biting down as electricity crackled along her nerve-endings, making her tremble.

"No," Vin ordered. "I told you, no holding back. I want to see your pleasure. I want to hear it. Do as you're told."

He pinched her nipple, tearing a groan from her throat before she could stop it. "Good," a soft murmur of approval, "that's what I want to hear."

Then he pinched her again and she made another sound, unable to keep them all inside. Taking away his hand for a moment, he licked his thumb then cupped her breast again, circling her nipple, leaving her skin slick, making it even more sensitive than it already was. Kara shuddered, her breathing hoarse and loud in her ears.

Vin's dark gaze shifted from the movement of his hand to her face, watching the effect of what he was doing. "You like that?" he asked, his voice soft and lazy. Seductive. "You like me touching you? You can speak."

But speaking was difficult. "Y-yes," she managed to force out.

"Good. Because I'm going to touch you some more." His hand drifted down her side, his fingers stroking over her skin and she couldn't stop shaking because his touch felt like a naked flame, burning her. Scorching her. There'd be marks on her tomorrow, she was sure of it.

At least, she hoped there would be.

Vin caressed her hip, unhurried, slow, then her thigh. Watching her as he did so, looking at her. "Beautiful." His hand shifted, moving inward, sliding up her inner thighs. "So beautiful, slave. You please me very much."

Her muscles clenched as she reflexively tried to close her legs but she couldn't because his hard body was sitting between them. God, she'd never had anyone touch her like this before. Never had anyone touch so slowly, stroking, exploring. The intensity of the pleasure scared her. Made her feel so vulnerable.

"V-Vin..." She shifted on his lap, suddenly uncomfortable. "I don't want you to...to..."

But the chain pulled tight as he wrapped it tighter around his wrist, his stormy gaze catching hers. Holding it. "You're a slave, baby." Reminding her of her role. Reminding her that she could use it for protection. "You don't get to choose."

She tried to swallow. "But you said—"

"That's different. If you're scared, tell me no and I'll stop." Vin this time. Not the master.

And for some reason, spread across his thighs, naked, she found this even more threatening.

She wanted the role-play. It felt much, much safer. Paradoxically, being the slave made her feel freer than being Kara.

"I don't want you to stop," she said.

"You sure?"

"Yes."

Vin stared at her. Into her. Gauging her reactions. Then his hand moved, fingers pushing through the curls between her thighs, sliding over the slick flesh of her sex.

She gasped, her body arching. Oh God... His fingers found the hard bud of her clit, circling, stroking. Kara closed her eyes, her head falling back. Pleasure rose inside her, swamping her, and she groaned with the intensity of it. Flames leapt behind her eyes as she felt him begin to push a finger gently inside her.

"Vin..."

"Don't move," he whispered. "Don't think. Just feel."

Kara screwed her eyes shut tighter as he eased his finger deeper inside her.

"You're tight. And hot. So fucking hot." He moved beneath her, the heat of him closer and she thought he must have sat up straighter, but she kept her eyes shut. She didn't want to look at him. This was too much. Way too much.

His finger eased out then back in again, a gentle, insistent motion that drew a helpless moan from her. Then his thumb circled her clit and she felt herself begin to burn.

"Oh...God..."

"You like that, slave? You like my fingers in your pussy? Tell me. Tell me how much you like it." His voice was rough, the sound of it as erotic as the blunt words he used.

She arched helplessly as his thumb circled again, pleasure catching fire inside her. "I l-like it..."

"Yeah, you do, baby. I can feel it. You're wet. Ready for me." He eased another finger inside her and she groaned, sensitive tissues stretching. "You're ready for your master, aren't you?"

She shuddered, unable to speak. Because it felt so good. So incredible. She began to lose her grip on the world around her. On her nervousness. Her fear. Even the sense of exposure and vulnerability had vanished, lost beneath the feelings racing like a forest fire through her. Need and desire. Heat and desperation. And pleasure. So much pleasure.

Kara moaned, her hips moving in time with his hand, the rhythm he set up becoming unbearable. It felt like he was pushing her to the edge of a cliff but holding her back from falling. And Christ how she wanted to fall.

"Please," she gasped. "Please..."

"You ready to come, slave?" The movements of his fingers

inside her had become slow, languid. Teasing her.

She shifted around, trying to get him touch her more. Harder. "Yes...yes...please...Oh, God, please..."

"Please what?"

"Please...m-master."

"I like how you beg. That's good, baby. So good." His body moved beneath her again and she gave a cry as his thumb pressed suddenly against her clit. "Come, slave. Come for me."

All it took was a little movement, the slick glide of his fingers, a slight pressure from his thumb and she felt the world explode around her. She cried out, only dimly aware of Vin's arm around her back, holding her as the orgasm ripped through her. Making her shudder and tremble in his arms.

Heaving in a shattered breath, she tried to pull herself together but couldn't. A heavy, sensual sensation was creeping through her limbs, weighing her down. So she gave up, letting the feeling wash through her, her heartbeat still racing.

When she at last opened her eyes again, she found him staring at her. Intense. Hungry.

"This isn't over," he said. "I haven't finished with you yet."

She should say something but she didn't know if she could even begin to form the words, let alone complete an entire sentence.

Vin pulled something out of the pocket of his jeans. A foil wrapped package. Then he flicked a glance down to his groin and back to her again. "Take my cock out."

This time Kara didn't pause. Didn't hesitate. As if her body had been obeying him for years and knew exactly what to do. She leaned forward, reaching for his fly. Her fingers fumbling a little with the button at the top but having no problem with the zip, pulling it down. Then she pushed her hand inside the denim, pulling down the cotton of his black boxers, closing her fingers around the hard length of his cock.

He didn't move as she took him out, but his eyes glittered, a raw hunger in them that made her breath catch. She looked away, unable to bear his gaze, glancing down at what she held in her hand instead. He was long, hard, his skin smooth and hot against her palm. And Jesus...he was really, really big.

"Put the condom on me," he ordered.

Kara's jaw tightened. She'd done this kind of thing in school, in sex-ed classes. Putting a condom on bananas and stuff. But she had a feeling putting a condom on an actual man was another thing entirely. Her hands shook as she ripped open the foil packet. And she fumbled taking the condom out, nervousness taking over once again.

"I can't—" she began, feeling like an idiot. But the words stopped in her throat as he put his hand over hers where it circled his cock and pushed down, both of them rolling the latex over him.

"On your knees." He pulled on the chain so she knelt upright. Then with his other hand, he gripped her hip, positioning her over him. "Slide down on me, slave. Nice and slow."

There was no time for protesting. Or hesitation. Or fear. Or anything in the way of thought at all.

There was only Vin. Only what he told her to do.

So she did what he told her, lowering herself onto him, feeling the unfamiliar pressure of his cock inside her, stretching her. There was pain and it was sharp, and she gasped, shaking.

The hand on her hip tightened, pushing her down hard so he filled her completely, and for a second all she could do was move to ease the discomfort.

"Keep still." He gripped the chain tight. "Breathe. It'll get easier."

And sure enough it did. The pain left her, the discomfort fading as she adjusted to the feeling of him inside her.

Kara looked up at him as he leaned back against the couch. He didn't look so lazily relaxed this time. His whole body was tense, holding himself absolutely still.

"Are you okay?" she croaked.

"That's my line, baby." Slowly Vin began to wind the chain around his wrist, pulling her closer and closer. "And no, I'm not okay. You're pleasing me a little too much." They were so close now, his mouth was almost touching hers. "You're so fucking tight, slave," he whispered. "You're making me lose my mind."

And then he was kissing her, deeply, slowly. Beginning to move inside her.

Kara put her hands on his chest, helpless against the pull of irresistible pleasure. Somehow her body knew what to do. As if this was familiar. As if she'd done this with him before many, many times. It was easy. Natural.

She kissed him back, so hungry for the taste of him, all her anxieties gone. Wanting only to please him. And for a little while she lost herself in the kiss, in the slow movement of their bodies.

Until Vin pulled away despite her protests. "No, I want to watch you." And he leaned back against the couch again, his dark eyes on her, the hand on her hip encouraging her to keep moving. "Please me, slave. Show me how beautiful you are."

She didn't feel exposed this time. Or threatened. She felt as beautiful as he'd told her she was. She was a slave, doing her master's bidding. And her pleasure was his.

Kara threw her head back, pressing her knees into the couch, moving on him faster, harder. She heard him mutter a curse but by then it barely registered. She was nothing but a creature of sensation, of pleasure. And when her climax hit her, she threw herself into it with abandon. Screaming with the sheer, overwhelming ecstasy of it.

Time lost all meaning for a while afterwards and when she next opened her eyes, she found herself swaying in Vin's lap, barely able to keep herself upright.

He didn't say anything, merely easing out of her. Then he wrapped an arm around her and shifted her gently so she was sitting on the couch instead of on him. Still saying nothing, he got up and disappeared down the hallway.

Kara sat there, dazed. And as her thinking processes resumed, all her vulnerabilities and fears began to come creeping back.

Where had he gone? What was he doing? And what the hell did she do now? Or even say? After that?

She had no reference point. No prior experience to make it easier. She felt as if she were freefalling without a bloody parachute.

Footsteps over the wooden floor. Vin returning.

"On your knees," he ordered.

Kara obeyed without a protest, sliding off the couch and kneeling on the floor. It was so much easier to be the slave at this particular point in time.

Fingers gripped her chin, pulling her head up so she could meet his gaze. She couldn't read the expression on his face but then one corner of his beautiful mouth lifted in a faint smile.

And her heart contracted strangely in her chest.

"Well done, slave. You pleased me very much." His thumb traced the bottom of her lip. "Perhaps I'll buy you again for another night."

Kara opened her mouth to say something. Anything. But he shook his head. "Don't speak. And don't move. Not until I'm gone."

So she stayed like that as he picked up his keys. As he

went down the hallway. As the door closed.

And when it shut behind him, she leaned forward so her forehead rested against the couch.

Jesus Christ. She'd just lost her virginity to Vincent Fox.

And she'd loved every second of it.

Chapter Five

Vin came out of the family meeting with the psychiatrist so angry he could barely speak. Despite the guy's assurances, despite what they'd agreed on earlier, he'd been informed they were going to have to release Lillian. She wasn't able to stay in hospital because technically she was better and the bed was needed.

Technically. Such a ridiculous term.

Lillian had schizophrenia. She wasn't ever going to get better. And once again it meant he was going to have to scour her belongings for knives. Once again he was going to have to make sure the police were notified. Once again he was going to have to visit Lillian every day to make sure she took her meds and she was okay.

And once again the fear for Ellie's safety would lodge itself in his gut like a piece of barbed wire.

Jesus, he wasn't ever going to get a fucking break, was he?

Vin got into the Corvette in the hospital car-park and slammed the door. Then he leaned back in the seat, his head against the expensive leather, and shut his eyes for a second, trying to get his anger under control so he could at least drive without wanting to run someone over.

Ellie would be gone in three weeks. Then he could finally let out the breath he'd been holding for the last fifteen years. The one he'd taken the day his father had at last washed his hands of his wife's mental illness and walked away, leaving his son to pick up the pieces.

Just three weeks. Okay, so no, Lillian being released now

wasn't ideal but there wasn't anything he could do about it. He'd already pushed as much as he'd been able to and that had done nothing but get the doc as pissed with Vin as Vin had been pissed with him. So he'd just have to deal with the situation as it was. He'd managed this long—another three weeks wasn't going to make much difference, was it?

From out of nowhere came a memory he'd been very carefully ignoring for the past two days.

Kara. Naked, apart from her slave chain. Sitting in his lap with her head thrown back. Her beautiful curvy body all flushed and pink. The heat of her as he moved inside her. The intense, incredible pleasure...

Christ, why was he thinking about that? Now? Because he didn't want to, no, he didn't. Had been actively trying to forget about it in fact.

"Fuck," he whispered into the silence, his body tightening as the memory got a grip on him and refused to let go.

Vin opened his eyes, reaching for the key in the ignition, hoping the sight of the hospital car-park was enough reality to banish the memory. He couldn't think about it. He couldn't afford to. There was other stuff he had to do. Important stuff. Besides, it was just sex, nothing more.

But images of her, the memories of how good it had been swamped him. So good it had shocked him. Better than anything he'd ever had. So much better than the reality of Lillian's imminent release.

He sat there, mouth dry, cock hard, reliving them. The moment she'd opened her coat in the pool bar to reveal her costume, and he'd made the decision then and there that if she wanted to lose her virginity, she was bloody going to lose it to him. Then in her apartment, seeing her nervousness, her fear. Wanting to make it okay for her, help her out by taking charge of the situation. Making the decisions so she didn't have to.

Except it had gotten out of hand and words had come spilling out of him. Orders. Demands. He'd never treated a woman like that in his whole goddamned life. Never thought that ordering her around, telling her what to do, and having her obey him would be so good. So fucking good. He hadn't been able to stop himself. Because he'd never had anything in his life that was just for him before. For his pleasure alone.

The last fifteen years had been about putting other people first. Ellie. His mother. His business. He'd done nothing for himself. Even the affairs he'd allowed himself had been hurried one-nighters while he'd been away on business, or a few dates here and there with women he met through work. Sex to satisfy his body, nothing more.

But having Kara had satisfied something hungry in his soul.

You're my property...

Jesus. He'd said that to her. To the woman he'd known since she was thirteen years old. Snarky, sarcastic, *virgin* Kara. He'd just taken control, turned her into his sex slave. And initially he'd done it to make it easier for her, giving her the benefit of his expertise. But the deeper they'd gone into the fantasy, the more a very male and primitive part of him had taken over. Oh, he'd given her opportunities to tell him no, he was sure he had. But had she really understood that she could? It had all been new to her and he'd...he'd...

He'd taken everything. And then at the end, he left her naked on her knees as he'd walked out.

You prick.

"Fuck," Vin murmured again as a coil of self-loathing tightened inside him.

Had she really wanted it? Or had he fooled himself into thinking she did? He should have called her, apologized. But he hadn't. Because even though a part of him was shocked at his own behavior, that primitive part had reveled in it. And that part wasn't sorry. Oh no, that part of himself didn't regret a single bloody thing.

In the car-park outside, a door slammed, the sound jolting him. Making him aware he'd been sitting there navel-gazing for the past five minutes.

The anger was still simmering away inside him and going over what he'd done with Kara in all its Technicolor glory didn't help. But he started the car and pulled out of the car-park anyway.

He'd planned on heading straight back to Fox Chase but soon found himself going in a different direction and parking in the upper part of town. Even then he couldn't work out what he was doing there until he saw the sign.

Manga Café Xtreme. Kara's café.

Vin parked the car, trying to figure out why the hell his subconscious had brought him here. Though of course, deep down, he knew.

He wanted her again. Wanted those moments again. Where he had something that was his. Utterly and totally his.

He knew he shouldn't be doing this. That he'd done what he'd told her he'd do, taken her virginity, and that was it. But still he put a hand to the door and still he went inside.

The place was full of university students and other weirdoes. Lots of gothic clothing and piercings and strange hair. Chicks wearing odd, flouncy dresses and guys who...well, looked like chicks. He didn't judge people, they could wear whatever the hell they liked as long as they weren't his sister. Each to their own, even if it was bizarre.

But he ceased to notice all the other bizarreness as he spotted the woman making coffee behind the counter.

Kara. Her blue hair had been pulled back in a ponytail high on the back of her head. She wore an over-sized black T-shirt with a wide neck that fell off one shoulder, exposing smooth golden skin, and a denim mini-skirt. With striped stockings complete with black suspenders. And Doc Martens.

Christ, she was weird. And strange. And sexy as hell.

He found himself unable to breathe, unable to move. Staring at her as she made the coffee, her movements quick, efficient and professional. How could making coffee be so damn hot? How could he feel himself getting hard just watching a strangely dressed, beautiful blue-haired woman work?

Kara looked up suddenly and he met her gaze—not purple this time but bright green—watching as a tide of color began to creep up her neck, washing over her face, flushing her cheeks. Her mouth opened, that sweet, full mouth he'd tasted not two nights ago.

And everything abruptly became crystal clear.

For fifteen years what he'd wanted had come secondary to everything else and for fifteen years he'd put up with it. Well, no more. He'd had a taste of what it was like to take pleasure for himself and had found a certain freedom in being selfish. He wanted that again. As much as he could get for as long as he could get it. If he was going to spend the next three weeks worried out of his mind about Ellie and his mother, then shit, didn't he deserve it?

The rest of the café faded away as Vin strode up to the counter, his gaze locked onto Kara's.

She'd frozen into place, green eyes wide in her flushed face, bringing to mind all sorts of delicious memories.

"I want to talk to you," he demanded without preamble.

Her throat moved, her gaze darting away to her customers then back to him again. "I'm kind of busy, Vin."

"Then I'll say it here." He was sick of games. Impatient with pretense and denial. "What we did two nights ago I want to do again."

Her flush deepened, became scarlet. But there were sparks of anger in her eyes. She put down the metal milk jug she was holding, banging it on the counter. "Jesus, you can't just walk in here and—"

"If you don't want it, just say no and I'll never bother you again."

Kara, her mouth still open, blinked.

Every muscle in his body pulled tight, waiting for her to answer.

Please, God, say yes. Please.

"Vin, I..."

"Tell me, Kara."

She let out a breath and looked away from him.

No. It was going to be a no. The disappointment was so bitter he could almost taste it on his tongue.

"Yes," she murmured, her voice so low it was almost inaudible. "I do want it."

For a second he didn't quite understand, so sure he'd been of a different answer. Then, as disappointment became something else, a satisfaction so deep he wanted to reach over and grab her there and then, he put his hands in his pockets to keep from doing just that.

"Good," he said, trying to keep his voice level. "Text me when you're ready."

Then he turned and left without another word. Needing to get out of her immediate vicinity before he did something stupid like haul her away from her café and into his car. Into the backseat where he could pull up her skirt, rip off her panties and bury himself inside her.

Instead he went back to his office, feeling better than he had in weeks. Which was weird since the prospect of sex didn't normally affect him like this.

Then again, it wasn't just ordinary sex, was it? It was sex with Kara. And he didn't know why that should make it different but it did.

He told himself he didn't care when she texted him, but he kept checking his phone the rest of the morning all the same.

Tonight. He hoped it would be tonight. And that she'd want to do again what they'd done two nights ago.

His slave. His property.

Vin scowled at his computer screen and reached down to adjust the hard-on that had made itself unwelcome in his jeans.

This was crazy. If Kara didn't text him soon he'd have to go back to the café again. And this time perhaps he *would* haul her away from the counter and into his car instead of just thinking about it.

Someone knocked on his office door then opened it without waiting for him to speak.

"For fuck's sake," Vin growled, irritated with the interruption. It would either be Hunter or Ellie since no one else just barged into his office like that. "Could you wait—"

The words died away the instant he raised his head to see who it was. Because it wasn't either Hunter or Ellie.

It was Kara.

He stared at her with a certain amount of shock as she closed the door behind her then leaned against it. She had her long black coat wrapped around her, incongruous in the summer heat, and there was a spark of defiance, of challenge, in her eyes.

Vin's breath caught, his body tensing. "What the hell are you doing here?"

She ignored the question. "First of all," she said, her voice breathless and a little shaky, "you should know that I don't want a relationship. All I want is sex. So whatever is between us doesn't mean anything, okay?"

He opened his mouth to tell her that yeah, shit, that was fine with him but she held up a hand. "Wait. Let me finish. Second, this can't get in the way of me and Ellie being friends. Her friendship is too important to me." She took a ragged breath and pushed herself away from the door. "And third, if we have sex, then I only want to do it if we do it like this." As she said the words, she opened her coat, letting it slip from her shoulders to reveal what she wore underneath it.

The slave costume.

Instantly he was hard as a rock, his hands gripping the arms of his chair tightly.

Holy Christ. She'd liked what they'd done. She really had.

"Are you sure?" he demanded hoarsely, because he had to know.

"Yes. I'm sure." The sun coming through the windows sent a path of light over the pale golden skin of her stomach and thigh, and he wanted that bikini off. Leave her in just the collar.

His fingers tightened even further on the arms of the chair. "You want to be my slave? Do what I say?" There could be no doubts here. None. Because he hadn't realized, until he'd seen the costume, that he'd wanted it to be that way too.

His slave. His alone.

"I'm in the costume, aren't I? Doesn't that tell you what I want?"

"That's not enough. I want to hear you say it."

Her eyelashes, long and thick with blue mascara, fluttered. Her throat moved. And he knew that saying the words was difficult for her. But her gaze when it met his was steady. "I want this," she said clearly. "I want to be your slave, Vin."

He felt something shift inside him. A key in a lock.

Slowly he pushed himself out of his chair and came toward

her. She didn't look away, didn't move from where she stood by the door, but he could hear her breathing become faster the closer he got to her. And when he put his hands on the door on either side of her head, he heard her breathing get faster still.

She smelled so sweet, like flowers with an edge of musk. And she was so warm. He remembered the feel of her skin beneath his fingers, like fine satin. The taste of her in his mouth, heady as a good wine.

She'd backed up against the door so he surrounded her, caging her against the wood. He liked that. Liked feeling he overwhelmed her. He shouldn't, he knew he shouldn't, but he did all the same. He wanted her overwhelmed by him. Wanted her panting and flushed, that snarky, sarcastic front gone.

"Are you my slave now?" he asked softly.

Her chin came up. "Of course now. Why do you think I've got my costume on?"

"It's the middle of the day, baby girl. In a building full of people working."

He knew the patronizing endearment would annoy her. And sure enough, a flash of the Kara he knew lit her unnaturally green eyes. "Why? Does that bother you? Oh my God, Vin. At least I have an excuse for not being adventurous."

She was taunting him. Of course she was. And it hit him that she was right.

He'd never been bad before. Never done anything crazy or wild. With a little sister and a sick mother to look out for, he couldn't afford to. Teenage rebellion—shit, any sort of rebellion—had been completely out for him. He'd always had to be responsible. Do the right thing.

Well, not today. Here he was, contemplating fucking a beautiful woman dressed in a slave costume, in his office, in the middle of the day. It was all kinds of wrong but he didn't care. He'd earned the right to be bad. To be wild. After fifteen years of toeing the line, he'd cross over it if he goddamn wanted to.

Vin reached down and locked the door. Then he took the end of her slave chain in his hand and stepped back from her. "You want it now, you'll get it now. Take off your clothes, slave."

He heard her breath catch. "What about you?" she asked. "Don't I get to—"

"I didn't give you permission to speak."

"But I don't—"

"You can't accuse me of not being adventurous then wimp out, baby. It doesn't work that way." Wrapping her chain around his wrist, he pulled her toward him so her heat and scent were right up close. "You came here to push me, Kara, don't pretend you didn't. So consider me pushed. If you don't want the consequences, then now's your chance to leave."

He didn't want her to leave, but he had to give her an out if she wanted to take it. Because he was afraid that another five minutes and he wouldn't be able to.

She stared at him for a moment, hesitating. "I'm not going to leave. But...I'm your slave, aren't I? Yours."

There was an expression in her eyes he couldn't read, a hint of desperation in her voice. As if she wanted an acknowledgement of some sort. So he gave it to her, gave it to them both. "Yeah, you're mine. Now do as you're told and take your clothes off."

The words must have been what she wanted to hear because her posture changed, became more relaxed, looser. Accepting. Her fingers went to the fastenings on her costume and a minute later she stood there in his office, the sun gliding a golden hand over her beautiful, naked body.

Calm spread through him, a tension he didn't even realize he felt leaving him. He had her now. His slave. For his pleasure alone. And now it was time to take it. Take something for himself.

Kara kept her gaze down as he led her toward his desk by the chain. He could hear her breathing fast and sharp in the silent room, and the sound made him harder.

As he sat in his chair, he watched her face, studying it for anything that would indicate fear. Saw none. Only the blush in her cheeks.

Christ, she was lovely. Blue hair and weird green eyes yes, but still so beautiful. What would she be like without the color in her hair? Would it be the same gold as the curls between her legs? And what about the natural color of her eyes? It had been so long since he'd seen her without contacts he couldn't even remember what color that was.

"On your knees," he ordered. Then he spread his thighs as she knelt, tugging her forward so she could kneel between them.

He held her chain tight, his heartbeat thudding. "Get my cock out."

Like she had two nights ago, she reached for the button of his fly then pulled at the zip. But this time her fingers didn't shake, nor did she fumble as she reached inside his boxers. And he nearly groaned as she touched him, the breath hissing in his throat as she drew him out. She flicked a startled glance at him as she did so and he didn't look away.

He hadn't two nights ago. Had wanted her to see how she affected him because it had so clearly turned her on too. So he didn't bother to do so now.

And when her color deepened still further, it satisfied him on a level he couldn't name. Turning her on was such a rush.

"Don't look so surprised, slave," he said softly. "You know how hard you make me. But now you've got to do something about it. So how about you wrap that beautiful mouth around my cock and suck me off?"

He'd chosen his words as much for her pleasure as for his,

knowing how she'd got off on his dirty talk the last time. And he wanted to shock her. She'd been pushing him since day one. Time to reciprocate.

Slowly Kara came up on her knees, the warm pressure of her body against his thighs making him ache. She hesitated. "I don't...I don't know..."

Vin put a finger beneath her chin and tilted her head back so he could see her face. Her green eyes darted away, her cheeks flaming scarlet. She'd gone tense.

"You don't know how to do it?" he asked. "Is that what you're trying to say?"

"I..."

"Answer me, slave."

She still wouldn't look at him. "No, I don't."

That surprised him. She'd been so sensual, had responded so completely to him two nights ago, he'd been sure she'd had some sexual experience.

Well, it didn't matter. He wasn't going to complain about having to teach her how to give head.

"Look at me." He used the same tone of command he did on the building site when the apprentices were out of line, and it had the desired effect, her gaze coming to his instantly. "Remember what I said about the saw? If it didn't cut then that it was my fault I didn't sharpen it? All you need to do is what I tell you. And if I don't like it, it's my fault."

Her throat moved. "Okay."

"Now, run your tongue around the head, slave."

Kara bent her head, no hesitation this time, and he felt her tongue touch his cock, at first tentative then, slowly, with more confidence. His breath caught. "Open your mouth. Take it inside." The order came out sharp but he didn't care. He just wanted more.

She did as she was told, the heat of her mouth engulfing him and he groaned as a shock of electric pleasure went straight down his spine. "Fuck...that's good." Vin closed his eyes for a second, leaning back in his chair as she began to move her mouth on him. She wasn't experienced but that in no way detracted from the intensity of the sensation. In fact there was an element to her hesitancy that made it even more intense.

God, she was going to blow his head off at this rate.

With his free hand, he grabbed her ponytail, coiling the softness of it in his fist, directing her movements. He looked down, watching as she knelt between his legs, sucking him off.

It was the most erotic thing he'd ever seen his life.

Outside in the hallway he could hear someone speak, the sounds of work continuing on around him. But not in here.

In here his beautiful slave was giving him a blowjob, and afterward he was going to flip her naked body over his desk and fuck the living hell out of her.

So wrong. Selfish of him.

The thought made him so hard he couldn't think, and suddenly he wanted to be inside her. Have the fantasy right now. And why the hell not? She was his to command, wasn't she?

His hand tightened in her ponytail as he eased her mouth off him. She blinked. "Did I... Did I do something wrong?"

"No, you did exactly what I wanted. I just changed my mind. On my desk, slave." Kara got to her feet then backed away slowly to the desk, putting her hands behind her on the wood and pushing herself up and onto it. She didn't look at him but he let himself look at her.

She was all pink skin and exquisite curves. Her hard little nipples were a deep rose color and he remembered the taste of them. Remembered the sounds she'd made as he'd sucked on them. Christ, he'd never thought a woman so soft and vulnerable could be so desirable.

Getting out of his chair, he went over to the desk, pulling out his wallet from his back pocket as he did so. Found the condom he kept in it, the one he'd had to replace after that first night with her. He got it out and ripped it open. Then he gave it to her and this time she didn't need instruction. She unrolled it down on his cock, her fingers firm, applying pressure, making him want to growl as fire flashed along his nerve-endings.

"Lie down," he said roughly and when she did so, he nearly growled again. The sheer eroticism of having her naked on his desk in the middle of a work day was like a punch to the gut. Smart, snarky Kara in a slave collar. Ready to do his bidding. "Spread your legs for me."

Her eyelashes fluttered closed as she did as she was told, letting her knees fall open. Letting him see how pink and wet she was. Ready for him.

He couldn't wait. Gripping her hips, he pulled her to the edge of the desk, positioned himself then thrust inside her.

She gave a soft cry, her body arching. He hooked his arm underneath her knee, drawing her leg up and around his waist, leaning forward, pushing deeper. Then he stopped, letting the incredible heat of her body seep through him. Into him.

He looked down at her, lying back on his desk amongst the boring detritus of work, the sun illuminating her. Gold and blue and pink. Like a rare and precious work of art made especially for him. Her eyes were closed, her mouth slightly open.

He thrust again, harder, listening to the sounds she made. Christ, she felt tight as a glove. Perfect.

"You feel so good, slave," he murmured. "I love how tight you are."

She gasped, her hands pressing down on the wood of the desk beneath her, her hips lifting in time with his.

"Do you like this? Do you like being naked on my desk?" The words spilled out of him, he couldn't stop them. Raw and hot and erotic. Words he'd never said to anyone else. "Being fucked in the middle of the day, where anyone can hear you?" He hauled her leg higher, pushing deeper. "I can make you scream, baby. Scream so everyone can hear how hard I can make you come."

Kara groaned, her body shivering as he moved inside her, faster now, harder. Pleasure uncoiling inside him like a whip.

Distantly he heard someone knock on his door and he said something—he didn't know what—and the knocking stopped, but somehow the knowledge of what he was doing and who he was doing it with, came back to him. An erotic tidal wave of knowledge.

Kara Sinclair. Who'd agreed to be his slave. Who he was screwing in his office in the middle of the day.

Bad. And yet so very, very good.

Vin gripped her hips tightly, moving faster. Driving himself and her closer to the edge and as he went over, he was conscious of only thing.

They had to do this again.

Chapter Six

Kara lay on Vin's desk feeling as if the world had ended. Outside the office she could hear people talking, the sounds of reality continuing, but inside all she could hear was Vin's breathing and hers, fast and ragged.

Oh God. She couldn't believe what had just happened, what she'd just done. That they'd ended up having sex on his desk.

Oh come on, really? You showed up here in the slave costume. What did you expect would happen?

She swallowed, her eyes still shut, trying to take a breath, put herself back together again.

Yeah, she'd expected this to happen. Wanted it to. Wanted to take his orders, lose her self-consciousness and her vulnerability in the role of his slave.

And also she'd been pissed at the way he'd just appeared in the café out of the blue, telling her he wanted her again. Embarrassed and pissed. She hadn't expected to hear from him again. Hadn't wanted to hear from him again. In fact she'd just wanted to forget the whole slave episode in her apartment. Her behavior had been so out of control, so unlike her that it had embarrassed her even to think about.

Until he'd pinned her to the spot in the café with those stormy blue eyes of his, making her thoroughly aware of every part of her he'd touched. Every part of her that wanted him to touch her again.

Possibly she should have waited to contact him when she'd got home that night but dammit, he couldn't have it all his own way. She'd wanted to push him so she'd made sure she had cover at the café and then had gone and got the costume again. And turned up at his office.

The look on his face as she'd taken off the coat had made it worth doing that alone.

But then he'd taken it much further than she'd ever expected.

Who knew that straight-arrow Vin would have taken her on his desk at work?

Who knew you would let him?

Cautiously she opened her eyes.

He'd moved away from the desk and was now in the process of doing his jeans up. She could see the sun coming through the office windows lighting bronze sparks from his dark hair, following the lines of his striking face.

Jesus, he really was quite phenomenally hot.

Kara sat up, too busy staring at him to remember she was naked apart from her slave chain. The second time they'd had sex and he still hadn't taken off his clothes. She'd seen him half-naked on the building site though, knew the lean, hard lines of his chest and abs.

She licked her lips, the taste of him sitting heavy and thick in her mouth. Salty and musky...delicious. She'd never gone down on a guy before. It had always sounded vaguely disgusting. But going down on Vin hadn't been. And when he'd taken her ponytail in his hand and directed her movements...

His head came up abruptly, blue gaze meeting hers. She felt the shock of it go right down through to her toes.

He didn't say anything, coming over to the desk and putting his hands on her hips, easing her down from the edge to stand on the floor. Then he went to the door of his office, picked up the remains of her discarded costume and the coat that lay on the floor, and came back over to her.

"It's okay," Kara began. "I can—"

"I didn't say you could speak," Vin interrupted. "I'm going to dress you, so don't move."

The thought of him dressing her made her uneasy for some reason. Totally insane when the whole desk-sex thing hadn't. "I can dress myself."

Vin's gaze pinned her to the spot. "You're speaking. Didn't I tell you not to?"

Kara's mouth shut with a snap. Oh she would have loved to tell him where to stick that but they were still role-playing, and some part of her wanted the fantasy to continue.

When she remained silent, he gave a little nod as if in approval. "You remember you're only here for my pleasure? Well, dressing you gives me pleasure. So shut up and stand there and let me do it."

She shut up and stood there and it was kind of humiliating to be dressed by a grown man when most of her life she'd been the one dressing other people. Her little brother and sister almost as soon as she knew how buttons worked. Her mother when the combination of work and alcohol had gotten to be too much. And yet a part of her—that part that loved this fantasy of having someone make all the decisions for her, take away all the responsibility—also liked having someone dress her. Because he did it so gently, carefully, with all his attention as if this task was the most important thing he'd ever done. As if she was precious.

No one had ever dressed her like that. Taken care of her.

A lump rose in her throat, unwanted, unasked for and she felt a weird prickle behind her eyes.

She swallowed then blinked fiercely. *No, please not tears.* Not fucking crying because some guy just happened to be gentle putting her clothes back on.

Christ, what a loser. What a pathetic loser.

"Vin," she began.

"Shut up. I haven't finished." He picked up the coat, eased her arms into it, drawing it around her mostly naked body, doing up the buttons with single-minded purpose. Right up to her chin. "There," he said, sounding satisfied. "Now, I'm finished."

For a second he gazed at her as if surveying his handiwork. Then he leaned forward and his mouth brushed hers, a fleeting warmth. "Thank you, slave. You did well. But you have to remember that I'm the master here, and I say when you're required and when you're not."

Kara blinked, the warmth of that kiss still whispering over her skin. Then she realized he was waiting for a response, a question in his eyes. He wanted to do this again, that much was obvious, and he was waiting for her to okay it.

Again? Did she want to do it again?

The small, vulnerable part of her wanted it. But the hard, outer shell, the one she'd been carefully building up for years, wasn't so sure. Behind the arrogance, the take-charge attitude, there was a gentleness to Vincent Fox she hadn't expected. And really, really didn't want.

But then again, it wasn't her who had to accept that gentleness, was it? It was the slave. And the slave had nothing to do with her. Nothing at all.

"Yes," she heard herself say.

"Yes, what?"

"Yes, master."

"Good." He stepped back, giving her room. "Keep your phone with you. And be ready. You are dismissed."

But he kept looking at her and didn't stop looking as she went to the door.

And she could still feel the pressure of his gaze on her back as she turned the handle and went out.

Kara squinted at the panel she'd just sketched out, yet another installment of the cartoon she was doing for Ellie based on the computer game her friend had created. Dark Shadow, the heroine, was in the process of fighting the villain, Iron Wolf. A villain that once again was looking more and more like a certain man of her acquaintance. A blazingly hot, kinky man.

Jesus Christ. Why was she drawing Vin all the time? She seriously had to get it to together. Ellie was going to recognize him and wonder why on earth Kara kept turning her precious Iron Wolf into her brother.

Uh yeah, sorry, Ell. It's because I've been screwing him every night for the past week and now I can't stop thinking about him.

Sure she could say that. It was the truth after all.

Kara dropped the pencil, staring at the image she'd just drawn, with Dark Shadow on her knees before Iron Wolf, head bowed...

Crap. She picked up the eraser and got rid of the image. No. Way. It was bad enough thinking about what she and Vin got up to every night, let alone drawing it.

Letting out a breath, she leaned back on the couch, reflexively checking the counter for customers. But there was no one. Most of the people in the café were hunched over the computers or talking.

Then she checked her phone, sitting beside her sketchbook. But there were no texts either.

And no, she wasn't disappointed about that. Not at all. Despite the fact that he'd told her last night that he'd want her again tonight. And that she'd frantically whizzed out to get a brand new box of condoms especially for the occasion.

Despite the fact that she'd bitten the bullet and shelled out to buy the slave Leia costume instead of keeping it on constant hire. A bit ridiculous considering he had her wearing just the collar and chain within seconds of arriving at her apartment. Still, he did seem to like taking the bra and panties off. Or watching her do it...

Kara cursed under her breath as a prickling kind of heat washed through her. Man, what was wrong with her? Did all virgins get like this after their first taste of sex? Like they couldn't get enough? Here she was, sitting at work and getting all hot and bothered at the thought of sex with Vin. Craving it like an addict craves a fix.

"Are you on a break?"

Her head jerked up at the sound of a familiar voice. And then the prickling heat turned into a bonfire as she saw who was standing in front of her.

Vincent Fox. In a suit. A very fine, expertly tailored suit. He wore it with no tie, his white business shirt, in crisp contrast to the dark navy jacket, open at the neck, revealing smooth tanned skin. Was it possible for the man to get any hotter?

Kara blinked at him. "What are you doing here?"

"I want a coffee. And this is a café. Apparently."

She blinked some more, struggling to fit his presence in her normal, day-to-day life. They only saw each other at night, as master and slave. Out of that context it was...weird.

"Oh, okay. I can do that." She quickly pulled a magazine over the pages of her sketchbook and got to her feet. But his sharp gaze caught the movement, lingering on the obscuring magazine. Goddammit.

"Where have you been?" She came around the side of the coffee table, closer to where he stood, hoping to distract him.

"You look very..." *Fucking sexy.* "Professional."

His gaze flickered back to her again. Then down at himself. "I've been to the bank. Meeting with one of their business managers."

"Ah. Didn't think you went around nailing things in a suit."

And just like that, the air between them thickened, the look in his eyes becoming hot, intent. "I could," he said softly. "If you wanted me to."

Oh for Christ's sake. How could he get her so breathless with just a look and mild double entendre?

She swallowed. "I thought I didn't get a say in what you did?" Because there was no doubt as to what he was referring to.

"Do you want one?"

Kara looked away from him, not expecting the question and strangely uneasy with it. Having a say might upset the delicate balance they'd found between them. Disturb the role he'd given her. She was quite happy taking orders in the context of their role-play, being told what to do and when to do it. Being taught the things that made him moan. Made him gasp her name. Made him curse harshly in her ear.

Having a say would require her to drop the slave mask. Be Kara. Be herself.

A whisper of her old vulnerability slid under her skin, cold and sharp as a paring knife.

"No," she said. "No, I don't." Turning, she began to move toward the counter. "So, how about that coffee?"

Busying herself behind the counter with the espresso machine, Kara tried to ignore him as he followed her over, leaning one hip against the edge of the counter and folding his arms.

She knew she should say something sharp and snarky but

she didn't know what. For some reason she couldn't quite divorce Vin the master from Vin Ellie's-older-brother. Which was disturbing.

She didn't want him to have any effect on her outside of the context of their fantasy. She didn't really even want him to acknowledge it.

"The bank, huh?" she said at last, grasping for a subject, any subject. "What's with that?"

Vin, on the other hand, seemed to have no problem dealing with her outside the context of their fantasy. The bastard. "I'm getting financed to expand the business."

"Expand? How?"

"Green construction. That's where the money is. And it's a growing market in New Zealand."

She stared at him for a moment, nonplussed. He didn't seem the type of guy who'd give a shit about green building practices, it had to be said.

Vin stared back. "What?"

"I'm just a little startled by the word 'green' in conjunction with the word 'construction'. Out of your mouth."

"Why? Construction's my business."

"Yeah but…" She stopped, realizing something.

That she didn't know anything much about Vin Fox. Oh she knew he was protective and liked to be in control a lot. That he cared about Ellie. That he worked hard. And she knew what got him off, what made him hot. But that was it. She didn't know his hopes or his dreams. The plans he had for the future or even where he wanted to be five years from now.

She didn't even know why he was into construction in the first place. Which kind of made her unqualified to comment on his lack of understanding about the whole green movement.

"But what?" He raised one dark brow.

You want to know. You want to know about him.

No, piss off. She didn't. She didn't want to know anything about him apart from when they were going to meet and where.

"Nothing." She turned on the machine, hoping the conversation would be lost under the noise of brewing coffee.

"What were you drawing back there?"

Bugger it. Looked like she wasn't going to get out of that either. Kara met his gaze, folding her arms. "Hentai manga."

"What's that?"

"Hardcore sex comics."

His brows rose. "What?"

"I think you heard me."

"I heard hardcore sex comics, yeah. But don't tell me you're drawing them."

"And why shouldn't I, pray?"

"I've never heard of a virgin writing that kind of thing."

"Shows you how many virgins you know. Besides, news flash, I'm not a virgin anymore."

He frowned. "You're really drawing hardcore sex comics?"

Kara opened her mouth, a snarky denial at the ready.

"Show me."

Her mouth closed with a snap. "What? No way."

"Why not? Sex isn't anything to be ashamed of. Besides, I didn't even know you drew stuff."

Kara began fiddling around with the espresso machine, pulling knobs and clanking around with metal jugs. She didn't want to talk about her drawing. Didn't even want him knowing about it. What would he think of it anyway? He was a guy who built houses for Christ's sake. He'd probably think her art was stupid, like most other people did. Or not even worthy of the term art.

"Kara."

"No." She jammed the metal jug full of milk under the nozzle for steaming and turned it on, the noise effectively rendering any further conversation pointless.

Vin's gaze however was inescapable.

Eventually, when the milk had been heated and keeping the machine on would only scald it, Kara was forced to answer. "Look, Vin," she said belligerently. "You and I do one thing and one thing only. We screw each other. Okay? You don't need to know about my drawing and I don't need to know about your company. We don't need to know anything about each other at all. And I'm happy with it that way." She poured out his latte, put the plastic top over the takeaway cup, and shoved it in his direction. "Here's your damn coffee. I'll see you tonight."

He said nothing for a long moment. Then he looked down at the cup. "I wanted an espresso not a latte."

"I don't care. Just go away and stop bothering me at work."

"I'll bother you wherever I goddamn please." He glanced back at her, eyes glinting, a storm gathering.

She refused to be intimidated. Or turned on. "Go away, Vin."

He leaned on the counter. "Why? Am I getting to you, baby girl?"

"No." *Yes.* "Stop being an asshole. I'm at work for God's sake."

He just looked at her and she felt stripped bare, more completely than she ever had as his slave. Then, before she could do anything about it, he picked up his cup and took a step back. "Yeah, you're right." His voice was neutral, the storm passing. His face guarded and blank. "Screwing. That's all we're doing. In which case, tonight. Seven thirty. You'll expect me."

She didn't speak as he turned and walked out of the café.

Nor did she want to acknowledge the emotion that slipped through her as he left.

An emotion that felt a lot like disappointment.

Vin strode out of Manga Café Xtreme then stopped, staring belligerently at the traffic going by him in the street, angry for no good reason.

The coffee in his hand was burning his palm so he glared at that instead of the traffic. She hadn't even asked him what kind of coffee he wanted, just gone ahead and made him a latte without asking. Well, he didn't want a latte. He wanted a fucking espresso.

It's not the coffee, dick.

No, of course it wasn't the stupid coffee. It was why the hell he'd even gone into Kara's café in the first place. There were dozens of other cafés near the bank where he'd had his meeting, but he'd walked right by all of them, coming here instead.

Why? When the need for coffee wasn't really all that pressing?

Vin's jaw tightened. He hadn't been thinking when he'd stopped outside Manga Café Xtreme, he'd just pushed the door open and gone right in, and then he'd seen her.

Sitting on the couch at the back of the café, bent over a coffee table. Totally absorbed in what she was doing. Her face screwed up in concentration, her glasses on the end of her nose. Her bottom lip caught between her teeth.

And in that instant he'd been seized with the almost overwhelming desire to know what she was doing. So he'd come inside and was down at the end of the café near her table before he'd even had a chance to put thought into action.

Drawing. She'd been drawing. And he was betting it wasn't

hardcore sex comics, no matter what she said.

He didn't know why he wanted to know though. And he didn't know why her insistence on them not sharing anything other than their bodies irritated him quite so damn much.

Because it shouldn't. He was quite happy with their present arrangement. Having her as his love slave, doing what he wanted when he wanted it and enjoying the hell out of it, satisfied a need in him he didn't even realize he had.

In fact this whole week he'd been a lot calmer. Dealing with the shit of having to take Lillian home from the hospital and getting her settled back into the council apartment he leased for her. Doing his usual sweep for sharp items and making sure she took her meds, at the same time as making sure Ellie was okay. Then there had been Fox Chase and a few last minute problems with getting the finances sorted for the expansion.

Knowing he had Kara made things easier. That when he got to her place, she'd be there for him. And she wouldn't give him any grief. She'd just do what he said, and he'd make her feel good.

Yeah, that had made the whole week better. So why he should feel annoyed because she didn't want to talk about whatever the hell she was drawing was anyone's guess. He and Kara had something good going on. Had an understanding. Why fuck it up with talking?

Reflexively Vin lifted the coffee and took a sip, pulling a face at the milky taste of it. Yet underneath that, he could also taste hints of what was probably excellent coffee. Man, if he could stomach this latte, she'd probably make a mean espresso.

He swung back round, glancing through the windows of the café. Kara was still behind the counter, fussing around with something. As he watched, she glanced up and met his gaze, glaring at him.

Well, shit. If she didn't want to talk, she didn't want to talk and he was good with that. But she couldn't tell him where to get his damn coffee. And if he wanted to get it from her café then he would.

Satisfied by the thought, Vin gave her a grin just to annoy her, then turned and started in the direction of his office.

Kara pulled the door to the café shut and locked it, stuffing the key in the old, worn leather satchel she usually carried with her. She stood outside for a minute, not knowing quite what to do with herself.

Fucking Vin. She was still feeling deeply unsettled and more than a little annoyed about his visit that morning. With all his questions and crap. And that cocky smile he'd given her as he'd stood outside on the sidewalk. Like he was sure of himself and sure of her. It grated. She hadn't thought much about boundaries when she'd agreed to continue with this...*thing* that was going on between them. Hadn't thought she'd need to. But his conversation with her earlier had crossed a line she didn't want crossed. Sex. That's all it was and that's all it had to stay. She didn't want anything more.

Around her the sidewalks had begun to fill with people all making their way home, the city streets slowly clogging with rush hour traffic. And she should be going home too. Back to her apartment where she'd quickly swallow some kind of makeshift dinner before getting herself ready for him. A shower, body lotion, prettying herself up like a good slave.

She scowled at nothing in particular, conscious of the anticipation already knotting in her stomach. Her body was, apparently, quite keen on the idea. But for some reason her head was telling her the opposite. That she should pull back, not exacerbate the hold he already had on her. Set some boundaries.

From the depths of her satchel came the sound of her phone signaling a text message. God, was it Vin already? Sighing, Kara pulled it out and glanced down at the screen, an odd kind of trepidation joining the anticipation. But it wasn't him. It was a text from an artist friend, asking her if she wanted to go out for a drink that night.

She bit her lip. Yeah, shit, maybe she should go out. Have a night off being Vin's sexual slave. He wasn't her master outside the bedroom and clearly, given their conversation earlier, he needed a small reminder of the fact. And perhaps so did she.

Deciding, Kara texted her friend, agreeing to meet up with her then sent off another quick one to Ellie, asking if she wanted to come out as well. Then she texted Vin. *Can't do tonight. Sorry.*

He'd be pissed off probably—or who knows? Maybe he wouldn't—but whatever, that was too bad. The more she thought about it, the more she didn't want to see him tonight. Like she had to put some distance between them. Make sure her armor was firmly in place.

She was only just putting her phone back in her bag when it chimed again with another text. From Vin. *You're kidding. Why not?*

Kara set her jaw and replied. *I don't need a reason. I'm not your girlfriend.*

Vin's reply was just as quick. *No, you're my slave. So do as you're told.*

Her heartbeat quickened, a shiver going down her back. Already her body was responding to his commands, which made it even more important that she assert herself in some way. *I'm not your slave tonight. So go play with someone else. Or better, go play with yourself instead.*

A small twinge niggled at her at the thought of him finding

someone else but hey, it wasn't as if they were exclusive.

A second later his response came back. *I don't want someone else. I want you.*

Kara stared down at the screen, her throat feeling strangely tight.

No, she couldn't give in. It felt important to hold her ground, maintain her independence. Especially around such a control freak as Vincent Fox. Give him an inch and he'd take a mile, and he'd already taken way too many miles around her. No, if she was going to set boundaries then now was the time to do it.

Her thumb moved decisively on the keypad. *Too bad.*

She sent the text then switched her phone off and put it back in her satchel.

Vin couldn't believe how pissed off he was. It was all he could do not to throw the fucking phone at the wall. All his earlier good feelings and calm had drained away the moment Kara's text had come through. Not tonight? What the hell? She'd been so adamant before that they were only screwing and he'd been good with that. Shit, he'd been more than fine with it. So why was she saying no now?

Was it because he'd overstepped the mark with his questions earlier? Was this some kind of punishment?

He got up from his desk, shoved his chair away, strode to the window and back again, restless and edgy. It shouldn't matter. It shouldn't matter that she didn't want to see him tonight. It shouldn't matter that he didn't get to have his way with her beautiful body. Tell her what to do and when to do it. He'd been fine before she'd come along so why things were different now was anyone's guess. Really, he should be shrugging his shoulders, grabbing Hunter and going out for a night at the pub on the piss.

He stopped by the desk, glaring at his phone. Her text was still sitting there. *Too bad.* He'd texted her again then, when he hadn't got a response, had tried calling her. But she wouldn't answer her phone. Calling her again would be stupid. And desperate. And he wasn't desperate.

"Fuck," he said to the empty office.

Those moments with her, in her apartment, where she knelt at his feet, were the only moments in his life where he had any control. Where life would do what he said for a change instead of feeling like he was at life's mercy. And they were good moments. Shit, they were *vital* moments. He didn't want to lose even one of them. But what else could he do? If she wasn't into it then he couldn't make her. He may take control with her in the bedroom, but out of it he wasn't the type of guy who forced women into doing what he wanted.

Go play with someone else...

Vin ran a distracted hand through his hair. Yeah, but there was a small problem with that; he didn't want someone else. He couldn't even imagine explaining what he wanted with some other woman. Oh, he knew there were places to go where he could get that whole master/slave dynamic if he wanted. But he didn't want it with just anyone. It only worked with her. There was just something about her, the way all her guards fell when he told her what to do. When her wariness dropped away and her snark vanished. When she let the pleasure he gave her overwhelm her. It made him feel like a god and hell, what man didn't like that?

Vin scowled at the phone, still displaying, *Too bad.*

Too bad his ass.

He had to know what had changed her mind. He had to. If she had good reasons for blowing him off then that was okay. It would suck but he'd deal with it. But he had to know what those reasons were. See what had changed between them.

She was his. She was his slave. And it was about time she learned that what was his, stayed his.

Chapter Seven

Kara swallowed the last of her wine and put her empty glass back on the bar. Ugh. Cheap chardonnay was not her favorite. It tended to go all acidic and sit uncomfortably in her stomach, and God knew she didn't need any more reasons to feel uncomfortable since she already felt uneasy enough as it was.

"Another glass?" Lincoln, the guy she'd met in the bar, slid an arm around her waist, leaning in close.

She resisted the urge to pull away from him. "Uh. No thanks. I'm good."

He nuzzled her ear. "Perhaps we should head out then?"

Head out. Yeah, they should. She'd been anticipating this moment from the second Lincoln had approached her an hour or two ago, but now that it was here she felt uncertain and didn't know why.

After a couple of wines with her friends, she'd come to the conclusion that not seeing Vin wasn't the only boundary she could set. That maybe she needed to set a few sexual boundaries as well. Like the fact that finding another guy would be a good thing for her, assert her sexual independence and all that. After all, she wasn't a virgin anymore, which hopefully meant that weird vulnerability thing she'd had going on before should have been well and truly put to bed, so to speak.

And hell, maybe she could even have sex like a normal person. Without the slave costume and the orders. But the only way to do that was to find a guy she could do it with. A guy who wasn't Vin.

Kara flashed a glance back at the table where some of her friends were sitting. One of them gave her a big thumbs up. And why not? Lincoln was hot and he seemed to be into her. Plus he seemed as normal as they came which was always a bonus.

But...

Jesus, it would have been good if Ellie had been able to make it, but her friend had had packing stuff to do in preparation for her trip and hadn't been able to come out. A pity since Kara could have used an unbiased opinion about Lincoln and whether going off to spend a night with him was really a good idea.

You don't need Ellie to tell you it's a crap idea.

Kara shook the thought off. No, God, there wasn't anything wrong with the idea. It was something she wanted to do. Needed to do. If only to get Vin out of her head because even now, even sitting with Lincoln, all she could see was how he wasn't as tall as Vin. Or as broad. That his jaw line wasn't as straight and his gaze didn't have that burning, fierce look like Vin's sometimes had. And he certainly didn't have Vin's air of absolute authority that made her want to...

Shit. She had to stop thinking about bloody Vin.

Lincoln's heavy arm tightened around her waist. "Come on, Kara. Let's go."

Yeah, definitely they had to go. If she stayed here too much longer she'd lose her nerve and that wasn't the point of the evening. The point of the evening was to grab back some freaking independence. Put some distance between her and Vincent Fox.

Kara slipped off the bar stool, reaching for Lincoln's hand and threading her fingers through it. He grinned at her in the darkness of the club, the bass of the music so heavy she could feel the beat in her chest. He was a good looking guy. Really good looking.

But he's not Vin.

Like her brain hadn't told her that fifty million times already. Bah. She didn't want Vin. Not tonight.

Turning, Kara began to lead Lincoln through the dancers, heading for the exit.

In the corridor outside, he pulled her back into his arms, one arm around her waist, holding her close. The move was unexpected but she went with it, trying to relax her tight muscles, tipping her head back to meet his gaze. He grinned and leaned down for a kiss, his mouth brushing over hers.

But there were no sparks. No fizz of desire. Nothing.

Shit. Shit. Shit.

His arms tightened, his mouth becoming more demanding. And Kara felt...uncomfortable. Like she couldn't breathe. She pushed against his chest and to give the guy credit, he lifted his head, loosening his arms and frowning. "What's up?"

Kara struggled to get a breath, the unease closing like a fist around her ribs. "Uh...nothing. I just...needed some air."

"You still good to go, baby?"

"Don't—" *Don't call me baby. Only Vin gets to call me baby.*

"Don't what?"

"Nothing." Christ, why couldn't she breathe? Why did she feel as though she had to get away? Like she had with every other guy she'd ever initiated things with.

Every guy except...

"Hey, if you're not—"

"I am." Kara reached for his hand again, tugging him with her as she began to head up the corridor toward the exit. She *was* going to do this. She had to. Otherwise what she'd be left with was dressing up as a slave every night for Vin Fox. Reliant only on him for her sexual pleasure. Which was crazy and so not happening. Relying on anyone for anything was so not happening.

Outside the footpath was full of people waiting to get into the club, or leaving it. Music thumped. People yelled at each other. Teenagers moved in packs catcalling and stumbling over each other.

A strange kind of fear began to replace her unease. The usual fear. Of going back to this complete stranger's house and getting naked with him. Of stripping herself bare. Being exposed. Vulnerable.

She swallowed, gripping his hand. Then she turned round suddenly, facing him. "When we get back to your place, I want you to take control. Okay?"

He frowned. "Take control? What?"

She could feel herself beginning to blush. Oh Jesus, she should never have said anything. And yet there was only one way she knew of that gave her some measure of protection for herself—being someone else. Being the slave. "I want you to call the shots in the bedroom. Like I'm your..." She stopped, unable to say the S word.

Lincoln apparently didn't need to hear it because he gave a disbelieving laugh and said, "You're kinky? No, scratch that." He gave her a quick once over, clearly taking in the skintight black mini dress, fishnets and combat boots ensemble. "Of course you're kinky."

Painful embarrassment flooded through her. Was the master/slave thing a kink? She supposed it was. There wasn't anything normal about it. People might have a role-play thing going on in their sex life, but it wasn't usually the only way they could have sex.

Trying not to let her embarrassment show, she lifted her chin instead. "Kinky or not, you're seriously turning down the chance to order me around when you get me home?"

His grin turned into something that was probably meant to

be suggestive, except she didn't find it anything but predatory. "Shit no. If you're into that, I'm more than happy to help."

You're actually going to go home with this guy? Strip naked in front of him? Give him all the control? Like you do with Vin?

Instinctive denial shot through her but she ignored it. She had to ignore it. This had become a battle. A battle she wouldn't let her need for Vin Fox win. "Come on then," she said decisively. "Have you got a car?"

"Sure. This way."

But they hadn't gone more than a couple of meters along the sidewalk when a prickling sensation crept over the back of Kara's neck. She turned her head and the breath squeezed tight in her chest.

Beneath a streetlight, leaning back against a familiar red Corvette, was Vin.

She stopped, frozen to the spot as their eyes met. And locked.

What the hell was he doing here? Her heartbeat began to race, adrenaline singing like a choir in her bloodstream. There it was. The fizz, the spark. The dizzying rush of desire. All the missing pieces of the puzzle that if the world had any justice, should have been there with the man she'd wanted to go home with tonight.

But they weren't.

"What are you doing, Kara?" Vin didn't move, leaning against the car with his arms folded, relaxed almost. But he wasn't relaxed. The ferocity of his gaze and the leashed energy in his posture told her he was angry. Very, very angry.

Her own anger flared. "I could ask you the same thing."

"Why do you think I'm here? I was looking for you."

"Well, now you've found me. What the hell do you want?"

"Kara?" Lincoln had begun walking back down the

pavement toward her. "What's going on?"

Vin's gaze flicked to the other man then back to her. And her breath caught. He knew. He knew what she'd been going with Lincoln to do.

Something ignited inside her. Part anger, part fear, part excitement. She held his gaze, determined not to look away. Determined to let him see the boundary she was putting between them. That in the bedroom she may be his slave but she wasn't out of it.

"Hey," Lincoln said as he came closer. "Who's this guy?"

Kara opened her mouth to say no one in particular but Vin cut across her. "She's mine," he said with complete and absolute authority. As if stating an incontrovertible fact.

The words died in her throat unsaid. He'd claimed her in the privacy of her apartment but out here, in front of someone else, it was a whole other story. No one had ever said she was theirs, not publicly. She'd never belonged to anyone.

"Hey, she's not yours, mate," Lincoln said. "She's got a mind of her own."

Slowly, Vin pushed himself away from the Corvette. "She's mine," he repeated in the same hard voice. "And she's coming with me." He didn't come any closer but then he didn't need to. A cold anger radiated from him, leashed violence in every line of his body. "Get in the car, Kara."

She didn't want to get into the stupid, freaking car. She couldn't let him and her own ridiculous desire win this. But the word no seemed to have vanished from her vocabulary the instant he'd said *she's mine*.

Lincoln looked at her and the expression on her face must have given her away because he said, "Kara, if he's bothering you, I can—"

"He's not bothering me," she managed to get out. "And I'm sorry." Because she knew, she fucking knew with every single cell of her being, that she couldn't go home with Lincoln. Couldn't take her clothes off in front of him. Couldn't have sex with him. Because at the sound of Vin's voice something inside her had gone quiet and still. Like prey going limp in the jaws of a predator, knowing it was caught. That fighting was useless.

Lincoln frowned. "You're not going home with me then?"

"No," Vin said. "She's not. Now get in the car, baby."

And she found herself turning and moving toward the Corvette, not looking at Lincoln. Drawn by the other man standing beneath the streetlight.

Vin opened the car door for her, standing aside as she got in, and soon as the door closed behind her, the unease vanished and relief flooded through her veins like a tide. She fought it, tried to hold onto the anger instead. Because, God, she'd gone ahead and meekly obeyed him without even an argument. What the hell was wrong with her?

The driver's side door slammed shut, the interior of the car filling up with Vin's intense, electric presence. She could almost taste the anger in the air between them, like sparks from a firework.

"What the hell, Vin?" she demanded. "Giving up construction and trying stalking instead?"

He put his hands on the steering wheel, his knuckles white. "You were going to go have sex with that bastard, weren't you?"

"What? Lincoln? Yeah, as a matter of fact I was." She threw the words at him like stones. A challenge. Part of her wanting to see what he would do, how far he would go.

Slowly, he turned to look at her. His blue eyes were almost black. "No." The denial was flat, hard. "I don't want you sleeping with anyone else but me."

"Like you get a say. I'm not your girlfriend. I can sleep with whoever the hell I want."

He stared at her and it felt like he was peeling back the layers of her anger, opening them up to the core of aching vulnerability that was at the heart of her. She swallowed, her heart racing, wanting to run, get away from him.

"Go on then," he said. "If that's what you really want, do it."

It was like he'd pulled the ground out from under her feet. She'd been expecting him to get all possessive and forceful, and part of her was longing for it, craved it like a woman living in the dark craves a small taste of sunlight. And he *was* being forceful in that he was forcing her to make a choice. A choice she didn't want to have to make.

Don't you want me after all? Don't you want to fight for me?

Her lips clamped shut on the words. No, she wouldn't say that. Wouldn't be so pathetic. "I'm not your girlfriend," she repeated instead.

"No. You're my slave."

The breath caught in her throat. "Not outside the bedroom, Vincent."

"So is that what that prick was for?" He gestured out the window to where Lincoln had been standing. "A show of independence? A punishment for crossing the line this morning?" There was lightning in that dark gaze of his. Jagged lightning. "Get this straight, Kara. While you're sleeping with me you're no one else's but mine, so if you want to play games and screw around, you'd better find someone else to play them with."

She found she was shaking. Jesus, what was the matter with her? "What does it matter to you what I do? Why should you even care?"

"Like I told you, you're mine. Not his. Not any other bastard's. You're mine and I'm not sharing you."

"So why did you tell me to go just now?"

111

"Why did you tell me no tonight?"

She blinked, anger tangling up inside her, knotting with the relief and the weird thrill his possessiveness sent straight down her spine. And the truth spilled out of her before she could stop it. "Because I needed some goddamn distance, Vin. And because you needed to hear the word no."

"You can tell me no anytime."

"Oh sure, and you won't track me down and stand under a streetlight beating your chest and marking your freaking territory."

He didn't look away, didn't flinch. "It's why I'm telling you to go if you want to. You always have a choice with me, Kara."

"Yeah, well what if I don't want to have to make a choice? What if I want someone else to make it for me?"

"You wanted that guy to make it for you?"

"Sure, why not?" She tried to sound defiant, ignoring the hollow sound of the words.

"Then why are you still sitting in the car with me?"

Oh shit. Of course Vin would realize. And know what it meant too. Her defiance was a sham. A façade. Because she wasn't going to get out, wasn't going to go chasing off down the sidewalk after Lincoln. She wasn't going anywhere.

She couldn't. There was only one man she'd ever give control over her choices and that man was in the car next to her. She trusted him in a way she'd never trusted anyone else.

The thought scared her and she looked away so he wouldn't see the fear, out the window to where the crowds around the nightclub heaved, people calling out and screaming, laughter and shouting.

Until Vin's strong fingers took her jaw in his hand and forced her head round so she met his steel blue eyes. "No other men," he ordered, his voice hard. "Not while you're sleeping with me."

She wanted to jerk her chin out of his hands, wanted to pull away, but his fingers were warm on her skin and she couldn't control her shiver of reaction. "Yes," she said hoarsely, unable to give him any other answer because, shit, there wasn't any other answer she could give. With another man she'd have to be Kara, and she couldn't be Kara. The slave was what she had to be and there wasn't anyone else she trusted enough to be that with. "But the same goes for you. No other women."

His thumb moved on her jaw, a stroke that set every nerve ending she had alight. "Possessive, baby girl?"

She met that gaze. Held it. "Fair, asshole."

That jagged lightning flashed in his eyes, the anger she'd sensed in him still there. Still just beneath the surface. But the thumb that caressed her was gentle and the contrast made her nearly tremble. "I'm always fair. You know that."

Of course she did. Yet she wasn't going to give in so easily. "Say it."

He didn't hesitate. "I would never screw around on you," he said in the same, flat, hard voice. "Why would I? When I have everything I need right here."

Oh, bugger him. Sometimes he said stuff that made her want to punch him and sometimes he said stuff that undid her completely. Her eyes felt dry and tight. Like they were going to fill with tears. But of course they wouldn't because crying wasn't something she was able to do anymore.

So instead she blurted out the words she'd never meant to say. "Why did you find me?" Her voice had gone husky. "Because if you're into slave kink, you could have gone to one of those clubs. You don't need me."

Silence fell in the car. And she wished she hadn't said anything, revealed so much.

But he didn't take his hand away, his thumb keeping on

with that maddening caress. "I'm not into slave kink. That only works with you."

"Why?"

"I don't know," Vin said, the rough edge to his voice pronounced. "Probably because you're so fucking oppositional all the time and having you do what I say for just one goddamned minute is such a relief." Then his gaze slowly lowered to her mouth and that maddening thumb moved to trace the outline of her lower lip. "But mostly because apart from this Corvette, you're the only thing I have that's mine."

The dry, scratchy feeling behind her eyes intensified. God, she was so pathetic how that got her off. How desired it made her feel. Wanted and, Jesus Christ, safe. It had been so damn long since she'd felt safe...

"Vin," she began, wanting to pull away, the old need to protect herself kicking in.

But his fingers tightened on her jaw, holding her still. "No. You don't want to have to make any choices? Then put on your seatbelt, baby, because tonight you won't have to make any."

The apartment door shut behind them and Kara turned to shrug off the bag she wore on her shoulders, dumping it on the hallway floor. His hands itched to grab her, pull her close but he kept them by his sides. That would be giving her what she wanted right away and he wasn't going to give her what she wanted, not right away. Not after tonight.

A cold, clear anger burned in his blood. He'd never been a possessive sort of guy—protective, hell yeah, he'd kill for those he loved—but the sight of Kara going off with that prick at the club had ignited a jealousy he hadn't realized was in him.

Shit, during the day she could do what she liked, but going off with other men while they had this thing going on between them? No fucking way. She *was* his. And maybe he shouldn't have revealed so much by telling her what that meant to him but part of him wanted her to know. So she'd understand it was important to him. That he didn't consider what was happening between them something he could get anywhere else. And because, he'd sensed, she'd needed to hear it.

But he also needed something for himself. And tonight he was going to get it. Tonight he was going to show her how completely his she was. Make her feel it. Make them both feel it. So she didn't go off with some other fucker again.

Kara didn't speak, just tipped her head back and looked up at him. Her hair was pink and blue striped today, glittering piercings in her eyebrow and nose. She wore a tight black dress, ripped tights and combat boots. An aggressive look to match the purple contacts she wore in her eyes.

He didn't wait, got straight to the point. "Get naked. But don't put on the slave collar yet."

Uncertainty flickered in her eyes. "I'm not doing this without the collar."

"Didn't I tell you that you didn't get a choice tonight?"

Her beautiful mouth opened, the uncertainty deepening on her face. But he held her gaze, daring her.

"Vin—" she began.

"You think I'd ever hurt you, slave? Is that what you think?"

Her throat moved. "I... No."

"No," he echoed softly. "So I gave you an instruction. Now go do it."

Her gaze slid away from his, dark, mascaraed lashes fluttering down. She was still and he found he'd curled his fingers into fists at his sides.

Give this to me, Kara. Please.

A couple of seconds passed. Then she turned and went down the hallway to her bedroom without a word.

Thank fuck. Relief caught him by the throat, a thrill of primitive satisfaction pulsing down his spine.

He hadn't realized how much her willing submission had meant to him until now. Until he'd seen her nearly walk off with some other man. He'd said she didn't have a choice but that was a lie. She always had a choice because he'd never force her into this if she didn't want it. And that made him as vulnerable to her as she was to him.

Vin leaned back against the wall, ran a hand through his hair, his heartbeat already accelerated, the vicious twist of desire coiling like a snake in his gut.

Distance. She'd wanted distance. And shit, she was probably right. He probably could have done with a bit of distance himself. Except...he didn't want distance. He wanted her. On her knees in front of him. Doing whatever he told her to do. Completely his...

Christ, this was fucked up.

The bedroom door shut and Kara came back down the hallway. She'd taken off her tight black dress, ripped stockings, and platform boots. Now she was as he liked to her be—naked. All soft, feminine curves and golden skin, long pink-and-blue striped hair with its blonde roots in a candy-colored shower over her shoulders.

Lust punched him hard in the gut. He loved that contrast to her. All her hard edges and sharp angles stripped away to reveal such incredible softness. Full breasts. Exquisitely curved hips and thighs. Graceful waist. He couldn't even remember now why he'd wanted all those fit, muscled women when there was Kara. Kara who only ever revealed this side of herself to him.

He pushed himself away from the wall as she came closer,

the slave collar held loosely in her hands. Then she stopped right in front of him, purple eyes wide. Uncertainty still lurked in them, the pulse at the base of her throat beating hard.

He knew why she was worried. Why she wanted the collar. It was the same reason he wanted her to wear it: so they didn't have to be themselves. So he could be the master instead of a man with a mother who was sick. Who had a business he had to work his butt off to keep going. A man constantly working to keep the shit life kept piling on top of him off his back.

But now he wasn't that man any longer. With Kara he could be the master, the man in complete and utter control. Whose only worry was the pleasure he'd take from his slave girl.

"Give me the collar," he ordered and held out his hand.

She didn't look away. Maintained eye contract as she handed him the cheap piece of faux leather, daring him in the same way as he'd dared her in the car. And he knew why—he was changing the rules and she didn't like it. But that was too bad. Tonight he didn't want her challenging him. What he wanted was her complete obedience. Her acknowledgement that she was his to possess in any way he wanted.

He closed his fingers around the collar. "You're defiant, slave," he murmured. "I'm not sure I like it."

A spark glowed in her eyes for a second. But then her lashes came down, her gaze averted. "I'm sorry," she murmured in a thick voice.

"I'm sorry what?"

"I'm sorry...master."

"That's better. You're already up for one lesson tonight, baby. You don't want to make it any worse. Now turn around."

She did so without hesitation, her back to him.

Gently he pushed the striped fall of her hair over one bare shoulder then looped the collar around her neck. And as he began to do up the buckle, he leaned forward so his mouth was near her ear. "Remember this, slave," he murmured. "This collar is a reminder of who you belong to." He pulled the buckle tight. "Me."

In the silence of the hallway he heard Kara's breath catch. "You like that?" He put a hand on the back of her neck, ran it down the elegant curve of her spine in a long possessive stroke, feeling her shiver beneath his palm. "You like belonging to me?"

"Y-yes." Her voice was a hoarse whisper.

Vin slid an arm around her waist, bringing her hard up against him. The softness of her butt pressing against his groin was like petrol thrown on an open fire, desire flaring inside him, his cock already pushing against the zip of his jeans. The soft warmth of her body and the scent of her was skin was like a drug he didn't even know he'd been craving.

"You stuttered, slave," he said softly, brushing his mouth over the vulnerable skin of her neck. "Tell me again how much you like belonging to me."

Another shiver went through her and she tilted her head slightly, exposing more of the bare curve of her neck in blatant invitation. "I like it."

"Like what?" He didn't kiss her again, keeping one arm tight around her waist. But he moved his other hand, spreading his fingers on her stomach so that the tip of his middle finger almost brushed the curls between her thighs. "Say it for me. Say it to your master."

"I like..." She took a ragged sounding breath. "Having you make the decisions."

He let his fingers curve lower, gently brushing her curls, feeling the tremble that went through her go through him as well. He wanted this. Had to have it. Her acknowledgement. Her choice. "And who do you belong to?"

Her head fell back against his shoulder, her body arching,

pushing against his hand. "You, master," she said thickly. "I belong to you."

Satisfaction uncoiled inside him, a primitive feeling that would have felt wrong in any other context. It quieted something in him. The part of him that was always fighting, always watchful, always vigilant. It let him rest.

This moment was his and only his. And so was she.

Vin tightened his arm around her, his palm flat to her stomach, applying pressure to keep her butt hard against his groin. "Yeah," he said roughly. "You do. Because I'm the only one who can give you what you want. What you need. I'm the only one who knows you, slave. And don't you ever forget that."

Kara couldn't breathe. But it didn't have anything to do with the collar around her neck. Every sense she had was focused on the hot palm that rested on her stomach. On the fingers that pushed through the curls between her thighs and stopped just short of where she desperately wanted them to go. If she didn't breathe then perhaps he'd move those fingers down just a little bit more.

She was held tight against him, all that hard, hot male power a wall at her back. The brief spark of anger she'd felt when he'd told her not to put the collar on yet had gone, vanished beneath the weight of her need. The sheer relief of being here with him and knowing she didn't have to fight. Didn't have to do anything but let him do whatever he wanted.

I'm the only one who knows you...

Fear twisted inside her, a reflexive fear, pushing through the wall she'd erected between herself and the slave. But it was gone before it had a chance to settle. A slave didn't have to be afraid of being known by her master because there was no rejection here.

No, there was only ownership. Belonging. And it was such a

relief. She didn't have to hide. Or fight. Didn't need to defend herself. She only had to be.

This was about more than not having to make choices so she could have sex. This was about giving her absolute trust to another person and feeling safe to do so. She couldn't allow herself to do it as Kara just yet, but she could do it as the slave.

Because the slave had nothing to lose.

Kara closed her eyes as his fingers twisted in her curls, tugging gently, and she shifted, restless and aching. She wanted more than gentleness. God, she wanted to feel owned. Possessed. "Please..." she said hoarsely. "Please, master. I need..."

"Stop it." His voice was a growl in her ear. "You were going to do this with another man tonight which means you don't get to ask for anything." The heel of his hand slid down a little more, stopping just above her aching clit, pressing down.

She shuddered. God, he'd barely even started touching her and already she was shaking, her body coiled and tight with desire. The combination of his arm holding her, the heat of his body at her back and the hot, spicy scent that was all Vin was an overwhelming mix. "I know," she forced out. "I'm sorry, master. I'm sorry."

"I've already had your apology. It's now time for your punishment."

The word popped like an exploding light bulb in her brain. *Punishment.* She went utterly still, an old familiar feeling crawling through her. Would he...hurt her?

You want him to.

A kind of desperate anticipation caught in her chest but she ignored it. Shoved it away. No, that wasn't what she wanted here. She was over that now.

"What punishment?"

"You don't get to ask that either." He released her suddenly and far, far too soon.

She began to turn, only to be stopped by his hand on the back of her neck, a heavy, sure, dominant grip. "No. Go into the lounge."

His hand dropped away and instinctively she moved forward through the doorway ahead of her into her little lounge.

"Stop," Vin ordered from behind her, a darkness in his voice that made her breath catch and her heart race.

She obeyed without thought. Without hesitation.

"On your hands and knees. Stay like that."

Again she obeyed, sinking down onto the multicolored rug. She stared at the bright threads beneath her, struggling to breathe, every sense focused on the man standing behind her. Shaky excitement and the lazy heat of desire tangling around one another at the thought of what he would do next. What he would say.

A footstep behind her and she wanted to turn to look at him but somehow she knew that wouldn't be allowed so she stared hard at the floor instead. She seemed to be sensitive to everything, from the corrugations of the rug under her palms and knees, to the faint breeze from some open window across her bare skin, to the ache between her thighs.

No more sound came. No touch. Was he still even there? Had he gone? Was this going to be her punishment? Left naked, on her hands and knees, shaking with need?

The moment drew out, the silence deepening.

Kara's breathing became ragged. If he'd gone she didn't know what she'd do. But she wasn't bloody going to check if he was there. If this was a test then she would pass it.

A hand settled suddenly on the curve of one buttock, stroking. The heat and the abruptness of the touch made her gasp, the sound harsh in the silence of the room.

He hadn't gone. He was still there.

"I like you waiting for me," he said softly. "I like you on your hands and knees shaking for me." That stroking hand slid down to the back of her thigh then up again and she trembled, unable to help herself, a wave of heat prickling all over her skin. Everywhere.

"Yes," he murmured approvingly. "Now show me how much a good slave wants to belong to her master. And make me believe it."

She didn't even think about disobeying. The reflexive fear of rejection had utterly gone because the only thing in her mind was to show him exactly that. She wanted to belong to him with everything in her. For this moment in time there was no one else. No other way to exist but to be his.

Kara crossed her arms on the floor in front of her, pillowing her head on them, widening her stance. Allowing herself to be as open and as accessible as she could.

Please take me. Please. I'm yours. Oh God, please...

She heard the hiss of his breath behind her, the catch that told her just what the sight of her did to him. And then there was his hand stroking her thigh, her hip, the small of her back, the roundness of her butt.

"Good," Vin said thickly. "That's what I want. You open and ready for me." His hand slid between her thighs, tracing lightly over slick flesh. She shuddered, pressing her forehead hard against her folded arms, a whimper escaping her.

His hand settled on her hip, fingers curving around, holding her still. Then he slid a finger into her. She groaned, trembling. Pleasure spiked. She tried to push back against his hand because, fuck it, he wasn't moving and she so desperately wanted him to move or to move against him. But the fingers at her hip only curled tighter.

"Keep still." Vin's voice had deepened into a growl. "This is your punishment, slave. You take what I give you, take all of it." The finger inside her eased out slowly, then just as slowly, back in. "Without moving or making a sound." The hand on her hip slid around and over her stomach and down, fingers grazing her swollen clit, sending sparks along her nerve endings. "And maybe, I'll let you come."

He couldn't be serious. How could she do that? When every move of that teasing finger made her want to moan, cry out. Shake apart.

She wanted to protest but more than that she wanted to prove she could take whatever he had to give her. Be a good slave. So she closed her eyes and clamped her mouth shut as the finger inside her moved in a slow, sensual rhythm. As the fingers of his other hand circled her clit lightly. The barest of pressures.

Keeping still was difficult. Stifling the sounds he brought from her agony. The pleasure built and built, inexorable, a force of nature that couldn't be stopped or contained. Her body shook like the ground underneath her was moving, the blackness behind her eyes leaping with bursts of color. And when he added another finger, delicately stretching her, she thought she would break apart.

"Good, baby. Yeah that's good." Vin's voice was ragged and breathless, and beneath the agonizing pleasure, she felt a kind of deep satisfaction. Because this was what he wanted too. This was for both of them. And by taking it, by being owned by him, he was giving her a little piece of himself in return.

Kara opened her mouth against her arm, biting down as a moan threatened to tear free, determined not to break. But the sharp edge of pain, familiar and bright was too intense, too perfect, and she'd never allowed herself a release like that so she had to be satisfied with clenching her jaw instead. Which didn't help.

"Fuck," Vin said hoarsely, moving his hand a little faster, a little harder. "Can you feel how wet you are? You want me so badly, don't you, slave?"

The spiraling pleasure had become sweet agony. He gave her only so much and no more, not enough to release the intense pressure that increased second by second.

And just when she thought she couldn't take any more, he removed his hands from her, leaving her body teetering on the brink, screaming. She nearly moved. Nearly cried out. Because abandoning her like this was one punishment she couldn't take.

But then he rested a hand in the small of her back, a reassurance that he hadn't gone. A gentle touch. Yet the words he said weren't gentle.

"Beg me, slave." The dark authority in his voice was rough with hunger. "Beg me to fuck you. Beg me to make you come."

The words rushed out of her, heedless, falling over themselves now he'd given her permission. Raw and broken and desperate. "Please, master. Fuck me, master. Please, make me come. Please...oh...please....master..." She ran out of breath, drew in more in a ragged burst. "I need it...I want it...please... God, please..."

He didn't say anything but she felt him shift behind her, the sound of a zipper being drawn down. The rustle of foil as he got a condom out. Then his large, warm hands were gripping her hips and the heat of his body against the backs of her thighs, and the blunt head of his cock pushing slowly into her.

She bit her lip to stop from crying out, because he hadn't given her permission yet, but she bit it too hard and the bright burst of pain made the whole world explode. A dry sob tore from her throat, the orgasm crashing over her with all the weight of a concrete block dropping from a great height, flattening her. All she could do was press her forehead against her folded arms, her eyes screwed shut, feeling herself torn apart as he slid deep inside her.

Quaking, she felt him pause, lean over her, the heat of his body searing against her spine. "I didn't tell you that you could come yet," he growled in her ear.

"I'm sorry," she gasped, shivering and unable to stop. "I'm sorry, master. I'm sorry. I'm sorry." And the words kept coming, over and over as he began to move again, harder and faster, driving her toward another impossible climax.

She couldn't do it a second time. She couldn't bear it. But he slid a hand between her thighs, stroking her, forcing her to begin the climb again, his voice in her ear dark and rough, whispering all the dirty things he was going to do her. Punish her with. And, God help her, her body gathered tight with a second orgasm and when it took her she couldn't stop the scream that burst from her throat.

Behind her, Vin thrust deep and hard then stiffened, his harsh groan in ear, his breath rough against the back of her neck. Then his whole body seemed to surround her, his hands coming down on the floor on either side of her pillowed head, the heat of his body pressing against her back. "You're mine," he said, the words so rough they were almost unrecognizable. "Understand? Mine."

He'd said it before. Said it many times. Yet now, surrounded by him, this was the first moment she'd felt it. In her flesh, in her bones, and deeper. In her heart. In her soul.

Owned. Possessed. Sheltered. Protected.

And she wanted it to last forever.

Perhaps later she'd change her mind. Later, the guards would come up and she'd think what a pathetic mess she was that she needed a man's ownership. But it wasn't later. It was now. And now was all she wanted.

Now was the whole of her existence.

He remained like that for a long time, the searing heat of his chest and stomach pressed to her curved spine. And when he at last pulled away she wasn't ready. Almost told him not to go. But like she'd stayed silent in pleasure, she stayed silent now, locking her jaw against the words.

She felt him move, withdrawing from her, the loss of his warmth nearly painful. But she stayed silent. Stayed where she was.

Behind her came the rustle of clothing, the sound of his zipper. A silence then his footsteps receding. Leaving as he always did without a word.

As the door shut, her body began to tremble and shake, a weird rush of emotion surging through her. A release of some kind, though she wasn't sure what from or why she was experiencing it.

But she knew that the moment had moved on.

That now had become later. And just for a second she hated it.

Chapter Eight

Vin stopped outside the apartment he'd just viewed, cursing under his breath. It wasn't right. None of it was right. The whole apartment block was seedy and run down, the kind of place alcoholics went to drink themselves to death. Yet he didn't have a lot of choice. The halfway house his mother usually went to had closed down due to lack of funding and this apartment was the closest he could get to the Fox Chase offices. And it had to be close. One of the benefits of the halfway house had been a manager who kept an eye on the residents. And the manager of that particular house had always kept an eye on Lillian. Making sure she wasn't drinking, that she kept taking her meds, that the other residents weren't hassling her or encouraging her drinking. Which had helped and had the added bonus of giving him one less thing to do.

But not now. Now that had to be his job.

Jesus, he just couldn't even get just one fucking break.

He stared at the dingy, stained wallpaper of the hallway and the seething frustration and rage that always seemed to be just below the surface these days threatened to break free. He wanted to kick the wall. Kick a hole straight through it. Kick away the chains of responsibility that bound him, tied him down. Constricted him. Claw his way out of the suffocating mass of everything he had to do for other people. Be free just for one goddamned minute.

Vin closed his eyes, trying to breathe around the thick ball of emotion that sat in his chest, his hands closing convulsively into fists. He had to do something, get rid of this feeling somehow because he had a meeting in a couple of hours with the bank—some trouble with his loan application—and if he went to that meeting in this kind of mood, it was going to be all bad.

Christ, it was just one battle after another. His mother, his business, Ellie. And even after Ellie was in Tokyo, it wouldn't let up because no one else was responsible for his mother but him. And she wouldn't ever get better. Wouldn't ever recover. He would have to deal with hospitals and the crappy mental health system for the rest of her life, no matter how long that would be.

His jaw tightened against the rage that caught in his throat. Getting angry and frustrated was pointless, a waste of emotion. And yet still the emotions filled him, making him restless and aching and tight. Sometimes when he felt like this, thinking of Ellie helped gain some perspective and helped him remember who he was doing all this for.

Yet it wasn't Ellie his brain went automatically to now.

Kara, on her hands and knees in front of him, her body trembling. Waiting for him. Ready to do whatever he wanted. Whatever he said.

Who do you belong to?

You, master. I belong to you...

Since that night he'd picked her up at the club, she hadn't refused to see him again. Every night he went to her and every night she was there, waiting naked in her hallway, the slave collar in her hands to give to him. Ready to cede control. There was no more talk about boundaries or discussions about what they were doing. There were no discussions at all. They didn't need to talk. What they got out of those hours together went deeper than words, deeper than sex, and he'd come to crave it. Need it.

A few hours when he wasn't fighting anyone. When the

world operated according to his rules and his desires. When there was a person who was there for him. Who would give him the escape he needed without question. Without argument.

He'd turned from the shitty hallway before he was even conscious of doing so, making his way back to his car. Then he drove fast because he didn't have long—an hour at most if he wanted to make this meeting with the bank on time.

When he pushed open the door of the café, she was there, standing behind the counter dealing with a queue of people. It was the middle of the day so it must have been the lunchtime rush. She raised her head as he came in, blue-and-pink hair held back from her head with a black Alice band, her eyes a bright turquoise. She wore a little mini dress made out of some kind of purple stretchy material that molded to her generous curves, outlining them perfectly and all he could think about was ripping that dress in half. Tearing it off her the way he wanted to tear off the wallpaper in that hallway. Pushing her against a wall and drowning himself in her. Drowning the rage and the frustration in heat and softness.

Fuck, he needed this. Needed her. And he hadn't realized how much until now.

A crease appeared between her brows, a crease that got deeper as he ignored the queue of people standing waiting to order and went straight to the head of the line.

"Vin," Kara hissed. "What the hell are you doing? If you want coffee, you'll have to wait your bloody turn."

He'd taken to coming in every morning to get himself an espresso—purely because she made such good coffee, or so he told himself. She never gave him an espresso though, only a latte. It was a small power-play but one he kind of enjoyed. Except not now. Now he wanted obedience.

He put his hands on the counter, ignoring the filthy looks directed his way from the people in the queue. "I want you," he said flatly. "Now."

She blinked in surprise. "What? What do you mean now?"

"What do you think I mean? You really want me to explain?"

Her mouth opened then shut again. She glanced at the queue then back to him. "Tonight." She spoke quietly. "You'll have to wait."

"I can't wait. It has to be now."

"Do you not see my lunchtime crowd?"

"I don't give a shit about your lunchtime crowd. I need you."

An expression flickered in her gaze, one he couldn't interpret. The smart comeback he was almost expecting didn't eventuate. Instead she let out a breath, looking once more at her customers. "Yeah and so does my café."

She was going to say no, he could almost see the word forming on her luscious mouth. And if she said no... The rage shifted inside him, frustration burning a hole in his chest. He didn't want to have to explain his need or justify it or fight for it because shit, he was so goddamned tired of fighting.

So he leaned over the counter even farther, holding her gaze. "Please, Kara." He didn't often say please because he hated conceding power to other people. And yet she held the balance between them. Her permission was always necessary for what they did and if she didn't give him permission, he was screwed. And not—unfortunately—literally.

She went very still, staring at him as if he'd said something completely shocking. "Vin—"

"Please," he repeated. So she understood. "I need this. I need you."

Once again her expression changed, something in her eyes softening in a way that made him feel as if a weight pressed hard against his chest. "Back at my apartment?"

"Yeah."

"How...long?"

"An hour max." Behind him people were starting to get restless, muttering. He ignored them, watching her instead. He always seemed to be at this point with her. For all the power he had in the bedroom, she was the one who seemed to have so much outside it.

She put down the metal jug she'd been holding. "Well, okay. Give me five minutes to sort out cover."

Relief swept through him and he had to struggle not to let it show. "The car's in the street. Meet me there."

It took longer than five minutes though and by the end of it he was nearly climbing the walls. But just when he'd come to the end of his meager stock of patience, she came striding out through the doors, heading straight for the Corvette without hesitation.

"What's up?" she asked as she got in, closing the door behind her. "I thought you preferred evenings?"

"Not today."

She frowned. "And today...?"

"I thought we didn't talk," he said flatly. "Or have you changed your mind?"

Kara was silent a moment. Then she looked away. "No. Forget I said anything."

The car journey was silent, tension taut between them. Almost as if she could sense the desperation coming off him and was pulling subtly away. If so he couldn't blame her. Because he did feel desperate, hungry for what he wanted. The violence of it disturbed him. The past couple of times he'd felt so cool and calm, in control. And yet now... He felt like he was crawling out of his skin with need.

He didn't understand why it should be so bad now. He'd had setbacks with his mother before, this wasn't any different.

But you've never had anyone you could go to before.

No, he hadn't. Not like this. Before, he'd work on the Corvette. Or his house out at Piha, or go out to the pub with Hunter. But now he didn't want the slow careful work of putting something together or even the laidback dude chat he had with his friend. He needed something more. An escape. Pleasure. Control. And Kara was all of those things.

As he pulled up out front of her building and stopped the car, he made himself pause before he got out. Made himself ask. "You sure you're okay with this?"

Kara undid her seatbelt. "I wouldn't be sitting here now if I wasn't."

"I'm not..." He stopped, not wanting to alarm her and yet wanting to give her some kind of warning. "All you need to say is stop, remember?"

"Yeah, I remember." She gave him a sidelong glance. "Why?"

He met her gaze so she could see what was in his. "Because I'm not in a gentle mood."

A flash of something showed in her face and he didn't think it was fear. "Who says I need gentle?"

"You were a virgin, Kara."

"So? That doesn't mean I'm an idiot."

"I just don't want to scare you."

"Says the man who put me on my hands and knees and told me he owned me."

He scowled. "I'm trying to do the right thing here, baby. I don't want to end up hurting you."

Kara looked down at her hands. "You won't. But maybe I'd..." She stopped.

"Maybe you'd what?"

She turned, put her hand on the door handle. "Nothing."

"Bullshit. What were you going to say?"

"It's nothing, okay? Come on, you said you only had an hour." Without waiting for him to reply, Kara opened the door and got out.

Vin glared at her as she slammed the door. What the hell had she been going to say? It felt important somehow. But no, they never talked. They never needed to so why start now? Besides, he only had an hour before this thing with the bank and he wasn't going to waste it.

Getting out of the car, Vin then locked it and followed Kara up to her apartment.

She held the door open for him, let it shut as he came into her narrow little hallway. And as soon as the heavy sound of it closing echoed, the familiar, biting tension tightened between them. The anticipation of what was to come.

Kara dropped her bag onto the floor, her lashes lowering, not looking at him. Already going into slave mode. Normally it made him calmer, made him feel more in control. But not today. Rage burned in his blood, frustration eating away at him, and her submission only made him even more aware of just how thin his control was. His mouth had gone dry, his heartbeat loud in his head and something inside him was shaking the bars of its cage, wanting to be free.

Shit. He'd always been strong. Never let his anger out. He couldn't afford to, not with Ellie and Lillian to watch out for. And now there was Kara... What the hell was he thinking coming to her like this? This wasn't the master in control, calmly directing his slave. This was just him, panting like a fucking dog.

Clearly sensing his hesitation, Kara's lashes rose, turquoise eyes meeting his. And he had the impression she could see exactly what he was struggling with. A weird vulnerability wound through him, a sensation he hardly ever felt. It only made him angrier.

"Eyes on the floor, slave," he ordered roughly. "I didn't say you could look at me."

Instantly her too-sharp gaze fell. But then she said, "Please master, let your slave girl help you."

So, it was obvious then. He guessed it was. Christ, he couldn't do this. Not when he was this close to the edge, this wild. He didn't trust himself, could feel the violence of all his pent-up emotion like a storm inside him. Waiting to be unleashed. On her. And that wasn't right.

"I changed my mind." His voice was unsteady. "I'll take you back to the café."

Kara had gone very still, her attention on the ground. "Why?" The word sounded like a demand with none of her usual slave-deference, but he didn't bother to correct her.

"I'm angry," he admitted shortly, hating that he had to. "Too angry for this right now."

"So?" She still didn't look at him, her posture all deference and yet her voice nothing but demand. "I don't care if you're angry."

Vin raised a hand to shove his fingers through his hair. Then realized his hand was shaking. Fuck. What was wrong with him? "You should care," he snapped. "I could hurt you."

For a long moment she just stood there, staring at the floor. Then suddenly she dropped to her knees in front of him. "I'm your slave," she said in a low voice. "I trust you, master. You wouldn't hurt me."

His breath caught. The material of her stretchy dress had pulled tight over her thighs and he couldn't take his eyes off the hem. He'd only have to nudge it a little higher and he'd see what color her knickers were. But that was the problem, he didn't

134

want to nudge. He wanted to rip. Wanted to shove her against the wall. Hold her down while took her. Hard and rough. Let loose the rage, free the frustration. Give in to it and let her take it all.

"You don't know that," he said hoarsely. "I'm too out of control."

"I'm yours. I'm an insignificant slave, it doesn't matter what you do to me."

"Fuck that. It does matter. You're not—"

"I *am* insignificant," she cut him off fiercely. "I'm a slave. I'm your property. Your possession. You own me." She looked up at him then, her gaze sharp as cut glass, confronting him. "A possession doesn't need your control."

Something in her eyes reached inside him and clenched hard. "I take care of my possessions," he said. "I don't break them needlessly."

"That's why I trust you. That's why you won't break me." Her gaze held his, demand glowing in the depths of her eyes. A demand he felt himself respond to whether he wanted to or not. "Let me take your anger, master," she said, her voice soft and fierce. "That's what you want from me. That's why I'm here."

He wasn't the only one who needed this. Who wanted it. This was important to her too. And, Christ, wouldn't it be so good to let go? To let her take his anger. Push the boundaries, see where it took them. Because he hadn't, not with anyone. But he could with her.

She'd trusted him with this fantasy from the moment she'd walked with him out of the pool hall. Now it was time to repay that trust. Give her his in return.

"Stand up," he ordered, his voice gone hoarse. "Go and get your collar."

She rose, graceful with it, and disappeared off the down the hallway. A second later she was back, the collar in her hands, holding it out to him in the little ritual they'd developed over the past week. He took it and she turned around, holding her hair out of the way so he could put it on her. His fingers shook as he buckled it, brushing against the soft, vulnerable skin of her nape. Madness. This was fucking madness. And yet...

Trust her to handle you. Either that or you walk out of here and never come back.

Yeah, that was his alternative. And he couldn't do it. He just couldn't.

"Turn around," he said. "Keep your eyes on the floor."

She did what she was told. "Master, my clothes...? Did you want me...?"

Vin stepped close, looking down at her. They were inches apart, her head slightly bent. Submissive. And yet she wasn't. This slave had as much power over her master as he had over her. But now it was time to reclaim a little of that power back.

"I'll take your clothes off." He lifted his hands to the neckline of her dress, his breathing accelerating. "Do you like this dress?"

Her slight hesitation betrayed her surprise. "What? I suppose..."

"I'll get you a new one." He was hard, so hard right now. And he wanted to do something violent. Savage. Let out that anger. He took a breath. "If I frighten you, say stop and I'll stop." He hoped to fucking Christ he could stop.

"Yes," she said, her voice breathless.

He didn't wait. With a sharp, vicious movement, Vin pulled, ripping apart the fabric of her dress. She gave a soft gasp, shivering as he pulled the material free of from her shoulders.

Vin paused, looking at her. There was a flush to her cheekbones and under the black lace her nipples had hardened. She wasn't afraid and she hadn't said stop.

Adrenaline coursed through him. He reached out again, gripping the bit of lace that held the cups of her bra together then jerked them apart, tearing the lace. The ruined bra fell away, freeing her breasts. She wasn't wearing tights today so now she stood there only wearing a black lace thong and her platform boots. Another jerk on the waistband of the thong, and that tore and fell apart too, leaving her only wearing the boots.

Fuck, she was sexy. The vulnerability of her white skin and curves a delicious contrast to the aggressive black leather and buckles of her boots. Arousal built inside him, mixing with the burning anger and frustration, turning into something so intense he shook.

Trust her.

Vin gripped her shoulders, spun her round so her back was to him. Then he pushed her up against the wall, trapping her there with his body. She inhaled sharply, turning her head to the side, her cheek against the cracked paintwork of the wall. Then she pushed back against him, the softness of her ass pressing against his cock, driving him crazy.

"Are you wet for me yet, slave?" he growled in her ear, the scent of her bare skin filling his head. The scent of musk and flowers and sex. The scent of his slave. His.

"Y-yes," she said breathlessly.

He reached one hand down, pushing between her thighs, wanting to feel for himself and yes, she was. He slid one finger effortlessly inside her, the slickness of her sex closing around him. Wet and hot and tight. She gave a little moan, her lashes falling closed.

"Oh no, don't come yet, baby. Not until I say." He gripped the trailing slave chain, coiled it around his other wrist, pulling so her head bent back, her neck curving, the arch of her throat exposed. Her breathing came harsher now, her hips moving against his hand.

He took his hand away. "Legs apart, slave." He undid his pants and protected himself with a condom from his wallet. Then, gripping the chain tight in one hand and pushing on her hip with the other, he thrust hard inside her. Then he thrust again, even harder. She gasped and he waited for her to say the word but she didn't. There was nothing but heat and softness and silence from her. Like he could pour out the rage that lived in his heart and she would take it. Take it all away.

Vin closed his eyes. Began to move. Harder, rougher.

Fuck his life. His mad mother. His useless prick of a father. Fuck them for leaving him to carry this by himself. Because he was tired, so tired of having to do this alone. Tired of having no one to turn to. No one who would take it away from him.

No one except his slave.

So he gave it to her. Sunk his rage and his frustration into her, letting the pounding rhythm of it echo in his head, in the beat of his pulse, in his heart. Pushing them both to the limit as he drove into her, as the pressure grew, as the arousal pulled tight. He could hear her saying something over and over again, like a prayer, but he couldn't concentrate on it, not with pleasure pouring through his veins like liquid fire.

He gripped her hip tighter, thrust harder, shoving her against the wall, aware of nothing but the heat of her sex around him and the pleasure that blinded him. That pulled him apart.

And the sheer fucking relief of letting the anger test the boundaries of his control, just for a couple of minutes.

Kara couldn't stop shaking. Every nerve ending screamed for release but she held on through sheer force of will. "I promise. I promise. I promise," she whispered, ragged and broken, over and over again to remind herself.

Because there was a sharp bit in the wall that pressed

against her stomach, maybe the point of a nail or pin, and with each of Vin's thrusts the point dug into her, an exquisite counterpoint of pain.

Agony. It had been years since she'd used pain as a kind of emotional release and now it was so inextricably woven with the pleasure she had difficulty untangling the separate threads. No, pain wasn't allowed, like crying wasn't allowed. But, God, it was so hard to hold out against. When every part of her wanted the release, the combination of pleasure and pain almost impossible to resist.

So she had to keep saying the words. Keep reminding herself that she didn't need pain anymore. That she was beyond it. That she wouldn't use it to come.

You don't deserve it anyway...

Kara shut her eyes, almost sagging against the wall as Vin's hoarse cry sounded in her ear and his body stiffened against her back, his hold on the chain loosening. She couldn't stop the trembling, part of her wanting to scream at him to keep going, do her harder, use her, make it hurt. But she kept silent.

He didn't move for a long moment, his weight forcing her hard against the wall, the sharp point of whatever-it-was digging into her, and she had to hold herself exquisitely still to stop from tumbling over the edge of the climax that was just within reach.

Vin's weight eased, his arm circling her waist, tugging her back against him. "Did I hurt you?" he murmured in her ear, the rough edge in his voice making her want to tremble all over again.

"No," she managed to croak out. And it was the truth, he hadn't.

"What did you mean, 'I promise'?"

Oh crap, he'd heard her. "I...I was promising you that I wouldn't come." And that was the truth too. Kind of.

"You didn't either, did you?" There was nothing but lazy, satisfied heat in his voice now, the suppressed violence of earlier gone. "Good girl. That's very good. I might reward you for that." His hand brushed over her stomach and she glanced down. Jesus, she was bleeding and then he'd know. Know that he'd hurt her despite her promise to him.

"Master, please," she said quickly. "Let me clean myself up for you."

"Not yet." His arm tightened, his hand stroking down through the curls between her thighs. "You need a reward."

She shuddered as he touched her. Perhaps it would be okay if he did it while she was facing away. So he wouldn't see the blood. So she wouldn't have to explain why she hadn't told him to stop.

"Wait there," he ordered. "Don't move."

Kara waited as he released her and she heard him step away. But there was no time to do anything about the bleeding because he was back seconds later, turning her then easing her back against the wall before she could protest. He dropped to his knees in front of her.

Saw the blood.

"Fuck." He tipped back his head and looked at her, banked rage creeping slowly back into his eyes. "You told me I didn't hurt you."

"You didn't. It's nothing. Just a scratch."

His fingers brushed her stomach. "Jesus Christ, Kara—"

"Don't call me that. Not here. Not now."

Vin surged to his feet, the look on his face thunderous. "You lied to me, slave."

"No, I didn't." She leaned against the wall, struggling to get herself together. "There was a pin in the wall. It wasn't you. And it didn't hurt anyway."

"You're fucking bleeding."

"It's not your fault."

"It is my fault! If I hadn't—"

"Master, please." She said it softly, trying to bring him back to the fantasy. She didn't want him to regret this or doubt her. Because she'd loved the fact she'd got him to stay, to give her his anger. She had the feeling that Vincent Fox always kept a tight grip on it and the fact that he'd trusted her enough to use it to push them both had made her feel...well, she still needed to sort through it but she'd felt thankful. Needed. More his than ever.

"It's just a scratch," she went on when he didn't speak. "It's nothing."

A second passed, then a minute. Vin just looked down at her, the expression on his beautiful face utterly unreadable. Then he said, "What do you want?"

She stared at him. "What do you mean?"

"You gave yourself to me. So now I'm going to give something to you. What do you want from me? Anything. You can ask for anything."

"Anything?" she repeated blankly. He'd never asked her what she wanted before and she'd been more than okay with it because whatever he wanted usually seemed to suit her. And besides, she liked she didn't have to make any decisions. But somehow, now that he'd said it and given her this chance, she knew exactly what she wanted.

"Naked," she said. "I want you naked."

He turned without a word and stepped into the lounge, and as she followed, she saw him beginning to shrug off his suit jacket. And yet another need rose up inside her.

"I want to do it."

He paused, his hand on his tie, flashing her an enigmatic

glance.

"Please, master." Hell, she'd beg for this if she had to because he never undressed with her. Always, she was the one who was naked. She'd never minded because it felt right since she was the slave but the hunger had always been there. He was a work of art underneath his clothes and she wanted to see him bare. Touch him.

Her mouth had gone dry, the small pain of the scratch forgotten, unassuaged desire beginning to build again. Yes, she'd beg. A slave had no shame. "Let me undress you. Please."

He hesitated for a moment then slowly turned to her, lifting his arms from his sides and holding them out. Waiting.

She walked forward, coming right up to him, her hands pulling on the knot of his tie. God, he smelled good. That spicy aftershave he used and freshly laundered clothes. Sun-warmed skin and a hint of musk from the sex they'd just had. Her fingers shook.

Slow down.

She made herself breathe, made her fingers slow as she managed to get off his tie, folding it neatly over the back of the chair before coming back to him to start on the buttons of his shirt. Undoing them one by one, revealing bare, tanned skin beneath the white cotton.

He was looking at her, watching her as she did it, she knew because she could almost feel his gaze pressing down on her. But she didn't look up, didn't want to meet his eyes. Her hunger for him was obvious, she couldn't hide it, but still. He hadn't said she could look at him anyway.

She finished unbuttoning his shirt, remembered to undo the cuffs around his wrists, then drew it off him, hanging it over the chair so it wouldn't crease too badly. The intimacy of the gesture wasn't lost on her and yet she didn't mind when it was him on the receiving end. When it was her, it was different.

He didn't speak as she knelt to take off his shoes and socks. Or when she undid his trousers and took them off too, leaving him in only a pair of skin-tight black boxers which did nothing to hide his response to what she was doing. Clearly he liked it.

She knelt in front of him, hooked her fingers in the waistband and slowly drew his boxers down. As he stepped out of them, she felt one of his hands rest gently on her head, his fingers sifting through her hair and she had to stop, take a silent breath, her throat constricting at the gesture. She didn't want tender. It threatened something in her. Felt dangerous somehow. So she bent, running her hands down his muscular thighs and long calves, and his fingers curled tight, his hold not at all tender all of a sudden.

"Up," he said.

She rose to her feet, standing in front of him. Looking.

Beautiful. He was beautiful. His skin was a deep tawny brown, like oiled silk over the sharply cut muscles of his chest and abdomen. A body sculpted from hard work, sweat and sheer physical exertion. He was the sexiest thing she'd ever seen. She wanted to run her hands all over him, kiss him, taste him. God, do *everything* she could think of to him.

"Please," she heard herself whisper hoarsely. "I want to touch you, master. Please let me."

He said nothing, going past her to sit down on the couch then holding out a hand to her. "Come here."

She went without hesitation, without any thought at all in her head except that perhaps he would let her have this. And if he did then the agony of not being able to have that release would have been totally worth it.

Vin took her by the hips, tugging her down into his lap so she was sitting like she had that first night, facing him, her knees on spread on either side of his thighs. But this time he

143

didn't hold her, only sat back and put his arms along the back of the couch, watching her, his eyes dark. The sun from the windows threw shadows over the pure planes and angles of his face, highlighting the sheer beauty of him.

How do you deserve a man like this? You don't. Of course you don't.

She shoved the evil thought away, stuffed it back into the darkness. Because that thought belonged to Kara, not the slave. The slave got only what she was given to her by her master and her master was giving her himself. She couldn't refuse.

She lifted her hands, put them on his chest, felt heat, the fire beneath his skin. He was smooth and hot, the flex and release of his muscles beneath her fingers as she let her fingers trail down his chest to his abdomen, searching, exploring.

Unable to help herself, she leaned forward and pressed her mouth to his throat, where his pulse beat strong and sure. His skin tasted salty and hot and delicious. She licked him, rocking her hips, the rigid length of his cock pressing between her thighs, her hands stroking farther down. This was too much for her. This was too good. She'd been on the edge already and just a little more friction would push her over it.

But Vin pulled her hands away. "Not like that, slave," he said. "Go get me a condom."

She didn't want to have to get up but since this was obviously going to benefit her too, she did as she was told, thanking God she'd started keeping a stash of condoms in one of the drawers of the dresser near the door.

He let her handle the protection, staying right where he was on the couch, then lifted her up, only to lower her down on him, so she felt him slide deeply inside her. Her fingers curled on his chest, digging into his skin, the breath escaping from her in a harsh rush. His hand slid behind her head as he pulled her down for a kiss that caught her by surprise.

He hardly ever kissed her. Yet this...this was hot. Sweet. Hungry. Intimate. It did things to her. Did things she didn't want and yet she couldn't pull away. Her master was giving her something and so she had to take it.

She shuddered in his arms, his hands on her hips guiding her movements in a gentle rise and fall. Pleasure burst in her head, a wild explosion of light, and she lost herself in it. Put Kara and her demons away, and let herself revel in being the slave, with nothing but her master's pleasure to worry about. Nothing to think about but him. Doing his bidding.

So that when he whispered, "Come for me, slave," she did. Instantly. Shattering like a pane of glass before a sharp stone, her high, wild cries swallowed by his mouth.

And when his arms closed around her, holding her as she rode out the aftershocks, she didn't pull away.

That was the beauty of being the slave. She could have the things Kara would never allow herself.

"I can't tonight, Vin. I'm going out with Kara."

Vin stopped in the middle of the busy footpath, cell phone clutched in one hand. "Why?" The demand came out before he could stop it.

"What do you mean why?" Ellie sounded more than a little pissed off. "That's none of your damn business."

With an effort he contained his angry response. Which, he had to be honest, had less to do with Ellie not wanting to meet him for a drink and more to do with the fact that Kara had cancelled their meeting tonight. It had been him the night before—a problem with Lillian's accommodation he had to sort out—and now he was restless and aching, and wanting her. Looking forward to the moment when he could wrap that chain in his fist and pull her to him.

Fucking Neanderthal.

Vin clenched his jaw tight. "What I meant was, I'd like to see you a few more times before you leave for Tokyo. If you have time that is."

There was a pause. Then Ellie said, in a softer tone, "Ah, I'm sorry, Vin. I know I said I was around but it's Kara's birthday today. She doesn't like to make a big deal out of it but I do."

Kara's birthday? She hadn't said anything to him about it. Not a word. Then again, why would she? They weren't in the kind of relationship that celebrated that sort of thing and God knew he already understood what Ellie was saying about Kara not wanting to make a fuss. He'd already noticed she hated having attention lavished on her. In fact, the only place she allowed it was in the bedroom, as his slave.

After he'd ended the phone call, Vin stood on the footpath, scowling at nothing in particular. Because somehow the knowledge of Kara's birthday had lodged in his brain and he couldn't seem to get rid of it.

He should do something. Get her a present. A little thing to show his appreciation of her in some way because it felt wrong not to mark the occasion. They'd been intimate after all and yeah, so it was only physical but still.

Of course the really tricky thing would be to find something she would accept from him because he had the feeling she'd probably throw anything he gave her back in his face. Somehow he had to find a gift that she'd both like and find impossible to refuse...

It wasn't until ten minutes later, as he was passing a jewelry shop that he saw something that made him stop. That made him put his hands on the glass and stare.

That made him smile.

Because it was possibly the one thing on earth Kara

Sinclair would not be able to refuse him.

Kara heaved in a shuddering breath, the aftershocks of her orgasm still echoing through her. She was on the couch in her apartment, astride Vin's supine body with him still inside her. And man, she felt good. He lay on the couch beneath her, his eyes closed, the white business shirt he wore unbuttoned, the fabric spread wide.

Leaning back in his lap, her hands behind her, gripping his knees, she let her gaze run over him, hungry for the sight. Sweat sheened his torso, highlighting the chiseled contours of his chest and abdomen, gleaming at his throat. She wanted to lean down and lick him there.

Lick him everywhere.

Holy God but he was so very desirable. Even moments after an orgasm, when she should have been happy and sated, she wanted more.

"Master," she said huskily, "may I touch you?"

He didn't move, his eyes closed, long dark lashes fanned out on his cheekbones. "No. We're done for today."

Disappointment twisted in her gut despite the fact that she knew the middle of the day visits were always going to be limited by their jobs. Tom, her assistant, was fine over a lunch hour but any longer and he started to get anxious. He was great with keeping the computers going and dealing with any tech issues but when it came to the coffee making, not so much.

"Oh." The word slipped out without her permission and she cringed inwardly, hoping he wouldn't hear the disappointment edging it.

His eyes flicked open and he lifted his head, one of his rare, perfect smiles hovering around his mouth. "Is that disappointment I hear, slave?"

Bugger. "Yes."

His smile deepened and she couldn't work out which was worse, the way his smile made her chest feel tight or the way him knowing she was disappointed made her feel exposed. Lifting a hand, he lazily reached for a lock of her hair, winding a strand through his fingers. "Good."

It was pathetic how much that simple touch excited her. Quite pathetic.

His gaze drifted to the lock of hair he'd wound around his hand. "The blue is fading. I like it. See that you don't dye it again."

Kara shifted on him, uncomfortable. She'd gotten sick of the blue herself but had been meaning to try out a new purple shade she'd seen in a shop the day before, not go au natural. Her real hair color reminded her of too many bad things. Too many bad feelings.

Being different, being someone else was always easier.

She took one hand off his knee and reached out to pull her hair out of his grip. Only to have his fingers close around her wrist.

"What are those?" He was looking at her wrist, his voice losing its lazy, sensual edge, becoming sharp, demanding.

Oh fuck. Had he seen the scars?

"Nothing." She twisted her hand out of his grip. No, she was not going to answer questions about those. Master or not, no effing way.

He said nothing but she could feel the weight of his stare. Pressing down on her.

Don't ask. Please don't ask.

His fingers released her. "On your knees, slave."

Oh, thank God.

She kept her gaze averted so as not to betray her relief, slipping off his lap and onto the floor, settling into the position that by now felt natural to her. At his feet.

"You've been keeping secrets from me."

Her shoulders tightened. Shit. Of course it was too good to be true.

"It was your birthday yesterday and you didn't tell me."

For a minute all she could do was stare at the floor in confusion. Okay, so not the scars but her birthday? What the hell did that have anything to do with it? And how did he know it had been her birthday anyway?

She heard Vin move, getting up from the couch, taking a couple of seconds to deal with the condom and put himself to rights if the sound of his zipper was any indication.

"I'm sorry, master," she said. "It wasn't important."

"Correction, slave." His long fingers gripped her chin suddenly, tipping her head back so she had no choice but to look up at him. There was a fierce expression in his gaze, intensity burning in the depths of his eyes. "I own you. Which means anything that concerns you also concerns me."

She wanted to deny it, refute it. But that was Kara talking and she wasn't being Kara right now. She was the slave and his.

"Yes, master," she said thickly. "I'm sorry."

His thumb caressed her lower lip. "I have something for you. For your birthday."

Oh Christ. Please don't say he'd bought her a present. A weird heaviness settled in her chest. Like a lump of clay sitting there, thick and large and immovable. She hated the sensation. How fragile it made her feel. As if she was made of glass and would shatter at a touch. She could handle a drink with Ellie, an offhand jokey toast to the suckiness of birthdays and how crap they were. But this was different. This was Vin, staring at her, giving her a gift. When no one had ever bought her gifts before.

She opened her mouth to say she didn't want it, break character completely, but his thumb settled over her lip, pressing down, silencing her. "You'll take it." There was nothing but finality in his voice and how he knew she wanted to refuse she had no idea. "Remember, slave, you don't get a choice. Now..." He took his hand away and stepped back. "Stay there. Don't move."

God. Kara waited on her knees, her heart beating oddly fast, watching as he turned and went out into the hallway, coming back a moment later with a long, flat box in his hand. The heavy lump in her chest got heavier.

Without any hurry at all, Vin opened the box and took out something, holding it up between his hands so she could see. A mesh collar of gold and bronze wires, intricately woven together, the clasp a small gold padlock. It glittered in the light through the windows as he carried it over to her, delicate and beautiful and like nothing she'd ever possessed in all her life.

"No." The word spilled out of her before she could stop it, thick and hoarse with denial. Because she couldn't accept it. Didn't want it.

But Vin ignored her, coming over to where she knelt before dropping to his haunches in front of her. "Do you see this?" He turned the collar so she could see the padlock clasp. See the word engraved on it. *Mine.* "You'll wear this because I'm your master and you're my slave. Because you belong to me."

Her eyes felt gritty, like there was sand in them. Her throat tight and raw. Kara could never accept this. But the slave could. The slave had to.

Fuck the slave. You want it, too, don't deny it.

She closed her eyes, shutting out the sight of the collar

glittering between his hands, too overwhelmed and conflicted to speak.

Mercifully he let her have her meager self-protection, not saying anything, but she felt the slave collar around her neck loosen and fall away, to be replaced by cool metal. Heard the click as he shut the padlock clasp.

Mine...

"Hold out your hand," he ordered.

She did so and felt him press something into her palm. Cracking open an eye, she glanced down to see a small golden key sitting there. Clearly the key to the padlock. Which meant he was handing her the power to wear it or not.

You want to wear it. You never want to take it off.

God, she did. So much. The collar around her neck had a weight to it that had nothing to do with the metal. It was the weight of ownership, of claim. It felt like his hand resting there. Choosing her.

Mine.

That one word had so many meanings. It didn't only refer to her being his but her *choosing* to be his. Her choice to wear this collar. Make it her own.

Mine. Hers. Kara's.

She couldn't speak, didn't trust her voice. He'd given her a gift and given it in the only way she could let herself accept it. And she couldn't even speak to tell him how much it meant to her.

A long silence fell but she kept her eyes closed, her fingers clutching the key in her palm, struggling to breathe.

Then she heard him exhale softly. "You're so goddamn beautiful, slave. Next time you'll wear that collar and nothing else."

Luckily she knew there was no response required so she

just knelt there until she heard the sound of the front door slam.

After he'd gone, she let out a breath she hadn't known she'd been holding, then opened her eyes and got to her feet. Still clutching the key, she went down the hall to the bathroom and stood in front of the mirror, looking at the delicate web of precious metal around her neck.

He was right, it did look good. She reached up a hand and touched it, brushing her fingers over the intricately woven mesh. It was so lovely, it really was. She'd never had anything so gorgeous.

Ah God, she'd always hated birthdays. Hated being given things. Hated any kind of attention or fuss made of her. It made her feel so vulnerable and she hated that too. And yet this collar didn't make her feel vulnerable. No, she just felt...owned. Claimed. Like for the first time in her life she truly belonged to someone.

She leaned against the vanity, noting suddenly the dark circles under her eyes and a certain pallor to her skin. Weird. She'd been sleeping quite well the past few weeks and she'd put that down to getting regular sex. Especially since before she and Vin had started screwing, sleep had been difficult.

Absently stroking the collar around her neck, she looked down from the mirror to the box of condoms on the vanity. The empty box of condoms. Dammit, had they gone through that box so quickly? She had that stash in the lounge, but it wouldn't hurt to double check that she didn't have any more under the sink. Crouching, she pulled open the cupboard, poking around amongst the loo rolls, cleaning fluids and tissues, looking for any spare boxes she'd missed.

No condoms. But there was an empty box of tampons. For a moment she stared at it, trying to figure out if she needed to get those as well. How long had it been since she'd had her last period? She wasn't the most regular chick in the world and didn't keep track of it much.

Okay, so she'd had it a couple of weeks before the NZ Con with Ellie which made it...six weeks.

Kara swallowed. No, shit, that couldn't be right. Could it? The last time she'd had wicked PMS not helped by yet another return to sender letter from her mother, so she and Ellie had gone out and got drunk. She'd got her period in the bar and had had to bug Ellie for some change for the tampon dispenser.

And yeah, that had been about six weeks ago.

She frowned at the tampon box. So she wasn't all that regular but she'd never been quite *that* late before. What the hell was going on?

Are you sure you don't know?

A lump of ice suddenly collected in the pit of her stomach. Oh no. Oh please God no. She and Vin had been careful. Every single time they'd used a condom. Every. Single. Time.

She couldn't be pregnant. She just couldn't be.

Kara stood, cold all over, forgetting entirely about the collar around her neck, feeling like she'd been in an earthquake and the ground hadn't stopped moving yet. There was, obviously, only one way to check.

Half an hour and five pregnancy tests later, there was no denying it.

She was pregnant.

Happy fucking birthday.

Chapter Nine

Vin stared down at the plans spread out on his desk. As the door of his office shut behind Hunter, he let out a breath and cursed.

He'd spent all morning getting Lillian settled in her apartment, then he'd had to do shitloads of running around for the bank, not to mention getting his application into Auckland University's School of Architecture in time for the deadline, and he now felt fucking exhausted.

It didn't help either that he'd begun to feel pissed off with Hunter for getting to spend so much time with Ellie. At first he'd been grateful to his friend for providing somewhere for Ellie to crash before she flew out to Tokyo. But as time had gone on, and his own work had piled up, he'd begun to feel irritated about it. Okay, so maybe more than irritated. Possibly Hunter's accusations about that making him jealous were right.

Vin kicked back his chair and sat, still staring sightlessly at the plans for his house. The house he'd been building when he could find the time. Between Lillian and his business, work had fallen behind majorly.

Just like his plans to spend some time with Ellie. And now he was jealous of his friend because Hunter was the one spending time with her when it should have been him.

And guilty because he was also looking forward to Ellie leaving since then he'd finally be free of the constant worry for her that always dogged him when Lillian was out in the community.

And pissed off because he felt guilty.

Christ, he was a moody bastard.

Vin leaned back in his chair with his hands behind his head. Shut his eyes.

His mood was so not helped by the fact that the more shit he had to do, the more he wanted to shove it all aside and go spend time with Kara. Lose himself in her. Indulge himself in the one thing in his life he had total control over.

He was still buzzing from the orgasm he'd had not a couple of hours earlier, could still picture her on him with her head thrown back, her lovely face lit up with ecstasy. Could still feel her body around him, holding him tight.

The scars on her wrist...

He frowned, the memory at odds with the hot sexiness of the moment. They hadn't been big scars, just a few white lines. And she'd been extremely prickly when he'd asked her about them, making it obvious she didn't want to talk about it. But then that was Kara, wasn't it? She didn't want to talk about anything. And that was okay, they both knew exactly what this relationship was all about. A fantasy. An escape. Being someone else for a time. So why he should want to know where those scars had come from was anyone's guess.

What *had* been truly momentous though had been when he'd put that collar around her neck and pressed the key into her palm. The gold and bronze had looked amazing next to her skin, just as he knew they would. So beautiful and his, all his...

He shifted in his chair, hardening for her already.

God, he couldn't wait till tonight. To see her greet him wearing nothing but that collar. Some days the promise of seeing her was the only thing that got him through the day.

There was a knock on his door.

Vin cursed again and opened his eyes. "Come in." It was probably Tina with yet more issues with the electrical subcontractors. Man, he so wasn't in the mood to deal with that crap today.

But it wasn't Tina. It was Kara.

Instantly his whole body leapt into screaming life, hard and ready for action.

He put his hands on the arms of his chair and was up and out of it before he quite knew what he was doing.

"No, Vin." Kara shut the door and held her hand up. "That's not why I'm here."

He stopped. Because she wasn't wearing the long black coat she normally wore when she came to his office for a little bit of master/slave play. Instead she was in jeans, black skinnies and Docs. A bright pink T-shirt in sugary counterpoint to all the black. And her face was dead white. She didn't have any contacts in at all and behind the lenses of her glasses her eyes were brown, huge and dark, shadowed with something that looked a hell of a lot like fear.

Something was wrong, that much was obvious. Very wrong indeed.

"What's up?" he asked sharply.

Her throat moved, her gaze sliding away from his. "I need to tell you something."

"What?"

Kara's hands clenched at her sides, T-shirt pulling tight across her full breasts as she took a breath. She looked almost ill. Her mouth moved but nothing came out.

"Kara?"

She took another breath, leaning against the door as if she needed it for support. "I just...gimme a minute..."

He took a step toward her, an unexpected strand of anxiety twisting inside him. "Are you sick?"

"Uh...not really."

But she damn well looked sick.

"Sit down, Kara."

"No, it's okay I can—"

"Christ's sake, sit down before you fall down." Taking her by the arm, he gently steered her toward his chair.

She made only a cursory attempt to pull away which in itself was reason enough to worry.

As she sat, Vin leaned back against the edge of his desk, looking down at her.

She had her hands clasped tightly in her lap, long golden hair in a riot around her shoulders. There were still a few hints of blue to it, but most of the tint had almost gone, leaving her with her natural color. Streaks of caramel and toffee, lighter gilt and deeper gold. It was beautiful, like he'd known it would be.

He wanted to put his hands in it, wrap it around his wrists as she went down on him.

Fuck's sake. Get your head out of the gutter. This isn't the time.

No, it so wasn't. Not when her knuckles were white as they rested in her lap.

"Kara," he said. "What's wrong?"

For the longest moment she didn't say anything, her head bent, like she was praying or something. Then suddenly she lifted her head and her dark eyes met his. "I'm pregnant."

At first the words didn't make any kind of sense. "What?"

"Please don't make me say it again."

But he still couldn't seem to work it out. "You're pregnant?" he repeated stupidly.

"Yes." Her voice was clear and cold, as fragile as a shard of glass. "And if you ask me who the father is, I'll cut your throat out with a spoon."

The edge of the desk dug into him and he could feel the sun coming through the windows on his back. A false sense of warmth and comfort.

Pregnant. Kara was pregnant. And he knew for a fact the only person she'd been with had been him which meant that...

"Fuck," he said as realization began to hit, the world tilting on its axis. "Oh fuck."

Kara gave a short, mirthless laugh. "Yeah, you could say that."

Shock began to move through him. Like he was standing in an icy lake in bare feet, the cold creeping slowly up through his legs. He had to grip the edge of the desk for support. "But how the hell did that happen?"

"How? Oh the fucking Archangel Gabriel descended and told me that lo! I would bear a child." The cold edge to her voice shattered. "How do you think, Vin?"

His thoughts wouldn't work, shock freezing them solid. "But we used a condom. Every single time. And you're on the pill—"

"I didn't start on the pill until last week. And condoms aren't failsafe."

No. Of course they weren't. But he'd never had any trouble with them before.

You never think it'll happen to you...

Vin pushed himself away from his desk, needing to move. Needing to get away from her. As if doing so would lessen the shock. Make it less real. Less so completely not what he wanted.

Jesus. Ellie was just on the point of leaving. His last responsibility apart from Lillian, gone. And he had all these plans. For the business. For himself. He'd been going to spend time on study, on turning Fox Chase into a totally green construction company. On building the house he'd been planning for years. On finally having a goddamn life for a change.

But this news... This would change everything.

He realized he was standing in front of the office windows, looking out over the harbor. Watching the boats sail away.

You thought after Ellie left you'd be free. You fucking idiot.

Because he was never free. Always there was something else that life kept piling on top of him. Always there was shit he had to deal with.

Anger smoldered to life inside his gut. A slow burning, deep rage at the injustice of it all.

He'd spent his whole goddamned existence looking after people, being responsible for people, putting his life on hold in order to make sure other people were okay. Putting himself second.

And now he would have to do so again.

It was like watching that house he'd built with his own hands catch fire and burn to the ground. All the dreams he had for the future, all the work he'd put into finally being free, to finally have a life that was his and not lived for someone else...

Gone.

Because he couldn't walk away from his responsibilities. He'd never been able to. To do so would make him as big an asshole as his father had been.

"Say something, Vin."

He turned from the window.

Kara was on her feet, staring at him. White-faced.

"What the fuck do you want me to say?" he ground out.

"I don't know. Anything."

"That I'm thrilled? That I'm ecstatic? That I want to marry you and settle down to have two point five kids in a house with a white picket fence and a fucking dog!" His voice had risen.

"No, of course not!" A flash of something terribly vulnerable crossed her face. "I don't expect anything."

Of course she wouldn't. She'd never accept any help from him.

Perversely that made the anger inside him flare, a brushfire out of control and burning anything that got in its way.

"Then why the fuck did you tell me?"

"Because you're the father, Vin! I thought you'd want to know."

He took a step toward her. "No. I don't want to know. This is the last thing on earth I wanted, Kara. The last fucking thing!"

"Don't you dare shout at me. It's not like I wanted this either!" Raw anguish glittered in her gaze. "This isn't my fault!"

A thick, tense silence fell.

He struggled to contain the rage. Failed. "We should never have done this. We should never have slept together in the first place. I knew it was a mistake. I fucking knew it!"

She blinked. "A mistake?" An expression he couldn't read crossed her face. "Yeah. Yeah, you're right. It was a mistake."

He'd hurt her. Christ, he was a prick. "Kara," he began.

"No," she said shortly, cutting him off. "Don't say anything else, Vin. I know where you stand. But don't worry, I won't be asking you for anything. At all."

"Kara, wait."

But she didn't. She crossed the office, flung open the door and went out before he could move.

Vin didn't follow. He didn't want to be around her while he was like this.

He needed to chill out, settle down before they decided what they were going to do. And shit, having someone to talk this out with before that happened would be good too.

Hunter. He needed to find Hunter.

Kara left Vin's office and headed straight back to the café. Given the fury burning inside her, probably going home would have been better but then she'd have nothing to do but think.

Think about the complete fucking mess she'd made of her life.

But then this wouldn't be the first time she'd screwed up. Oh no. She'd done it before and many, many times since.

The café was crowded when she got there and she was able to push reality aside as she went about making coffees and heating muffins. Making smoothies and getting Tom to troubleshoot a couple of people having technical difficulties.

Easy, this stuff. Things she'd done a thousand times before.

She put her mind on autopilot, buried the anger and the gut-wrenching fear. The horrible déjà vu this whole thing had brought back. Especially seeing Vin's face as she'd told him. The anger he hadn't been able to hide. The knowledge that hers wasn't the only life this had ruined.

But she couldn't think of that now. She couldn't. She'd fall apart right here and that was not allowed. Falling apart wasn't ever allowed again.

The rest of the day was a blur. When the time came to close up she dawdled over it, chatting mindlessly to Tom until he made noises about having a bus to catch and that he'd be late if he didn't leave now.

Eventually she found herself having to make her way home, the city streets full of people doing the same thing. Returning to their lives after a hard day at work. All of them with homes to go to, friends to catch up with. Lovers to embrace. Wives or husbands to talk about the day with.

But she didn't. She didn't have anyone. And she'd never felt so alone. Even the day the social workers had told her she'd be going to a different home than her brother and sister, she hadn't felt this isolated.

She desperately wanted to talk to Ellie but fear stopped her from making the call. Her friend had been really preoccupied the past couple of days, something obviously going down with Hunter, and Kara didn't want to disturb the delicate balance with her own crap. And anyway, what would her friend say about the fact that Kara had been sleeping with Vin? That she was potentially going to be an aunt?

Nausea shifted in Kara's gut as she let herself into her apartment. Dumping her bag on the counter in the kitchen, she went over to the fridge and pulled it open, staring blankly inside, not really knowing what she wanted since she wasn't even hungry. There was a half drunk bottle of wine on a shelf next to the milk and she'd already reached for it before she remembered.

Pregnant. Alcohol was a no-no.

Only if you want to keep your baby.

She dropped her hand from the wine, closed the fridge door and leaned her forehead against the cold metal, closing her eyes.

A wave of raw grief went through her. How the hell could she keep the baby? She had a business that was struggling, a shitty little apartment that she didn't own, a straight-out weird sexual relationship with the father, no family to speak of. Insane to bring a child into a life like this, especially when she couldn't support it.

It would be like repeating her mother's life all over again. She'd have to do what her mother had done, work three jobs just to survive. Leave the kids home alone for days at a time because she had no one to look after them. Hoping like hell they'd be okay. Then taking refuge in the bottle because it was the cheapest way to escape reality.

That was no life for her. It was no life for her child.

Her throat closed, something burning behind her eyes. But it couldn't be tears because she never cried. She'd lost the ability the day she and her brother and sister were taken away from their mother by social services. Or rather, she'd decided she hadn't earned the right to cry since it was her fault their family had been broken up in the first place.

Stupid, overdramatic kid that she'd been.

Forcing down the old anguish, Kara pushed away from the fridge. The nausea was still there. Shit, she needed to eat something. Nausea was not conducive to making decisions. And decisions clearly needed to made. Steps needed to be taken.

"I knew it was a mistake."

Jesus, that was an extra pain she didn't need. Vin's words had hurt. Hurt far more than they should have. Because what they shared together didn't feel like a mistake. Being with him felt so good. A chance to step outside herself. Be someone else. Not Kara Sinclair, weird owner of a failing Internet café and not particularly good aspiring manga artist.

And now she wasn't even that. Now she would be Kara Sinclair, solo mother.

Panic closed a fist around her throat. She struggled to take a breath.

Turning around, she strode to the counter and pulled her bag off the stained Formica. Digging around inside it, she grabbed her phone.

He would say no. He would. Especially now. But she knew she had to ask.

One night with her master. That's all she wanted. Just one

last night where she could be free of herself. Free of having to be Kara and be the slave instead.

Vin's hand shook as he pulled open the Corvette's door. There was blood on his knuckles. Hunter's blood. And in the garage behind him only silence. But he didn't turn.

He didn't want to see his best friend—the one he'd just beaten the crap out of—lying there in a pool of his own blood. Or his sister dressed only in one of Hunter's T-shirts, bending over said best friend. The friend who'd been screwing her, the fucker. His little sister. The one he'd been protecting all his life. The one he'd thought would be safe with Hunter.

But she wasn't safe. She'd never be fucking safe.

Vin got in, slamming the door after him, rage, thick and hot and electric, coursing through him.

Gravel sprayed as he accelerated out of Hunter's driveway, tires screeching as they hit the tarmac of the road.

He didn't know what to do, how to get rid of this feeling. This fury.

First the baby, then finding out his best friend was screwing his sister. The best friend who'd been abused as a teenager, now doing the same to Ellie.

You know that's not what's happening. You know that's not really what you're angry about.

Vin swerved as a cat ran out onto the road in front of him, and he nearly hit a car coming in the opposite direction. The woman in the car hurled abuse at him as she drove past.

Christ. He needed to calm down, get a grip.

Still shaking, he pulled the car off the road and stopped, sitting there gripping the steering wheel tightly as the engine ticked.

He shut his eyes, watching the scene in Hunter's garage play out all over again. Him trying to find Hunt because he had to talk to someone about the baby and his friend was the only one he trusted enough to talk to. Coming into the garage and seeing Ellie dressed in only a T-shirt, wrapped around his best friend.

He hadn't known how close to the edge he was until that moment. Until that sight had kicked him in the guts. Perhaps if he hadn't just had the news about the baby, he'd never have lost it like he had because violence wasn't his thing. But seeing Ellie and Hunter together had been the last straw. His friend was a good guy but Vin knew how screwed up he was. Not someone you'd want banging your sister that was for fucking sure.

His hand ached at the memory of his knuckles connecting with Hunter's hard jaw. The red mist that had descended in front of his eyes as he'd pulled the other man to the ground. He'd wanted to lash out, to hurt him. Full of rage at the betrayal.

But of course it wasn't only the betrayal, was it? The issue wasn't Hunter. Or Ellie.

The issue was himself.

He's just playing out a fantasy, Ellie. A sick, fucked-up fantasy where he gets to be the one in charge.

Vin had yelled those words at her. Careless, unthinking words. He'd meant them for Hunter but they could easily be applied to himself.

Because it was him and what he was doing that was the problem. He was the one playing out the sick, fucked-up fantasies. Where he got to pretend a woman—his own sister's best friend for God's sake!—was his personal property, to do whatever he wished with. Treating her as his sex slave. Getting off on her obedience. Indulging his possessive streak, that fact that she was his and no one else's. Giving her a collar with the word *mine* engraved on the padlock. Jesus.

Slowly Vin's grip on the wheel tightened even further, the blood on his skin stark against his white knuckles.

He was supposed to protect people. He was supposed to look after them, make sure they were okay. His mother. Ellie. Kara. And to some extent Hunter. But they weren't okay.

His mother was surviving in the community only barely. Ellie was opening herself to a world of hurt with a man who had more baggage than a 747 could cope with. Hunter had just stood there and taken the hits Vin had given him, as if he'd welcomed the beating. And Kara...

Kara was pregnant with his baby because he couldn't keep it in his pants. Because he'd put himself and his needs first.

Consequences. There were always fucking consequences.

His phone buzzed in his pocket. He didn't get it out immediately, a sudden foreboding twisting inside him that it would be Ellie telling him Hunter needed to be taken to the hospital or something because that was just the type of day it had been.

Getting it together, Vin finally pulled the thing out of his pocket and glanced down at the screen.

It wasn't Ellie. It was a text from Kara. *The slave requests her master's presence.*

Shit. No way. She wanted this now? After what she'd told him?

Without his conscious permission, his body began to harden, not giving a crap what his mind thought.

Vin bit off a curse. His hands were all bloody and he was still full of rage and self-loathing, and compounding what had been a giant mistake in the first place by going back and doing it again was the very last thing in the world he should be doing.

And yet he wanted to. Wanted to escape from all this shit by being the master. Take control of his slave girl.

Your pregnant slave girl.

Jesus Christ, this was so fucked up. He began to type out a refusal and yet somehow the text that he sent wasn't no. It was yes. And when he put the car into gear and pulled back into the traffic, he wasn't heading back to the office to crash, but to Kara's apartment.

She met him at the door in her slave costume and he didn't miss the fact that despite his last order to her, she wasn't wearing the collar he'd given her, only the cheap one that had come with the costume. She didn't say anything as he pulled the door shut behind her, only turned without a word and went down the hall to her tiny, chaotic little lounge. He followed her, finding her kneeling in the middle of the room when he got there, her head bent submissively.

His cock was already hard, the shaking in his hands no better than when he'd left Hunter's. All the rage seemed to have coalesced into a deep, raw hunger that felt like it had settled right down into his bones, become part of his DNA. A hunger that he would never be free of.

Kara knelt there, a figure painted in differing strokes of gold. Pale honey for her skin, rich tawny for her hair, gilt for the bikini she wore. Even the blue tips of her hair seemed stained with gold.

He didn't know why it should be this way. Why he should want a sexual relationship that was as far from right and normal as it was possible to get. Why he couldn't seem to escape the need when for years he'd managed to control himself. He'd never gone out to get trashed with the boys. Never spent his weekends getting laid or getting high. He'd never been able to and hadn't had a problem with it. He had too many other responsibilities.

Yet now he was face to face with his own personal crack—Kara Sinclair in a slave costume with him holding the chain.

"This is the last time," he said into the heavy silence. "I'm not doing this again."

"I don't please you, master?"

He'd almost never called her by her name while they were in their respective roles. But he did now. "Kara."

"Don't." She raised her head and he saw she still hadn't put contacts in. Her eyes were dark, the color disconcerting him. "I want the fantasy."

Yeah. The fantasy. Yet looking down into her eyes, somehow all he could see was the stark whiteness of her face as she told him she was pregnant. The fear there. The vulnerability.

And with that between them there could be no fantasy. Not anymore.

"We need to talk about this."

"No." The finality in the word was crushing. "I don't want to talk about it." She leaned forward, ran her hands up the backs of his thighs. "I want to be your slave. I want you to use me."

And of course his bloody dick hardened even more at her words, at the feel of her hands, at the press of her body against his legs.

Sick, fucked-up fantasy…

"This isn't the time."

"The hell it isn't." Her hand moved, pressing hard against the fly of his jeans, finding the hard ridge of his aching cock, squeezing.

Pleasure turned on like a light inside him, the thrill of it shooting straight down his spine, the breath hissing in his throat. "Kara—"

"I'm not Kara." She pulled at his fly, reaching for his zipper, tugging it down with one hand while with the other she loosened the tie of her bikini top, letting it fall off her.

And he, sick fuck that he was, couldn't stop looking at her. The curves of her full breasts as she freed them, tight, pink nipples. She looked up at him again, her fingers pressed against the cotton of his boxers, her thumb running up and down the ridge of his erection. "I'm the slave. *Your* slave."

He put his hand over hers, holding it down against his groin. Hard. So she couldn't move it. "No. This has to stop. Things are different now."

She stilled then leaned forward, her forehead pressing against his abdomen. "Please." Her voice was quiet, devoid of her usual snark. "Please. Just tonight. I need...I need this."

"Baby—"

She lifted her head and for a second he glimpsed desperation in her eyes. "Please. I'll beg if you want me to." Beneath his imprisoning fingers, her hand moved lightly over his aching shaft. "I just want a night."

The hunger inside him began to shift and turn like an animal making a home for itself. Settling down to stay.

You want it. Don't deny it.

Yeah, of course he did. Hell, he'd already made one catastrophic error with her—what was another? And shit, why not include beating Hunter to a pulp and nearly turning on Ellie too?

It wasn't like the day could get any worse.

He moved his hand, gathering the softness of her hair into his fist. Then he pulled and her head came back, the sound of her sharply indrawn breath loud in the room.

"One night," he said. "Then we talk."

"Okay."

"So what are you waiting for? Get naked."

He didn't miss the flash of relief that crossed her face as he released her and he didn't try to kid himself he didn't like that. Or the way her hands shook as she quickly undid the bikini bottoms she wore and stepped out of them.

His desire coiled tighter as she stood there naked. Soft and vulnerable and female. And all his to do whatever he wanted with her.

Yeah, it was sick. It was fucked-up. But it was his fantasy and he would live it one more time.

"Why are you wearing this?" He tugged on the chain attached to the cheap collar. "What happened to the collar I gave you? I ordered you to wear it."

She didn't look at him or offer any kind of explanation. "I'm sorry, master."

He could push but he wasn't going to. Not tonight. "On your back."

She obeyed without a protest, lying down on the multicolored rugs that lay all around the apartment, golden hair spread everywhere.

"Spread your legs."

Again she moved obediently, letting her knees fall open. She was looking up at him, eyes dark. She wasn't wearing her glasses today and for some reason he was very conscious of the fact. As if her glasses were a mask she'd taken off, showing him the woman behind it.

He swallowed, his throat thick with an emotion he didn't want to name.

God, she was so vulnerable. She hid it well beneath her snarky, prickly exterior but he knew. He saw just how vulnerable she was. And tonight he seemed to be even more conscious of her vulnerability. They'd pushed the boundaries with his anger once before but now it just didn't seem right.

She deserved more than to lie on the carpet with her legs spread, waiting for him to screw her. She deserved to be looked after. Taken care of. Especially now. Because he had the feeling that Kara Sinclair hadn't been either looked after or taken care of much in her life.

Vin shifted, aware that his hand was aching. That the rage had seeped away, leaving him feeling empty and tired and weirdly lost. He didn't want to be the master, ordering her around. For the first time what he wanted was to wrap his arms around her and hold her soft warmth against him. Make love to her. Not screw her on the carpet.

Slowly he dropped to his knees. "Sit up."

She blinked, then frowned. "What—"

"Don't question me. Sit up."

Kara pushed herself into a sitting position. "Master, I don't—"

He pushed his fingers into her hair then leaned down and covered her mouth with his. She gave a little sigh, leaning into the kiss, lips parting, letting him taste her. He kept things gentle, kept it sweet, his tongue tracing the line of her lower lip. She tried to make it more intense, kiss him more aggressively but every time she did, he pulled back. He'd had enough of aggressive tonight.

Kara made a soft sound in the back of her throat. "More," she murmured against his mouth. "Harder."

He curled his fingers tighter in her hair, tugging her back again. "No. Not tonight." He freed one hand to stroke her bare shoulder, caressing her.

She stiffened. "I don't want that."

He didn't stop, his hand dropping down her spine, lightly stroking that too. "You don't want what?"

"Gentle. I don't want gentle."

"Why not? What's wrong with it?"

Her gaze slid away. "I just don't want it."

"This isn't about you, remember? You're here for me." He trailed one finger down her arm, moving lightly over her golden skin, watching the goose bumps rise as he did so.

She'd gone still under his touch. He let his fingers trail over the dips and hollows of her collarbone, the graceful arch of her throat. "You're beautiful," he murmured. "You know that, don't you? Kara, you're—"

"Stop." The word was hard and sure.

Vin paused. Looked into her eyes. And the expression in them was just as hard and sure as that word had been.

"You told me that if you did anything I didn't want, all I needed to do was tell you to stop, right?"

Oh yeah, he remembered. "Yes."

"Well, I'm telling you to stop."

Chapter Ten

Vin's eyes darkened and she saw something she could have sworn was pain flash through them. But she didn't back down. She couldn't back down.

Her whole body was trembling, fight or flight reflex kicking in. It was the sound of her name that had done it. She'd never liked it when he turned gentle. When he became tender. It made her feel threatened in a way she couldn't have articulated. But it hadn't been until he used her name that she'd realized she had to stop this.

It broke the fantasy. And tonight of all nights, she'd needed the fantasy. She'd even pleaded with him for it, for God's sake.

"Why?" he asked. "Did I hurt you?"

"No." Shit, if only he'd hurt her. She could use a little pain right about now. "But I'm not your bloody girlfriend, I'm your slave. I don't want to be treated like fine-freaking china."

His expression hardened. "Why not? You don't think you deserve to be treated like fine china?"

Kara turned away, the panic from earlier curling fingers around her throat again. "I just don't want it, okay?"

"Why? What's wrong with it?"

"We're not having this discussion." She got to her feet. "If you're not going to give me what I want then perhaps it's best if you leave."

Vin stared at her. Then he rose in one smooth, athletic movement, making her aware of how fluidly he moved and how much that turned her on.

Man, this was all so insane.

She was just like her mother, escaping reality with something that would only screw her up more. Only with her it wasn't alcohol. It was a slave fantasy with her best friend's older brother.

While she was pregnant.

Self-loathing twisted, the sharp edges digging into her. An old, familiar pain. Like whenever she got one of the letters she sent to her mother back again. Unopened. Unread. A silent, envelope-shaped rejection. A reminder of the guilt she never seemed to be able to escape from.

"I thought you wanted this," he said. "You begged me."

"Yeah, well, I changed my mind, okay?"

"Why? Because I treated you like a human being for once and not a slave?"

"Hey, you were the one with the slave fetish, Vincent. Not me."

His whole posture went rigid. "You didn't want it?"

She cursed under her breath. Because she couldn't lie. She'd wanted it. "I...I didn't mean it like that."

"Then what the hell did you mean?"

"I meant, we had rules with this...whatever we're doing. We had boundaries. And I was okay with that. I don't want it to change."

"Bit late for that now, don't you think?"

Kara took a breath. "Look, all I wanted was a quick, hard fuck. If you can't give that to me then piss off."

The look on his face had become unreadable. And she gradually became aware of the aura of leashed violence around him. That he had blood on his knuckles and circles under his eyes. He looked tired. Like he'd had something taken out of him. By force.

She'd always tried not to be curious about him. Tried to keep her thoughts of him purely sexual because that was easier. Safer. And yet now an unfamiliar and unwilling sympathy tightened her chest. What had he done after she'd delivered her bombshell? Where had he gone?

"Vin, I—"

"Save it." His expression shuttered. "You wanted me gone, I'm gone."

He turned then disappeared down the hallway and she heard the front door slam shut after him.

Pain bloomed inside her.

Fuck, it was always this way, wasn't it? She seemed to screw up no matter what she did. But how could she tell him that tenderness hurt far worse than violence? That gentleness cut far more deeply than being rough ever could? He wouldn't understand.

Her throat closed up, her eyes burned. But she wasn't allowed to cry. And the one release she used to allow herself she'd promised her favorite social worker she wouldn't do anymore.

For long minutes Kara stood naked in her lounge, as a familiar pressure began to build, the burning behind her eyes becoming more intense. A pressure there was only one way of relieving.

She hadn't had it this bad since she was sixteen.

Kara wrapped her arms around herself, suddenly cold. The pressure grew, pushing against her skin from the inside like a tire constantly filling with air, becoming harder, tighter.

There's razors in the bathroom.

Oh God, so there was. But she'd promised that social worker she wouldn't cut again. Promised she'd make a go of trying to fit in with the foster family she'd been placed with. And she had tried, getting rid of the razors, allowing the scars to heal. She hadn't touched one for ten years, using a razor only to shave her legs.

Only a couple of cuts. Ease the pressure.

Ten years, hell, that was a long time. She'd never even had a slip up. So would having one now be a bad thing? She'd feel better afterwards. She always did.

Kara turned and went down the hall to the tiny bathroom. She tried to avoid her reflection in the mirror as she pulled open the drawer in the vanity, but the movement of the stupid slave chain fastened to the collar around her neck kept catching her eye.

The pressure thickened, the burning sensation behind her eyes even worse.

She was such a mess. All she'd wanted was normal. That was all she'd been looking for. And what had she got instead? A master/slave fantasy where she got off wearing a collar and a chain and taking orders from her best friend's older brother.

Maybe she couldn't do normal. Maybe she'd never be able to do normal.

Some life you're going to give your baby.

The pressure constricted in her throat.

Of course she couldn't do normal. She didn't even know what normal was.

Tearing off the collar and chain so she stood naked in front of the vanity, she then took a new razor from the drawer and pulled open the packet. The metal gleamed in the light, comforting. She extracted it, holding it lightly between her fingers then turned her other wrist over. There were faint, pale lines on her skin, the legacy of her troubled teenage years. Her foster mother had seen them, thought she was doing drugs and had threatened to get rid of her.

If only it had been drugs. At least she'd have gotten some fun out of it.

Gently Kara laid the edge of the razor against the delicate skin of her inner wrist.

Like pricking a balloon...

That's what she used to tell herself. When the pressure behind her eyes and the pain in her heart got too much she'd feel like a balloon too full of air. All she needed was a way to release the pressure, let it out. A small cut and all the air would escape, the pressure would ease. She'd feel better.

Lightly she drew the razor across her skin, careful not to cut too deep. It stung but it was a good pain. An easy pain. She let out a shaking breath as red sprang up in a line across her wrist, the blood a rich contrast to the pale flesh beneath.

It felt a little better but one cut wouldn't be enough. It never was.

Kara laid the razor on her skin and cut again. The pain deepened. Just a little more maybe.

"What the fuck are you doing, Kara?"

She whirled around, her mind blanking with shock.

Vin stood in the doorway, a look of such incandescent rage on his face that she took a helpless step back. He moved, so fast she couldn't stop him. Clamping strong fingers around her bleeding wrist, he then reached for her other hand, twisting it so she gasped and dropped the razor.

"Are you trying to kill yourself?" he nearly shouted. "Is that what you're doing?"

"No! God, no, of course not." She hissed in pain as his fingers pressed down hard on the cuts. A line of red had run down her arm, dripping onto the floor. "Vin, stop it."

"Are you out of your fucking mind?" He hauled her close, staring down at her. "If you don't want the baby there are easier

177

ways to go about it!"

The pressure was back, as was the fierce burning behind her eyes, the tightness in her throat, her heart swelling up with guilt and pain and fear. "What are you doing here?" she croaked. "I thought you'd gone."

"Clearly you did. Is that what you were waiting for? Me to go so you could slit your fucking wrists in the bathroom?"

The stormy blue of his eyes had darkened into black, fury staining his high cheekbones red. An avenging angel. An angel with a sword sharper than any razor. "I-it's not what it looks like," she forced out, a wave of shame swamping her. Of all the people to catch her cutting it would have to be him.

"Then what the hell is it?" he demanded. "You have scars on your wrists. Scars you wouldn't talk to me about. Are they from a previous suicide attempt? Don't lie to me, Kara."

The humiliation was like acid, burning her. She tried to pull away but he wouldn't let her. So she did what she always did when she was threatened. She attacked.

"I'm not trying to kill myself, Vincent," she said, enunciating his name sarcastically.

"Then what are you doing?"

"I'm a cutter. You know what that is? I cut myself with razors."

Shock passed over his face. "Why?"

"Because I like it. Because it makes me feel better. Because I have to get this pain out any way I can!" The words spilled out of her like the blood out of her cuts, helplessly, hopelessly. Words she'd never said to anyone else. "Because it hurts. It hurts so much. I just wanted normal. I just wanted sane. But I'm not. I'm screwed up. I always have been, I always will be and now I've screwed up your life as well as my own. This kid doesn't stand a chance. And I can't cry about it. I can't even do that one, simple thing!" Her voice echoed around the tiny space of the bathroom and the shame of the admission was so intense she wished she could die of it. But there was no escape from herself or those piercing blue-gray eyes of his that stared into her, through her. Seeing her like no one else could.

"Don't look at me," she cried, desperate. "Don't look at me like that!"

For a long moment he said nothing. Then with a sudden, violent movement that took her by surprise, he turned her in his arms so she ended up facing the mirror, not him. He still gripped both her wrists, the hard warmth of his body pressing against her spine.

"I won't let you hurt yourself," he growled in her ear.

"Then go away. You don't have to watch."

"I want to help you."

"I don't want your bloody help!"

"Yes, you do. You need it. You need someone, Kara."

"Yeah, okay, you're right. I do need someone. I need someone to hurt me."

The statement had the desired effect. She could feel him go rigid behind her, the grip on her wrists faltering. Good. Perhaps he'd go away. Leave her to deal with it herself in her own way.

Oh yeah, because that way worked so well in the past.

"Hurt you?" Vin echoed.

"You said you wanted to help." She could see him in the mirror, the achingly beautiful lines of his face set and hard. His body tall and broad and powerful behind hers, somehow emphasizing her nakedness. Making her feel small and feminine and vulnerable. Defenseless.

She dragged her gaze away, looking down at the sink instead. "And that's what I need. I need pain. Because it makes everything else easier to bear."

He said nothing. But the warmth at her back didn't move.

Oh God, why wouldn't he leave? She'd been torn open, the darkest parts of herself spread out for him to see and now she was drowning in humiliation. Suffocating. And the pressure was still there, building and building. No way to escape it or release it.

Kara struggled to breathe, tried to pull away.

And Vin bit her.

Shock froze her to the spot.

He'd sunk his teeth into the sensitive cords at the side of her neck, sending a bolt of pain right down her spine. She inhaled sharply. His head moved and he bit her again, a little lower this time but no less hard. Kara let out a gasp because it hurt.

He released one of her wrists, the one that wasn't bloody, sliding his hand across her stomach. And down.

She stiffened. "What are you—"

"You want pain. So I'll give it to you. But I'm doing this my way. If you don't like it, all you have to do is say stop and I'll stop." His hand pushed through the tangle of curls between her thighs, long fingers finding her clit. Stroking her. And this time when she gasped, it wasn't because it hurt.

He moved his head, biting the other side of her neck, his fingers stroking, rubbing gently, around and around. And the pain of his bite began to mesh with the pleasure of his fingers on her. Becoming something else. Something even more powerful.

Kara couldn't stop the moan that tore from her throat. This wasn't right. Pain couldn't be pleasure. She wasn't allowed a release like that. She'd managed to stop herself from having it that day he'd screwed her up against the wall in her hallway but this, tonight, was different.

Tonight she was broken. Was raw and bleeding, and although she knew she didn't deserve it, she couldn't bring herself to say the word that would end it.

He bit her shoulder, dropping her bleeding wrist to cup her breast, pinching her nipple hard. Then the hand between her thighs moved, a finger sinking inside her. The pain and the pleasure twined around each other, making her cry out. Another pinch, another bolt of hurt. Another finger pushing into her, deeper, harder. She moaned helplessly.

Vin's thumb brushed over her clitoris, circling as his fingers moved inside her, and she found herself arching against his hand, panting. The pressure began to change, no less demanding, no less intense, but more focused. All it would take would be another brush of his thumb, another movement of his fingers. Another pinch to her nipple and she'd come.

Like the cut of the razor, the climax would bring such relief.

"Please...Vin...please..." She'd never used his name during sex before. But she was so far gone, she hardly noticed.

He said nothing. One hand came to rest on the back of her neck then pushed her forward and down, so she was bent over the vanity. The hand stayed there, a strong, dominant hold, keeping her cheek held against the cold porcelain of the sink.

She began to shake. Her neck stung where he'd bitten her and she knew she'd have bruises. God, she hoped so.

Behind her came the sound of a zipper being drawing down and her muscles tightened in response. Oh, Jesus, please let him take her. Use her. Hard and rough. The razor would never be enough now. She needed him. Needed the release only he could give her, an outlet for the anguish, the guilt and the shame that she never seemed able to leave behind no matter how hard she tried to escape.

The hold on the back of her neck eased as his fingers tangled ruthlessly in her hair, pulling her head back with a sharp jerk. Pain prickled all over her scalp and she gasped, the sound turning into a cry as she felt him spread her open with his other hand. Then the push of his cock into her, a harsh thrust rather than a slow slide.

He went still, deep inside her, the tiny bathroom space full of the sound of their ragged breathing.

The edges of the vanity dug into the tops of her thighs, her head pulled back so far it was uncomfortable. His fingers twisted tighter into her hair, tugging harder.

Kara shut her eyes, the pain and the discomfort merging with the feeling of him inside her, the heat of him against the backs of her thighs. The pleasure and pain of it promising a release that would probably break her in two.

Vin began to slide out then back in, a few shallow thrusts, teasing her. At the same time, he pulled her hair, increasing the tension, little barbs of agony piercing her scalp. Kara shuddered, light bursting behind her eyes, pleasure building like a fiercely burning fire.

His free hand slid around her front, stroking her clit as he thrust. So light and gentle in comparison to the punishing grip he had on her hair. The contrast brought strangled sounds from her, gasps and moans she had no control over.

He began to move deeper then, a hard rhythm that turned the sounds into something more raw and desperate. The pressure inside her crushing.

This was going to destroy her. Shatter her.

In some dim part of her brain, a warning screamed. Telling her to say the word that would end this before her defenses broke down. But it was too late for that. She was too far gone to turn back now.

She would fall apart when this was over and she didn't think she'd ever be able to put herself back together again.

It'll be okay. He's here.

She didn't know where the reassurance came from. But it was enough.

Kara squeezed her eyes tighter and ignored the warning, embraced the intensity of the physical sensations, throwing herself into them. The hard push of his cock inside her, the sharp edges of the sink, the pain in her scalp, the light brush of his fingers against her clit.

He slowed his movements and she moaned in protest, shifting restlessly against him, desperate now for release. But he ignored her, his touches becoming even lighter, delicate brushes that only prolonged the agony. Every inch of skin began to feel sensitized, the pull of his fingers in her hair the most delicious pain. He eased slowly out of her, so damn slowly she nearly screamed in frustration. Then back in, just as slow. She pushed back with her hips, wanting more.

"Keep still," he ordered in a low, guttural voice. "You wanted pain. I'm giving it to you."

Yes, this was pain. Caught on the cusp of an orgasm so intense she'd probably scream herself hoarse when it overwhelmed her. Pain and pleasure so inextricably twined she couldn't work out which was which.

She was shaking, her knees buckled against the vanity, only the press of his body keeping her there. The pain in her wrist was a dim memory compared to the agony of pleasure coursing through her now. And still he went on and on, building the ecstasy slowly but surely until she was mindless with need. A creature aware of nothing but her own, desperate hunger.

Someone was begging in a low, hoarse voice. Saying his name and please over and over again. Her.

"Kara," Vin said softly.

He gave one deep thrust that shoved her hard against the vanity then jerked her head back sharply. Her spine bowed as the pain shot down it. As the pleasure exploded like a magnesium flare behind her eyes, bright, shining. Incandescent.

She screamed as she fell over the edge. And screamed again as his fingers brushed her clit, the sensation so acute she almost couldn't bear it. A delicious torment that seemed to go on and on, overwhelming her so that all she could do was press her hot cheek to the cold porcelain of the sink as her voice ripped itself raw.

Broken, all right. Into tiny little pieces. Shattered beyond repair.

The deep, gut wrenching sob that welled up inside her seemed torn straight from her soul, wrenched into the light of day by the intensity of her release. She tried to bite down on it but it came out of her mouth anyway. A long, low moan that turned into a cry of pure agony. She had no energy to keep it down this time and it escaped, ten years of anguish finally given voice.

Vin's arms came around her, strong and sure, pulling her upright. Holding her tightly. And she couldn't seem to stop the sobs. Couldn't find the will to push him away even though every part of her wanted to run and hide.

He turned her so she faced him then pressed her head against his chest, giving her a measure of privacy and she took it. Sobbing and sobbing against his T-shirt. A never-ending well of tears that soaked the cotton.

She cried until her eyes felt swollen shut. Like she'd never open them again. Until her voice was thin and ragged. Until she felt empty. All the air inside her had gone, leaving her nothing but a hollow shell.

Vin said nothing. Instead he calmly turned on the shower, took off all his clothes and pulled her into it with him. He began to wash her gently, cleaning away the blood, the salt from her tears. Washing her hair too, his fingers massaging her scalp, easing away the pain.

She didn't want him to take care of her like this. It was dangerous. But she couldn't remember why and it was good having someone touch her so carefully. Good to feel as if someone cared. Especially him.

So she let him do it, let him dry her, put plasters on the cuts to her wrist. Let him wrap her in the blue Chinese silk robe she loved. Even let him pick her up in his arms and carry her back to the lounge.

She kept her eyes closed the whole time. She felt so tired. And when he finally sat on the couch, with her in his lap, she let her whole body go limp, relaxing into his warmth. Allowing herself the luxury, just this once, of letting someone else take care of her.

Silence fell. A deep, abiding silence that she felt no inclination to break.

And sometime after that, she fell asleep.

She felt so warm in his arms, the gentle weight of her relaxed against him in sleep. Vin looked down at her face now wiped clean of makeup. Of tears. Her expression peaceful, her breathing even. But still he could see the dark circles under her eyes, the lines of pain around her mouth.

He'd never hurt a woman like that. Not deliberately and never during sex. But he hadn't been able to think of any other way to help her. And he had to help her. He just had to.

She was a woman in pain. A pain he'd never realized the depth of until he'd seen her standing naked in her bathroom holding a razor, her wrist bleeding.

He'd come back because he'd known the moment the door had shut behind him that he couldn't leave her. That he should have remembered that when she got sharp and snarky it was because she was hurt and trying to protect herself.

Except he didn't know what he'd done to hurt her except try to be gentle.

Well, perhaps he understood a little more about that now.

Vin brushed aside a long golden strand hat had fallen across her face.

Pain. I need pain.

Why? What had happened in her life that she had to hurt herself in order to feel better?

I just wanted normal... I'm screwed up... It hurts so much...

A heavy, sharp stone seemed to rest just above his heart. He'd known she was vulnerable and yet he'd worked his own sick shit out with her all the same. Sure, the first time they'd been together it had helped her. But that's where he should have stopped. He should never have kept going. Kept using her to service his own needs.

He hadn't wanted to hurt her tonight, really hadn't wanted to. But he'd seen, perhaps for the first time, that Kara's needs were different. And that perhaps it was time to give her what she truly wanted. Help her the way she wanted to be helped.

So he had. He'd given her the pain she demanded. But he gave her pleasure too. Because whether she thought she deserved the pain or not, she had to have with it pleasure. She totally deserved that.

Kara shifted in his arms, turning her head against his chest.

And he had the odd impression he could sit like this forever, just holding her. And he wouldn't mind. Wouldn't mind a bit.

Vin settled back against the couch. Tiredness crept up on him. They had so much to talk about, so much to discuss. But now wasn't the time.

Tomorrow. It would have to be tomorrow.

He shut his eyes. Just for a moment.

Chapter Eleven

It was the sensation of feeling trapped under a heavy weight that woke her. Kara cracked her eyes open to find herself lying on her side on the couch, a heavy male arm snaking across her chest, holding her tightly, warmth like a fire against her back.

Vin. Who'd apparently stayed the night.

A strange sense of peace stole through her. She'd never slept with anyone before and she hadn't known how comforting it would be.

Not just anyone, girl. Vincent Fox.

Who'd discovered her shameful secret.

Who'd given her the pain she requested. Who'd held her as she'd broken apart afterwards. Held her as if she mattered.

Heaviness gathered in her heart. She hadn't mattered to anyone for years, not since the day she'd been told by her mother that she wasn't to come home. Her little brother and sister had been returned to their mother's care but Kara, who'd aged out of the foster system by then, wasn't wanted.

No one had wanted her. No one except Vin.

She'd been such a pathetic mess last night, yet despite all the provocation she'd given him, he hadn't turned around and walked away. He'd stayed. And more than that, given her something she'd never thought she deserved—pleasure with the pain.

She swallowed, suddenly breathless, that weird feeling in her heart squeezing tight. He seemed to have the ability to make her accept a lot of things she never normally allowed herself. Somehow he'd managed to get under her guard and after last night...

Kara shifted as the breathless feeling intensified. Man, she really could do with a bit of distance right now.

Untangling herself from Vin, she slipped down the hallway to the bathroom to relieve her aching bladder. Then, as she washed her hands at the sink afterwards, she stared at herself in the mirror.

Red-rimmed eyes, tangled hair, and yep, bruises on her neck. Dark ones. She looked like a freak show. Grimacing at her reflection, she waited for the inevitable shame to assail her. But it didn't come. Instead there was only an odd sense of...acceptance. Vin had seen all of this and hadn't turned away. Hell, he'd been the one to give her those damn bruises in the first place so was there really anything to be ashamed of there?

Slowly, she turned from the mirror and went into the bedroom, pulling open her wardrobe to grab some clothes. A tiny pair of denim shorts over black fishnet stockings and a tight, neon pink T-shirt. Heavy black biker boots. Her armor against the world.

Yet as she stood at her dressing table, putting her hair up in a ponytail and putting in some bright blue contacts, she realized that she hadn't been thinking of armor when she'd pulled on those clothes. She'd been thinking of Vin. Of what he liked to see her in.

Dressing for a man? What the hell was going on with her?

The breathless feeling returned and she found herself creeping back into the lounge, drawn to the man still lying asleep on the couch.

She couldn't stop looking at him. His face was relaxed in sleep and without its usual stern expression he looked so much younger. More approachable.

His mouth was curved slightly, hinting at a smile.

She hadn't seen that smile much. Most of the time he was so disapproving and stern. Even when she'd been younger and she and Ellie had first become friends, Vin had been the unsmiling, parental figure. No, they couldn't have their music turned up loud. No, they couldn't have one of his beers. No, they couldn't go into town after dark. Always the buzz kill, that was Vin.

She'd resented him then, taking on Ellie's own annoyance with his constant boundary setting. Thinking he took the whole father-figure thing way too far. But it must have been hard as a teenage boy. To have to bring up your little sister by yourself. No wonder he always looked so damn grim.

Yet he wasn't like that all the time. She remembered his smile yesterday as she'd sat astride him naked, a lazy hand in her hair. When he'd given her a collar for her birthday. A collar she'd taken off because stupid girls who got themselves accidentally pregnant didn't deserve nice things like that, did they?

Neither did they deserve pleasure with their pain. Or to be allowed to cry. Or to have someone wash them, dress them, wrap them up in strong arms and hold them while they slept...

Her eyes stung as she watched his beautiful face. As the ache in her heart clenched so tight she thought it might be crushed entirely.

She'd never been in love before but she had a horrible feeling she might be in love now.

And naturally, that was the moment Vin's eyes opened, catching hers.

She didn't want to blush but her skin didn't listen. "Oh, you're awake." She made herself hold his gaze. "Good morning."

He blinked. "What time is it?"

"Uh...eight, I think."

With a muffled curse, he sat up, scrubbing a hand through his dark hair. As he did so, she caught a glimpse of the scrapes on his knuckles, another reminder of the night before. And still the shame and humiliation she should be feeling didn't come. There was only worry, for him.

His hand slowed and she realized she was staring. Well, too bad if he saw. "You get into a fight or something?" she asked, glancing at his hand.

"Something like that." His gaze dropped to her neck, noting the bruises, blue eyes darkening. "Those are from me, aren't they?"

"Yeah. But it's okay. They don't hurt this morning." At least not enough to cause her too much discomfort.

His gaze kept going down her body. "You're never going to be normal dressed like that," he murmured with his usual bluntness.

Her words from the night before. Again she braced herself for the tide of embarrassment.

Vin lifted his gaze back to hers. "But I think you know that, don't you?" And there was no condemnation in his eyes. No judgment.

She swallowed and oddly enough there was only an echo of embarrassment that caught at her. Only a small twinge. A reflex. He'd seen everything last night. There really wasn't any more to her he could have seen. "Yeah, maybe I do."

He let out a breath, leaned back against the couch, studying her. "So the weird hair, the clothes, it's your armor, isn't it? A way to keep everyone at a distance."

Man, he saw so much. Too much. "Probably."

"Probably?" One dark eyebrow rose.

"All right, so it is. There's nothing wrong with wanting to

protect yourself."

"From what?"

"From other people's crap."

"No, nothing wrong with that." He was silent a minute, his gaze drifting down her body once more. "You know, I used to think you looked weird. And you still do. But you're so damn hot with it."

Her cheeks heated and it wasn't embarrassment she felt this time but pleasure. She was freaking pleased he'd noticed, for God's sake. Kara stuck her hands in the back pockets of her shorts, shifting uncomfortably on her feet. "Well, thanks."

A small silence fell.

"What happened last night, baby?" he asked. "Why do you have to hurt yourself like that?"

She'd been expecting the question but not the gentleness in his rough voice, and it made her feel even more uncomfortable. "I'm not...not your baby."

"Tell me, Kara."

"It's just...something I used to do when I was sixteen. You know, typical emo teenage stuff. I always was a drama queen."

"No," he said, and abruptly sat forward. "Don't minimize it. Don't dismiss it like that." He reached out and grabbed her wrist before she could stop him, turning it outward. The scars along it were so obvious she almost jerked her hand away, wanting to hide it. "There's nothing funny about cutting yourself with a razor."

She didn't want to talk about it. Didn't trust that gentle note in his voice. Last night, he'd seen her stripped of her defenses. Laid bare. Crying like a child.

But nothing bad happened, right? He drained the poison and took care of you.

Her heart felt tight and full. Yeah, he had. What he'd given her last night had been far more effective than any razor. More powerful than pain. And that deserved recognition. She owed him.

You love him.

Jesus, that too. But that was something she couldn't deal with right now so she let him hold her wrist, trace the scars with his finger. Then she said, "My life was fairly shitty when I was a kid. I was in foster care a lot."

He didn't look at her, thank God. As if he knew this confession needed privacy. "How come?"

"Oh, my mum was a single parent. She worked three jobs in order to support me and my brother and my sister. Meant she had to leave us at home by ourselves, sometimes for days. Then she'd come home and hit the bottle."

"What about your dad?"

"I never knew him."

His fingers tightened almost imperceptibly on her wrist. "So what happened?"

It shouldn't have been hard, after all, it had happened years ago. But still, getting the words out was difficult. "Mum worked all the time so I used to look after the other two. I tried really hard to make sure they both looked cared for because Mum was terrified we'd get taken by social services. But one day...I dunno, I think I was so worried about Liam and Rose that I must have neglected myself. Anyway, one of the teachers at school asked me if I was okay and whether things at home were okay. I said I was fine, that everything was good, but then she started asking me about Mum. About my brother and sister. Long story, but eventually social services were called. And we were taken into care." It should have been good for everyone. But it wasn't.

Vin's finger stroked along one scar, back and forth. He didn't say anything, staring at the movement of his finger. But she knew he was listening. "We got split up. Sent to different homes. I was able to stay in touch with them, but then Mum got solvent, gave up the drink and requested them back." This was the hard part. "At least she asked for my brother and my sister." She stopped. Even now it hurt, though she told herself it didn't.

"And you?" Vin kept his gaze on his finger.

"No," she said hoarsely. "I'd aged out of the system by then, but Mum didn't want me to come home. She said I'd 'disrupt' Rose and Liam from settling back in and it was best if I kept my distance. I believed her at the time. It wasn't until later that I realized she was punishing me for breaking up the family."

"Kara." His hand closed around her wrist, gently holding. "What happened to you?"

"In foster care? Nothing much. Just a series of families I never fit in with. Never wanted to fit in with, to be honest."

"And the cutting?"

She pulled her wrist out of his grip. "I don't want to talk about this, Vin. It's not important."

"Bullshit it isn't. If it wasn't important I wouldn't have caught you last night with a razor in your hands."

"Don't worry, I saw enough psychologists to last a lifetime. It's just my way of handling the guilt. And Mum's rejection. Yeah, I lost it last night and I'm sorry you had to see it, but I haven't felt that way for over ten years."

"So what was different about last night?"

"Uh, the tiny matter of me being pregnant might have had something to do with it."

Vin looked at her and she knew he saw through the bravado. He always had. "Yeah, you're pregnant with my baby. Which means if I catch you cutting again, so help me I will not be responsible for the consequences. If you want pain, you come to me and we'll do something about it. But no razors. That's over now. Understand?"

She looked away as another part of her gave itself up to him. "Yes. I understand."

"Good. And as to the pregnancy, we both had a hand in it, Kara. It's my fault too."

"I know. But neither of us asked for this."

"Whether we asked for it or not is irrelevant. The real question is what we do about it." Vin pushed himself up and off the couch in a swift, determined movement. "I'll give it to you straight. I won't ever abandon this child. Understand?"

His vehemence, not to mention his certainty, took her aback. Then again, knowing Vin as she did, she should have expected it. "Won't ever? You sound pretty certain about that."

"I am certain. I know all about fathers walking out on their kids, and it's not something I'd ever do."

Well, he probably would know, given his and Ellie's background. Her friend had told her a little about their father who had given up on them and their mother who needed to be committed every now and then, but Kara had never questioned her deeply about it. Hell, she never wanted to talk about her family crap, why would anyone else want to talk about theirs?

"That's good to know. But you're assuming I'm keeping it." She hadn't made any kind of decision yet, and she said it partly just to test the idea out, see how it sounded to her own ears because all options had to be considered. But she didn't like the sound of it. At all.

Vin's eyes narrowed. "You won't?"

Get rid of her child.

The way Mum got rid of you.

No damn way.

The decision settled down inside her like a stone settling

onto the bottom of a lake. Heavy, immovable. This would be hard and she would struggle, no doubt about it. But she wouldn't let this child be the scapegoat for her own mistake or let it carry the burden of blame.

Maybe she couldn't have normal, but she could make her own version of it.

Kara met his gaze. "Actually, I think I will. Keep it, that is."

Vin wasn't surprised. Smart, stubborn Kara—who never let a challenge go unmet—fail at this particular hurdle? No way.

She stood there all tough and weird, and goddamned sexy in her shorts and stockings get-up. Looking as if she wanted to take on the world and tell it go and sort its shit out.

Looking as if she could do anything.

It was a very convincing facade. Yet he knew that underneath all that toughness and snark, was a fragile, vulnerable woman. A woman who'd been hurt and hurt still. And no wonder given what she'd just told him about her childhood. About her mother.

It made him angry just thinking about it. And the fact that he'd joined in the hurting of her made him angrier still.

He'd hated to do what he had the night before because he'd never got off on hurting people. But he'd seen the pain in her eyes the moment he'd caught her with that razor, the naked anguish on her face. The desperation. She'd been at rock bottom and he couldn't walk away from her. Protecting people was such an innate part of him that walking away right then wasn't an option.

He didn't know what had driven her to that point, what made her want to find relief in pain. But one thing he did know was that she didn't deserve it. And that she should have more than pain.

He hadn't been expecting her to fall apart so completely at the end. But he was glad she had because he thought she needed to. And was glad that he'd been there to hold her. Take care of her. Because she needed that too. In fact she needed someone to look after her more often.

Vin stared at her, conscious of the relief that swept through him. He may not ever have intended to have a child but now he was, giving it up or getting rid of it was not an option. "I hope you're not assuming you're going to do this alone."

"I hope you're not assuming you can just take charge."

Well, shit, of course that's what he wanted to do. But he wasn't her master here. And with Kara, you couldn't assume anything. "No, of course not."

"Okay then. So neither am I."

"Fine. What are your plans in that case?"

She frowned. "I don't have any right now."

"Why not?"

"Why not? Jesus, Vin. I've only just made the decision to keep it."

"Then you'll need to start thinking about what you're going to do then, won't you? About where you're going to live. About how you're going to manage."

Her frown became a scowl. "Stop being so damn order-y. I'm only five weeks along, if that. We've got plenty of time to work all that crap out. And don't forget, lots of miscarriages happen in the first twelve weeks. No point making plans for something that may not even work out."

Vin gritted his teeth. His whole life had been about making plans, making sure everything was taken care of. Keeping control of his shit and everyone else's. He'd had to. Making mistakes was not allowed when even one missed pair of scissors or one overlooked kitchen knife could have led to disaster.

"You need at least to have a vague idea, Kara. And remember this doesn't just affect you."

"I know that," she snapped, a stain of red appearing on her cheekbones. "But give me some time to at least process it, for God's sake. Ellie's leaving in a couple of days too, and I can't think of anything else until she's gone."

Oh Christ. Ellie. Hunter.

A mental image of his friend lying on the ground, blood all over his face, loomed into Vin's consciousness. His knuckles ached in sympathy.

He was such a hypocrite. Getting on Kara's back when it wasn't like he was a paragon of virtue. Especially not after he'd let his temper get the better of him and had not only beaten the shit out of his friend, but fired him too. From the company he partly owned.

What a fucking mess.

"Yeah, okay," he said, feeling suddenly more tired than he'd ever felt in life. "But at least go and see a doctor."

"Why? So they can tell me what I already know?"

"Just do it, Kara."

She didn't like the order and he knew she was trying to think of some way out of it. So he added, because he didn't want to argue with her anymore, "Please."

Something changed in her face, the glint of temper fading. Her mouth, in a tight line, softened. "Okay," she said after a moment. "I will."

Kara came back from her doctor's appointment a few days later feeling mutinous. All the tests were positive. She really was genuinely pregnant. The woman had been lovely and understanding, shoving lots of pamphlets and free baby crap at her. Kara had dumped them all in her wardrobe as soon as she'd gotten home then dyed her hair rebelliously with the new purple dye she'd found in a pharmacy on her way home.

The streaks of purple looked good with the gold in her hair. Made her feel like her old self again.

Vin hadn't visited her since he'd left her apartment a couple of days ago and she was glad about it. The baby, not to mention what had happened in her bathroom that night, had changed things between them and no amount of telling herself she didn't miss what they had, made her miss it any less. Or him.

Yeah, she missed the sex all right. But mainly what she missed was Vin. Especially when she'd texted him after the appointment with the doctor and all she'd gotten in return was a *Good.*

Stupid love. She still hadn't fully processed that little emotion which was perhaps for the best since clearly it just plain sucked.

And when Ellie turned up on her doorstep the night after walking out on Hunter, she decided that she'd go on not processing it quite happily since Ellie's pain distracted her from her own. Besides, she'd always found it easier to give support to someone else than receive it herself, so she let her friend talk about what was happening with Hunter. And kept quiet about her own news. She didn't want to tell Ellie until it was certain. Until she had no choice.

Later that night, the pair of them went out to a bar for a few farewell drinks, Kara managing to do a bit of tricky water substitution for her vodka shots. Vin joined them a bit later but his presence only added tension to an atmosphere that really didn't need it.

He didn't say much, sitting in the booth seat nursing a beer, a dark look on his face. And of course her stupid body leapt into aching life in reaction. Images of that night in her bathroom unreeling like an erotic movie inside her head. The pain and the pleasure. And the exquisite relief. His arms around her, holding her...

She told herself to ignore him. To treat him the way she'd always done. Ellie's controlling big brother.

Who just happens to be the father of your child.

Kara found herself putting a hand over her belly under the table. And as she did so, she caught Vin's gaze from across the table. She lifted her chin. "Problem?"

He glanced over to the bar where Ellie was waiting to order another round of drinks, then glanced meaningfully at the glass in front of her. "That better not be vodka."

"What do you think I am? Stupid? I've been drinking water all damn evening."

He remained silent, long fingers moving absently up and down the side of the beer bottle. It was kind of erotic so she had to look away.

An awkward silence fell.

"You haven't told Ellie?" she said after a moment, desperate to break the silence.

"No. Should I have?"

"I wanted to wait until after the twelve-week mark. Until everything is...y'know, certain."

Another pause.

"What about Hunter? Have you told him?"

Vin's look darkened still further. "No. I haven't."

Kara stared at him, hearing the rough note in his voice. Oh man, was there trouble between the two of them? Certainly sounded as if there was. And there was only one reason for that: he'd found out his best friend had been with his sister.

Actually, now she thought about it, there'd been tension

between Ellie and Vin tonight as well. For the same reason?

"You know, don't you?" Kara said bluntly. "About her and Hunter."

Vin's expression became a hard mask. "Yeah, I know."

The movement of his fingers on the bottle stilled and Kara found herself looking once again at his hands. At the healing skin on his knuckles. And remembering the aura of leashed violence around him the night he'd come to her and found her in the bathroom.

Oh shit.

"You found out the day I told you about the baby, didn't you?"

"Yes."

"Vin, did you hurt him?"

"It's none of your goddamn business."

"So those marks on your knuckles came from something else. A wall maybe." She didn't know why it was important to get an answer from him. Perhaps because it seemed inconceivable that Vincent Fox would lose control enough to hit someone. Especially his best mate.

The expression on his face hardened even more. Which told her everything she needed to know. Yes, he had hurt Hunter. And yes, he was deeply ashamed of the fact.

"Vin—"

"I don't want to talk about it, Kara."

"Like I didn't want to talk about my bloody family. But I did. Because you asked me."

"You didn't have to."

"No, but I did anyway."

"Why?"

"Because after that night you found me in the bathroom, I

thought I owed you an explanation."

"Oh and now you think I owe you one?"

"Well, don't you?"

"I don't fucking think so."

But she refused to be daunted. "Why? You ashamed that you got angry? That you lashed out?"

His hands fell away from the beer bottle and he put them under the table. "This isn't the time, baby girl."

"I'm not a baby girl. I'm the mother of your freaking child."

Something flashed over his face. An expression she couldn't read. He glanced at the bar again. Ellie was leaning against it, talking to the barman.

"Yeah, I hit him," Vin said roughly. "I beat the shit out of him." His gaze came back to hers. "And yeah, I'm ashamed of it. Wouldn't you be?"

Sympathy twisted inside her. Because in his place, yes, she would have been. "The baby announcement can't have helped."

"No, but that's no excuse."

"Everyone makes mistakes, Vin."

He turned his head again, looking over at his sister who was returning with the drinks. "I don't expect you to understand. But mistakes are the one thing I can't afford to make."

Chapter Twelve

Vin walked out of the airport departures area to find Kara waiting for him, leaning against the Corvette in the drop-off zone. She had major panda-eyes, mascara running over her cheeks.

"What?" she said, looking defensive. "I'm crying. Big deal. My best friend—shit, my only friend—has just left for a couple of years overseas. So sue me."

"I thought you didn't cry."

"I didn't." Her chin lifted. "At least not until some guy bit me on the neck and screwed my brains out on my bathroom vanity."

He could see past the defensiveness this time. Could see the grief in her eyes. Shit, he felt it too. Only partly mitigated by the conversation he'd had with Hunter after the guy had turned up when Ellie went through the gates.

His best friend loved his sister. Was willing to give up everything to be with her. And man, the taste of humble pie was terrible. Still, he had to hand it to his friend. Hunter had some pretty dark stuff in his past but he'd faced it. Come through it. And all so he could be with Ellie. You had to respect a man for that. Even though it was going to mean yet more work for Vin in sorting out what was going to happen with the business. But then that's what he did, wasn't it? He sucked it up. Dealt with it.

"Did you want anything in particular?" he asked, leaning against the red metal of his car. Relief would hit him soon. Relief that Ellie was gone, that the worry that had been his constant companion for so many years would finally lift. But along with that relief would come the guilt, not to mention the fact that he was going to miss her.

Her and Hunter. In one fell swoop he'd lost the only family he'd ever had.

His throat felt tight, choked with something that tasted an awful lot like loneliness.

"I thought," Kara said softly, "that you might want some company. Seeing as Ellie's gone. Unless of course, you and Hunter—"

"Hunter's gone too."

Her eyes widened, a rim of dark brown showing around her deep gold contacts. "What do you mean Hunter's gone too?"

"He followed her onto the plane. I spoke to him just ten minutes ago as he went through the gates. I assume she doesn't know he's coming."

A grin turned her lovely mouth, making the blunt edges of the loneliness inside him feel sharp all of a sudden. "Damn. Guess he came through for her after all. God, I can just imagine her face when he turns up."

"Yeah. Wonderful."

Her grin faded. Shit. She must have picked up on the stupid, pathetic note in his voice. "Then you really must need company."

"I've got work to do, Kara. I can't afford to stand around—"

"Drop me off at the café. I'll make you an espresso."

For a moment, he didn't know what to do. He didn't want to be around her right now. Her smile. Her warmth. They were dangerous. Her sexy and naked at his feet, that he could handle. Her crying and lost in his arms, yeah, he could handle that too.

Her smiling at him and offering company? When he felt

lonely? Nope.

"Like I said, I have work."

Something flickered in her eyes. "Okay, so maybe I could use the company too."

"Kara..."

"Please, Vin."

So quiet he almost missed it. But the mascara tracks down her cheeks spoke for themselves as did the liquid shine of her tears.

He let out a breath. "Hop in then."

She grinned, brighter than before. And turned to get in the car.

"Wait," he ordered.

"What?"

"Your hair. It's purple." He hadn't noticed it in the dim light of the bar the night before but now, with the sun lighting up the rich gold, the dark streaks were obvious.

"So?"

"I don't like it."

Kara rolled her eyes. "Who cares whether you like it or not? We're done with sleeping together anyway, right?"

No.

The denial was instinctive and hit him out of the blue. Yeah, he hadn't been to see her the past couple of days but that was because Ellie was leaving and work had been a nightmare. Plus he'd already decided that the master/slave fantasy was over. He couldn't do it, not knowing she was pregnant. It felt wrong somehow.

But that didn't mean he didn't want her.

In fact, just looking at her now, leaning against the red metal of his car, her purple and gold hair loose down her back, she was so goddamned sexy. She wore a little pleated school-girl skirt today, along with a tight, white blouse. No tights or stockings, just long golden legs with black biker boots. She had a couple of buttons of her white blouse undone, revealing the purple lace of her bra. Not that the buttons needed to be undone in order to see that—it was obvious under the white cotton.

Weird and slutty, his better self said. His cock, on the other hand, was totally okay with her choice of outfit. Hot and sexy, it thought.

"Yes," he said aloud, because saying it aloud made it true. "We're done sleeping together."

Kara lifted a shoulder. "Great." And she opened the door and got in.

Yeah. Great.

If he told himself that often enough, then maybe his goddamned dick would get the message.

Kara put the takeaway coffee cup down on Vin's desk. "There you go, one black espresso, two sugars."

Perhaps she should have taken the hint and left him alone at the airport. But she hadn't been able to. The expression on his face as he'd said goodbye to his sister had been set and grim. And she'd got the idea by now that he looked like that when he was protecting himself.

And if she felt sad at Ellie's departure, then he must be feeling pretty shitty about it too.

So it made sense for them to feel shitty together.

At least that's what she told herself. Totally not anything to do with the fact that she missed him, a nagging ache that wouldn't seem to go away.

Vin grabbed the coffee and pushed his chair back, stretching out his long, denim-clad legs. "Who's watching the café then?" he asked as he raised the cup to his mouth.

"Tom. I'll have to go back in an hour." She watched as he took a sip. "Good?"

"Yeah." He took another sip, eyes narrowing as she hitched herself up on the edge of his desk. "Have you made any decisions about the baby yet?"

Kara let out a breath. Over the past couple of nights she'd thought about it, stressing about how she was going to cope with the café. The financial side of it already wasn't good, adding a kid to the mix only made it worse. She hadn't been able to bring herself to do the sums because she knew that whichever way she looked at it, unless she had a huge injection of cash, the business was going to tank.

She wrapped her hand around her latte, the heat of the cup warming her suddenly cold fingers. "No, not yet."

"Should you be having that coffee?"

Kara scowled. "I'm giving up alcohol. No way I'm giving up caffeine."

His gaze had dropped down to the bare expanse of her thigh, her skirt having ridden up due to her position on the desk. "And what about the café? How are you going to manage that?"

She liked the way he looked at her, no denying it. But she'd meant it when she'd told him they were done sleeping together. No point muddying the waters with sex. Especially the kind of sex they'd been having.

Wishing she'd worn a longer skirt, Kara pulled on the hem, trying not to look too obvious about it. "I don't know yet. But I'm sure I'll figure it out."

Abruptly his eyes lifted to hers, sharp and focused. "What do you need? Money? Extra staff?"

Her defensiveness kicked in, she couldn't help it. "Like I said, I'll figure it out."

"Don't be stubborn about this, Kara. If you need help, ask for it."

"I'm not being stubborn."

"Bullshit, you're not." He put his coffee down and leaned forward, elbows on the desk. "Do you even want to keep the café?"

She could feel herself beginning to bristle. "Of course I want to keep it. It's my business."

"Why? It's not like it's a roaring success."

"Hey, what the hell would you know?"

"You hardly have any customers and Ellie told me you're struggling."

Kara stared at him in shock. "Ellie told you?"

He didn't even have the decency to look embarrassed. "I asked her."

Making a mental note to kill her friend at the earliest opportunity, Kara gave him a disgusted glance. "Jesus, Vincent—"

"Don't be so bloody defensive," he cut her off with his customary bluntness. "I had to know because this concerns me too."

"Yes, but—"

"Your business is failing and you're fighting a losing battle. Trying keep it afloat at the same time as bringing up a child is a recipe for ruin. Believe me, I know this. I've done it."

Kara struggled with her outrage at his arrogance. And also with a strange sense of relief that she wasn't alone. That someone else knew exactly what she was going through. It wasn't something she experienced very often. "Oh yeah, and you're so ruined." She gestured at the office around them.

"Looks like one hell of a ruin to me."

Vin's hard gaze didn't flinch. "Because I took on a shitload of debt and worked my ass off. Because I didn't see my sister for years I was working so damn hard. Because I had Hunt to look after her. You want that for our kid? I sure as hell don't and I don't think you do either."

Well, no, of course she didn't. Her mother had given her such a great example of what not to do after all.

She swallowed and looked away from him, glancing down at the coffee in her hands. "Why me? Why can't *you* give up your bloody business?" Even as she said it, she knew how childish it sounded. Not to mention stupid. Fox Chase was successful and growing. He'd be mad to give it up.

"You think I'm not giving up stuff?" he said in a low voice. "I am. I'm going to have to can the architecture degree I planned to start this year."

She glanced back at him. "Architecture degree?"

This time it was his turn to look away. "Yeah. I want Fox Chase to be able to offer the total package. Design and build. And I wanted to specialize in green building. But I don't have the skills yet."

"You can't hire an architect?"

"No. I want to do it." A small hesitation. "It's something I've been wanting to do for a long time. I've just never had the chance."

And now he wouldn't. Thanks to their stupid affair.

She didn't know what to say. Looking back at her hands once again, she eventually said, "I don't want to give up the café. Because if I did..." She stopped. Because every little piece of herself she gave him felt like she was making herself even more vulnerable. "I'm not sure what else I would do."

He was quiet a moment. "What else did you want to do?"

"I...don't know." Slowly she turned the cup in her hands. "I liked drawing cartoons. That's all I was any good at in school. Just stupid little drawings. And then I got a part time job in a café and I got quite good at making coffee too. Then I read about the Japanese manga café culture so I thought I'd get one going here. Especially since it combined the two things I kind of enjoyed."

"That's not what I asked, Kara."

She bit her lip. "I told you. I don't know what I want to do. The café earned me some money and I was okay with that." At least she'd been happy. But now the status quo was upset. Now she would have to reconsider things. Her unease deepened. She'd never had much in the way of ambition at school. Never let herself have any. Because wanting something was too hard and she'd had too many rejections in her life to contemplate reaching for more.

The café had been a safe choice, she saw now. Because here she was, contemplating giving it up, and yet her fear wasn't about losing it, it was about not knowing what else to do.

"But it's not earning you money now and being okay with something is hardly a life." Vin's words were uncompromising and uncomfortable. "What about those cartoons then?"

"Sure. Like drawing manga is a smart career choice." She shifted on the desk. "It's a moot point. Since I'm going to have a kid, I won't be having much of a life anyway."

"Don't be stupid. It's not that cut and dried. Kids aren't the end of your life."

"Right back at ya, buddy." She put her cooling latte down on the desk. "Kids and architecture school aren't mutually exclusive either."

"But they are if you have a full time job and other responsibilities. And if you want to spend any time at all with them."

Kara stared at him. Once again she was getting the implacable mask. The one that said, *These are the facts. Suck it up.* "You really have all the answers, don't you? It doesn't have to be that way all the time, Vin. You can change your reality if you want it enough."

His blue-gray gaze stared back, unflinching. "So change yours, Kara. Stop shooting for *good enough.* Aim higher."

Unease twisted inside her. "What's wrong with *good enough?*"

"Nothing. But you're better than that. You're smart and you're clever and you're determined. You should want more."

His words went straight through her like arrows punching through tin foil. And she knew he meant every one because he never said anything he didn't mean.

"What if I don't want more? What if I'm happy with what I have?"

He saw so much. So much she didn't want him to see and yet couldn't seem to hide from him. "But you're not happy. Are you, baby?"

"Neither are you."

He let out a long slow breath. "I guess we can't always get what we want, right?"

A silence fell between them. Heavy with the weight of burdens they were carrying.

Then abruptly Vin got up from his desk, walked over to the windows, tightly leashed restlessness in every line of his tall, broad figure. "You know I'm building a house, right?" he said.

She did know. He'd been in the process of building it for a while now, doing the job himself. Ellie had told her it was because he was such a control freak he wouldn't let anyone else touch it. "What about it?"

"I've fast-tracked the building. It should be finished in a month or so. I want you to move in when it's done."

Shock moved like a cold wave over her. "You want me to move in?" she repeated blankly. "Why?"

He swung round to face her. "Because you're pregnant. And I need you close in order to look after you."

"I'm not sick, Vin. I don't need looking after."

"That's my child you're carrying. And I told you I'm not abandoning it. My job as a father starts now."

Kara slipped off the desk. No way was he starting into his control-freak stuff. Not with her. "No. You don't get to do that, Vincent Fox. You don't get to order me around like you own me. I'm not your slave anymore. And I'm not your sister either. I'm not even your freaking girlfriend. Yes, this child is yours but it's also mine. And you need to leave me alone to make my own decisions about how this is going to go."

Frustration crossed his face. "If you think I'm going to stand back and take a passive role in this kid's life you've got another think coming. I won't let you do this alone."

Oh crap, that's all she needed. Vin doing his protective thing. And he wouldn't back down about it. "That doesn't mean I have to move in with you."

"Fine. I'll sell the house and move in with you."

"You will bloody not!"

"Why not? You won't have to pay rent. And you'll have someone around to look out for you."

"I don't *need* anyone to look out for me." She'd been looking after herself for years now. Yeah, okay, so she loved him but she didn't need him, that was for sure. "God, next you'll be offering marriage."

His eyes narrowed. "Perhaps that would be a good idea. Kids need a family."

A weird kind of panic turned over inside her. Marriage? A family?

It's what you wanted, wasn't it? Normal?

Yes, it was. But him marrying her because he had to, because she was pregnant, that wasn't the kind of normal she had in mind. People got married because they loved each other.

What makes you think you deserve anyone's love?

Out of nowhere came the image of the collar, the one she'd shoved in a drawer the day she'd taken that pregnancy test. The one he'd given her for her birthday. A beautiful and precious gift, something you surely didn't give to a casual screw. Too good for her and yet, "*You belong to me,*" he'd said before giving her the key.

A pain settled in her chest, a sharp kind of hope she didn't want to acknowledge. Forcing the thought from her head, she chucked her cup in the bin beside the desk. "Well, I hate to disappoint you but I'm not the marrying kind. And as for all this moving-in shit, that's not going to happen either. Now if you'll excuse me, I have a café to run." She moved to the door, grasped the handle.

"Stop being so bloody stubborn, baby girl," Vin growled.

"And you respect my right to say no, asshole."

She didn't wait for an answer, slamming the door behind her as she left.

Vin looked down at the plans he'd had loaded onto his iPad then glanced back up at the building taking shape in front of him. The roof was on already—Hunter's fix for the roofline had worked a treat—and soon they'd be ready to do the cladding. The two new apprentices he'd just hired had been a little wild, but they'd already been nicely whipped into shape by the guy he'd taken on to replace Hunter.

Maybe he and Kara would be able to move in before the twelve-week mark.

Vin glanced down at the iPad again, checking his email, but there was nothing from her.

Not hugely surprising given how angry she'd been with him the day she'd walked out of his office. He'd decided after that to give her some space, and it had been a couple of weeks since he'd had more than a few terse texts from her telling him she was goddamn okay and to stop fucking bothering her.

Typical Kara. She must be really annoyed with him.

Of course he shouldn't have asked Ellie about her business without her knowledge. But then he had to do something. Had to feel like some plans were being made. Okay, so it was early on in the pregnancy but a little information gathering wouldn't hurt. And whether he knew or not didn't change the fact that her business *was* in trouble.

And he hadn't been kidding about her moving in. He wanted her close so he could make sure she and the baby were okay. She might think it was some kind of control- freak thing and yeah, maybe it was. But that's just how he operated. It was either that or he rang her every day, called in to see her every evening, and he didn't think she'd like that either.

You could just leave her alone.

Vin stared sightlessly at the iPad screen. No, he couldn't. She was having his baby. And she might act all tough and independent but she was vulnerable underneath it all. She had no one else to count on except him. And if she had another episode with the razor...

He went cold at the thought.

No, she had to be with him. Here. In his house. His home.

He looked up at the building again. This thing had been in

the planning stages so long. Ever since his father had told Vin to draw him a house. A house for their family to live in.

Well, he'd drawn that damn house only for his father to fuck off. But dammit now the house was real and his family *would* live in it.

If it killed him they would.

The iPad made a chiming sound. A new message. He opened the app to find a message from Kara. *Scan appointment. Tomorrow at 3pm. You want to be there?*

Stupid question. Of course he wanted to be there. *Yes. Send me the details.*

A second later and he had the place and the address. Another second and she'd added, *Thanks for giving me some space.*

Vin snorted. *Don't get used to it. Tomorrow we sort out what we're doing.*

She didn't reply.

Vin hit the off button on the iPad. He'd have this, by God he would. He'd have her close, where he could see her. Look out for her and their child. Make sure they were okay.

Touch her.

But he closed that thought down. No, they weren't going back to what they had before. He'd put his own needs first then and now they were dealing with the consequences.

There could be no more mistakes.

Chapter Thirteen

Kara fiddled with her ponytail then flicked over the page of the stupid woman's magazine she wasn't reading. Yet another Z-list celebrity with yet another "baby bump". She resisted the urge to check the time on her phone again. She'd already compulsively checked it twice since she got to the clinic for her scan appointment. Probably only a few seconds had passed since the last time.

Nervousness churned in her gut, worsening the faint nausea from the morning sickness. She'd woken late this morning and had had to skip breakfast in order to get to the café on time. It'd been unusually busy too and the muffin she'd had mid-morning, followed by half a cheese panini at lunch was all she'd managed to fit in today.

Not enough. No wonder she felt ill.

Although that may have been the leftover from her conversation last night with Ellie via Skype. Where she'd finally told her friend about the baby.

Ellie's eyes went wide. "What?"

"Do I really have to say it again?"

"Yes. Because I don't think I quite got it the first time."

"I'm pregnant."

"Fucking hell! But how? I mean...aren't you a virgin?"

The look on Ellie's face brought a reluctant grin out of her. "Clearly not anymore."

Ellie blinked. "Wow. I just...wow. You know you're going to have to tell me everything now. And I mean bloody everything."

"Actually, there's some details you may not want." Kara braced herself. "Considering the fact that Vin's the father."

Ellie's mouth opened but nothing came out.

"I'm sorry, babe," Kara said, rushing to get the words out. "I'm really sorry I didn't tell you. But it just kind of happened and I totally didn't mean to, and I know—"

"You've been sleeping with my brother?"

"Uh...yeah."

Ellie bit her lip then let out a long breath. "Okay, well, I gotta be honest with you. It's a little weird."

"I know. That's why I didn't want to tell you."

"I didn't even know you and Vin... That you guys... I mean, I thought you didn't like him?"

"I kind of don't. But I kind of do, too, if that makes sense."

"Not really, no. I'm still coming to terms with the thought of my best friend actually wanting to sleep with my brother."

"I hate to break it to you, babe, but he's hot."

Ellie held up a hand. "Ew, no. Please don't go there."

So she hadn't gone there. Especially not about the collar and the slave fantasy. But as she'd talked to her friend about Vin and the baby, about how he'd asked her to move in with him, a deep yearning had broken open inside her. Like a damned-up river finally being able to flow again.

That was what she wanted. What she'd desperately wanted all her life.

And yet not quite. Because in all her fantasies, the fantasies of a family she'd had as a lonely teenager, she was loved. And Vin didn't love her. The only reason he'd offered this was for the baby's sake.

Aim higher.

Maybe he could, with his successful company, the house he was building. The plans he'd made for himself. But she couldn't. All she could do was draw cute cartoons and make a mean coffee. Oh and rock purple highlights like a boss. There wasn't much else for her except the café.

You're smart and you're clever and you're determined. You should want more.

Vin's voice, the words directly confronting the feelings of worthlessness she'd always tried so desperately to hide from. He never said anything he didn't mean. So why didn't she believe him? Why shouldn't she want more for herself? Like a family for a start.

Kara stared unseeing at the pages of the magazine, fear turning over inside her, making her mouth go dry. The old fears of rejection, of failing, of making yet another mistake in her life. But fuck it. This was her chance. Her chance at a normal life. A chance of having the kind of family she'd always wanted for herself. A place to belong. Okay, so he may not love her, but he did feel something for her. He wouldn't have given her that collar, claimed her as his, if all he'd wanted was a screw. Surely?

Maybe she could move in with him. Accept that from him like she'd accepted his care that night she'd cut herself...

Abruptly Kara threw the magazine back on the waiting room table. There was no one else waiting, just her. She got up out of the chair and paced around, staring at the pictures on the walls. The stages of pregnancy. Examples of scans. Happy families.

She stopped in front of one poster of a mother holding her child. A normal looking mother in a white dress, normal hair, normal smile. Looking at her baby with such love.

Kara's heart felt tight in her chest, the echo of pressure building. She didn't look like that. Today she'd tried, put on some skinny jeans and a tank top. Put her hair up. Left her makeup behind. Left her contacts out. But deep inside she felt the same. Still the weirdo girl with the strange dress sense. Who didn't fit in. Who cut herself when she got sad. Whom nobody wanted. Pretty much the antithesis of the mother in that poster.

How could she be that mother anyway? How could she give a child love when she'd never had it herself?

The poster swam in front of her eyes. Stupid fucking tears. Crying. All the time she was bloody crying. She hated it. Man, sometimes she preferred the razor. It was less painful than the tears.

"Kara?"

A deep, rough voice behind her. Vin.

She stayed where she was, staring at the poster. Not wanting him to see her tears. Or the sudden leap in her heart that she was sure must show on her face. "Look at that woman," she said, hoping like hell her voice sounded level. "Who wears a dress like that? I mean, really."

Warmth behind her. The familiar, spicy scent of him. And an overpowering urge gripped her. To step back into his arms. Turn and press her face against his chest. Let him hold her like he had that night. When he'd helped her ease the unbearable pressure of all those years of grief and pain.

It wasn't a razor she wanted. Or tears. She wanted him.

Perhaps he wouldn't ever love her. But he'd give her his strength and his support. Ease her pain. And he'd do it without question. Without hesitation. Because that's the kind of guy he was. The kind of guy he'd always been.

When it came to giving support, he'd never reject her.

Kara didn't think. She turned and stepped close to him. Wrapped her arms around his lean hips. Laid her forehead on the hard wall of his chest. And whispered, "I'm scared, Vin."

He didn't move. Didn't step away. At first she felt him tense, then gradually he relaxed and his arms came around her. Holding her close. "I know." His voice rumbled against her ear. "But it'll be okay."

A hand rested on the back of her head. She closed her eyes a moment. "I don't know how I can do this. How I can give a kid love. I never had it when I was little. What if...what if I can't?" Fear twisted, heavy and dark. "What if I'm too screwed up?"

Gentle fingers gripped her ponytail, pulling her head back. The look in his eyes was so sharp, focused. "You're not screwed up, Kara. You just had a shitty childhood. But that doesn't mean you can't love. I had a shitty childhood too, but that didn't mean I couldn't love Ellie."

And God, that shitty childhood hadn't prevented her from falling in love with him, had it? It was a screwed up kind of love maybe, but it was love. She knew it, felt it in her heart.

"Yeah, I guess."

"And you said you had a brother and sister. You must have loved them."

Liam and Rose. Eating breakfast in the morning. Toast because that's all Kara could make and bread was cheap. Brushing Rose's hair. Wiping Liam's face when he got butter all over it.

"It hurt when we were taken away. When we were split up." Liam crying, Rose reaching out for her. Not for their mother. For Kara. "So I guess I did." She hadn't got to see them much while they were all in foster care and then, once they'd been given back to their mother, not at all...

Vin's fingers in her hair tightened. "You know that no one will ever take your child from you, don't you? No one will *ever* take our child?"

As if anyone would ever get past him. "I do. But actually...I think that's not really what I'm afraid of."

"Then what?"

The fear twisted again and she recognized it now. Saw it for what it was. "I think I'm more afraid I *will* love it. That I won't be able to help myself." She swallowed. "And love hurts, Vin. It hurts too much."

"Ms. Sinclair?" The radiographer was standing beside the reception desk. "We're ready for you now."

Kara wiped her eyes. Pushed herself away from him. "Come on. Let's get this over with."

Vin tried to tell himself he wasn't nervous. But no amount of telling himself that changed the unsteady feeling in his gut as the radiographer moved the ultrasound device over Kara's bare stomach. On the little screen a black-and-white image showed, full of strange shapes and moving blobs. The technician made a satisfied sound. "Ah, there it is. Do you see?" She pointed to one of the blobs. It pulsed. "That's your baby."

The unsteady feeling became an earthquake, the world moving under his feet. Resettling itself into a new landscape. An entirely different and unfamiliar country.

That tiny thing was his baby. His child.

Kara made a soft, choked sound. He was holding her hand and her fingers tightened sharply around his. He turned his head, looked at her. Found her dark eyes on his, full of fear. Full of something else too.

Love hurts.

Yeah. It did. It was huge and terrifying and painful. The responsibility of it crushing. Not something you'd want to share with anyone because the burden of it was easier to deal with alone. That way no one could take it away from you.

He wanted to tell her it was okay, that it would be all right. But he didn't know if it would be.

She blinked, turned her head away. Yet didn't let go of his hand.

Afterwards they walked out of the clinic with the envelope full of pictures of the little baby-blob, the unspoken weight of what they'd created between them hanging in the air.

"We need to sort stuff out, Kara," Vin said, halting just outside the clinic entrance. "I need to know what you want to do."

She stopped, put her hands in her pockets. "Well, I told Ellie about it."

"I know." His sister had phoned him the night before and had given him a lecture, telling him if he hurt Kara, he'd have to answer to her. His little sister was proving to have a bit of a protective streak herself. "But that's not what I'm talking about."

"You mean the whole moving in thing?"

"Yeah."

Kara gave him a look from over the top of her glasses. "I'll move in with you, Vin." A small hesitation. "But that's not all I want."

Well, thank fuck for that. He hadn't realized how badly he'd wanted her to agree until now. It would be one less worry he'd have to deal with. Make the burden a little lighter. "What else do you want then?"

She stared at him, stubborn determination in her brown eyes. "You mentioned marriage. Well, I want that too."

That, he hadn't expected. When she'd mentioned it before, in his office, the idea had appealed to him in a purely legal sense. It tied up loose ends. Made sure that if anything happened to him, his child and its mother would be looked after. No, he'd never intended to get married. Never intended to do the wife and kid thing. But since the kid part of the equation had happened anyway, the logical, protective part of him insisted that making her his wife made sense.

"Marriage, huh?" He met her gaze. "I thought you hated the idea."

"So? I'm allowed to change my mind."

"What changed it?"

She shifted on her feet, but didn't look away from him. "I want a family, Vin. A normal freaking family. And this is my chance to have it."

"You sure about this? I'm going to be a hard-ass about the moving-in part but you don't have to marry me."

"I'm sure." And there was no doubt at all in her face. "What about you?"

"Yeah. It makes sense from a legal standpoint. And it would give the kid a proper family."

"Exactly."

Yes. It was a good plan. A good idea. So why did he feel like there was something missing? That something more needed to be said?

"This hasn't got anything to do with love," Kara said suddenly. "Just so you know."

He stared at her, taken aback. Love? He hadn't said anything about love. Because what did love have to do with marriage? Nothing. His parents were supposed to have been in love and look what happened to them? Not much damn love in that relationship as far as he could see.

And yet there was something in her eyes, almost like a challenge. As if she was daring him to disagree. Which was weird because why would he? This didn't have anything to do with love on his part either.

"I didn't think it did," he said. "I didn't offer to marry you because I love you, Kara."

Her lashes fell abruptly, hiding her gaze. "No, I know you didn't." There was no change in her voice or her posture but somehow he got the feeling that he'd disappointed her. Failed her in some way.

A tight sensation settled in his chest. "Kara—" he began.

"I think we can discuss the details at my place," she interrupted, already turning away. "How about you take me home?"

Fuck.

They were halfway back to her apartment when Vin's phone went off. He glanced down at the screen then cursed viciously. "Sorry, but I'm going to have to answer it."

He pulled over to the side of the road and picked up his phone. "Fox. Oh...I see..."

Kara glanced at him. His face had settled into that impenetrable mask again. "What? No. No, I haven't. No, I understand." He turned his head, looking out the window, his expression hidden. He raised a hand, shoved his fingers through his hair. "Yeah, I'll do that now. Okay. I'll call you back."

"What's wrong?" Kara asked quietly.

"Nothing," he said curtly. "Just something else I have to handle."

"Bullshit, it's nothing. You look like you could chew through metal."

He put the phone down in the holder between the dash and the handbrake. Adjusted the aviator shades he wore, the ones that hid his eyes so she couldn't see them. "I have to go see someone. I want you to stay in the car." His words were flat and cold and suggested that arguing would be a mistake.

"Who?"

"My mother." He hauled on the wheel, pulling the Corvette back out into the traffic.

"Why? What's wrong with her?" She didn't know the details, but she was aware that Ellie and Vin's mother suffered from some kind of mental illness. Ellie didn't talk about it much. Another thing Kara hadn't wanted to probe too deeply into. Mothers were just uncomfortable subjects all round.

Vin didn't answer. Just drove. The car filled with a thick, tense silence that Kara wanted to break but didn't know how. Clearly questions weren't welcome, and she had a feeling that pushing wasn't going to help either.

Eventually they drove down a street full of run-down state houses, frayed washing hanging on lines, rubbish piled up in gardens, weeds hanging over fences. Cars in driveways standing on blocks. A collection of kids played in one driveway, staring as Vin parked the Corvette.

"Stay here," he said shortly.

"Why?"

"Because I fucking said so, all right?" He said the words so savagely that all she could do was stare at him.

He didn't say anything more, getting out of the car and slamming the door behind him.

She watched out of the window, her heart suddenly beating fast as he walked up to a big, two-storied building with green painted weatherboards. The place had clearly been divided up into apartments—she could see the balconies of several.

Foreboding gripped her.

She didn't know what was wrong with his mother but

whatever it was, it couldn't be good.

Vin had always seemed so self-contained. So strong. He gave the impression he could handle anything. But she remembered the look in his eyes when the technician had pointed out their baby on the screen. The shock in them. And her own fear reflected back at her.

She'd felt terrified. Terrified of loving that tiny blob on the screen and she knew he felt the same.

He was human, just as vulnerable and just as freaked-out as she was. A human being who needed someone. But he didn't have anyone, did he? Not now Ellie and Hunter weren't here.

The only person he had was her. And even if he didn't feel about her the way she felt about him—and clearly he didn't after the comments about marriage and love she hadn't been able to help herself from asking him outside the clinic—that didn't mean she was going to let him do this alone.

She got out of the car and walked up the path to the apartment block. Inside, she caught sight of Vin heading up the stairs to the second story. She followed him up, then down a long hallway, seeing him knock on one of the doors. She waited, keeping an eye on him. Not wanting to risk him yelling at her quite yet. Not when all she wanted to do was to make sure he was okay. That whatever he was facing, he didn't have to do it by himself.

After a moment, when the door didn't open, he pulled some keys out of his pocket and unlocked the door, disappearing inside.

Kara followed him, stepping into the tiny apartment. The place smelled of cigarette smoke and something sour, like old cooking oil left to stand too long. She went down the narrow hallway and came out into a small lounge area. The place was full of dirty plates and unwashed cups. Ashtrays full to overflowing. A couple of empty wine bottles beside a ragged sofa.

Then from one end of the apartment came a blood-curdling scream.

Kara's heart leapt into her mouth. What the hell was that? She rushed through the lounge to find a second even tinier hallway which led to a bedroom and a bathroom. The bathroom door was open. Inside a gray-haired woman in a dirty nightdress was crouched on the floor screaming. One hand was tied to a towel rail. Vin was crouched beside her, not touching her, the low rumble of his voice only barely audible beneath the screams of the woman. She was hurling abuse at him, telling him he was a fucking liar. That someone needed to die. That the demon wanted someone dead and she was powerless to stop him.

His mother. This broken, screaming woman was his mother.

For a moment Kara couldn't do anything, rooted to the spot with horror. Then she noticed that his mother's wrist was raw from the plastic tie she'd used to bind herself to the towel rail, blood beginning to seep down her arm. Jesus. She needed to be cut free.

Kara went back into the lounge and the small kitchen at one end of it, began pulling out drawers to find something to cut off the tie around the woman's wrist. But there was nothing. No scissors. There weren't even any kitchen knives. There was only plastic cutlery.

"I thought I told you to stay in the car."

Kara whirled to find Vin standing behind her, holding his phone. He didn't look so much angry now as tired. No, not just tired, exhausted. He glanced away, beginning to punch some numbers into the phone.

"I know but...I thought you might need help."

"I don't need help, Kara. What I need is for you to do as

you're told. I've got enough to worry about up here without worrying about you as well." He turned away as someone on the other end of the phone answered.

Kara took a ragged breath, watching him. He sounded so cool and calm, as if his mother wasn't just screaming her lungs out not a meter away, as if he did this kind of thing every day.

She swallowed, her mouth dry. God, he probably did. This was what he'd had to deal with for years and years. Ellie had told her a couple of times that her mother sometimes had "episodes". Kara had got the impression that Ellie didn't see her, that her mother was often "too sick" for visits from her daughter.

Well, she could certainly see why that was.

Vin finished his call. He put his phone back in his pocket, ran another distracted hand through his hair. Hair that was already standing up on end. "Go get in the car."

"But what about...your mum?"

"I've called the crisis team. They'll be here soon. And the police."

"The police? Surely you don't..." But she stopped, the words halted by the look on his face. Bone-deep weariness.

"She's violent when she's like this," Vin said. "The police are for everyone's safety."

Her throat tightened, her heart aching for him. "What happened?"

Vin lifted a shoulder. "Who knows? She's not supposed to drink but she does. She's not supposed to smoke but she does. She's supposed to take her meds but sometimes she doesn't. A collision of all three from the looks of things."

"This..." She gestured toward the bathroom. "She's like that a lot?"

Vin just looked at her. And in his stormy blue eyes, in the

exhaustion she saw there, she read the answer. Yeah. It was a lot.

"Please, baby," he said softly. "Please get in the car."

His demands wouldn't move her. But she couldn't resist him when he said please.

Wordlessly, Kara did what she was told.

It took a couple of hours to finish up with the police and the crisis team. Getting Vin's mother into a van so they could take her to hospital. Vin dropped Kara back to her apartment then left for the hospital himself.

For the next couple of hours she tried to busy herself with drawing, with TV, with anything really, but she couldn't stop thinking about it. Couldn't stop thinking about him.

The ache in her heart was like a splinter of glass digging in. Sharing the pain for what it must have been like for him, having to deal with his mother when she was like that, when he was only a teenager for God's sake. She remembered the times her own mother had got drunk sometimes after a hard day's work. The fear that gripped her. Because that drunk woman wasn't her mother. Was someone else. A stranger.

Did Vin feel that way? Had he been scared as a teenager? He must have been. Shit, she'd been terrified herself just today. And he'd had no one to help him, no one to turn to. He'd had to bear it all himself. It exhausted her just thinking about it.

She was at the point of going to bed when she heard the knock on her door. It could be no one else. And it wasn't.

When she opened the door, Vin stood on the other side of it. He didn't say anything, just looked at her, his eyes so dark and empty they looked black.

She said nothing either, pushing the door wide so he could

come in. And he did. Silently going into her lounge and sitting down on the sofa, his head in his hands.

Kara stood there not knowing quite what to do but wanting to do something for him. Anything. When Ellie had been like this over Hunter, she'd brought out the vodka. Perhaps it wasn't what he wanted but hey, someone had to drink the damn stuff since she couldn't now.

Getting a glass and the bottle, she poured him a shot. Put it on the table in front of him.

For a second he didn't move. Then slowly he lifted his head. Reached for the shot glass. Downed it. And she didn't need to be asked, she knew he wanted another.

So she poured him another. And another.

And a fourth.

Then he pushed the glass away and leaned back on the couch, his arm flung over his face.

Kara put the bottle down, came and stood in front of him. She so wanted to help him but she didn't know how.

Bullshit, you don't.

Once when she'd been broken apart, exposed and vulnerable, he'd held her. He hadn't said a word, just held her in his arms and it had been exactly what she'd needed.

Of course she knew how.

Kara dropped to her knees in front of him and wrapped her arms around his waist, and put her head in his lap and rested there. Giving him what he'd given her—the warmth of her body. The reassurance of her touch.

He didn't move. After a moment he put a hand on her head and Kara closed her eyes.

It was enough.

Vin felt heavy and slow, the vodka he'd consumed providing

a nice buffer between him and reality. He didn't want to move. Didn't want to think. He'd had enough of today. It had been shitty. Too many feelings he didn't want. Too many reminders of what he couldn't have.

Peace. Security. Freedom.

And it hadn't been until he'd gotten to Lillian's place, seen her screaming on the floor, that it had truly sunk home. He couldn't ever have that peace and security. Or the freedom. Not ever. Because he'd always have this. And even though Ellie had gone, the worry would never truly go away. If not for her, it would be worry for his child. Worry for Kara.

Perhaps his mother wouldn't hurt them but there were no guarantees. And it wasn't like she was ever going to get better.

No, he was stuck with it. With no one to help. No one to turn to. Hunter had helped to a certain extent but the guy had his own demons to deal with.

And now he was gone, Vin truly was alone.

Sometimes he didn't know what was worse, the sense of being a prisoner in his own life or the crushing isolation. An isolation he couldn't overcome because to do so would be to rely on someone else. Share the burden. And he couldn't do that. Not ever.

A couple of hands were pulling at him, the warm weight against his knees shifting.

He opened his eyes to find Kara standing over him. What was she doing here?

Oh yeah, that's right. He'd come back to her apartment after Lillian had been admitted to hospital. Why, he had no idea. But then she'd given him vodka.

Thank fuck for vodka.

"What is it, baby?" His voice sounded weird, slurred. Shit, he really was drunk. It was kind of unfamiliar since he didn't often get like this. But right now, he didn't much care.

"You need to go to bed. It's late and you need sleep."

"Yeah. Where are my keys?"

"You are so not driving."

Ah no. That probably wouldn't be a good idea.

Somehow he was on his feet, swaying gently. An arm snaked around his waist, a curvy female body pressing against him.

Not just any female body. Kara. She was so soft, so warm. He turned his face into her hair. She smelled like flowers. Sweet and musky. Familiar. "I love the way you smell," he said.

"Thanks."

"You're so fucking beautiful. You know that, right? You know how beautiful you are?"

"Yeah, you told me."

"It's true though. Even when you've got that color in your hair and your eyes are weird colors. Even then you're beautiful."

A light came on and he frowned, closing his eyes against it. Then she was pushing him and he felt something behind his knees. A bed. He sat as the light switched off.

Opening his eyes again, he watched as she reached forward to grip the hem of his T-shirt. "What are you doing?"

"Undressing you. You need to be in bed and asleep."

Sleep. Yeah, that sounded good. So good. And yet there was something even better about the soft brush of her hands as she pulled his T-shirt up and over his head. He reached out and took one, pressing her palm to the bare skin of his chest. Her touch burned. Licked him with fire.

"Vin," she said softly, her hand motionless.

No, it wasn't sleep he needed. Or vodka. He wanted, just

one more time, freedom from the worry. Freedom from responsibility. Freedom from all the fucking burdens he had to carry.

Freedom even from being her master.

For once in his life, he didn't want to have to make any decisions. He wanted someone to make them for him.

"Touch me," he said, his voice rough with the vodka and with sudden, desperate need.

In the dimness of her room, all he could see was her face, half shadowed by the bedside light. Clear skin, golden hair, wide dark eyes. Such beauty.

He was used to taking the control, but now the alcohol had loosened something inside him and it wasn't control he wanted from her. So it was easy to say, "Please. I need you."

Her expression changed. Became softer. She moved, pressed a kiss to his mouth, fleeting and soft. "Shall I change?"

And in his hazy, drunken brain, it suddenly became clear why he was here. He'd come for her. She'd seen what he had to deal with. She'd seen his mother screaming on the floor. She'd seen him exhausted and at the end of his rope. She'd seen everything. And he didn't have to explain or talk about it because she knew. Because she'd been there too.

He lifted a hand and touched her cheek. "No. I don't want a slave tonight. I want you."

"Me?" The word sounded almost shocked. "Are you sure? I could go get the costume—"

"I'm sure. Kara, please."

She stared at him and he couldn't interpret the look on her face now. Then she said, "Lie back."

He lay back on the bed, closed his eyes. And he felt her hands on his chest, on his arms, stroking him lightly, gently. Exploring him. Then her mouth at his throat, trailing kisses around his collarbone and down, the flick of her tongue against his nipples, light tracing fingers on his abs.

So good to be touched like this. So good be touched at all. The gentleness of her, the hesitancy of her touches, as if she wasn't sure she should be doing this. Then her growing confidence that sent a crack straight through his heart.

He kept his eyes closed, let her explore. And when she stripped his jeans and boxers from him, he lifted his hips to help her. She ran her hands up his thighs, wrapped her fingers around his cock, the touch tearing a groan from him. Then she squeezed and the groan became a growl. "That's right, baby girl. Just like that."

She stroked him, made him ache. Made him want to push her beneath him and bury himself inside her. Take control. But he didn't. Screw control. He didn't need it. Not tonight.

Kara moved, holding him. Then he felt her tongue on his cock, swirling around the aching head, delicate little licks like a cat.

The breath hissed in his throat and he arched back into the mattress, fire streaking straight up his spine. Then heat engulfed him as she took him into her mouth.

"Oh fuck, Kara." Pleasure hit him, a wave of it spinning him around, taking him away. Turning him over and over in a current made only of sensation. Of the wet heat of her mouth and the softness of her hair over his thighs.

Vin reached down, tangled his fingers in that softness, lifted his hips, driving himself into her mouth until it was so fucking good he couldn't stand it. "Baby, wait," he groaned, wanting to pull away so he could take her, too, but by then it was too late.

She took control, pushed him over the edge, pleasure exploding in his brain like a hammer blow and all he could was lie there as the climax gripped him tight, wringing him dry.

And afterwards, when the vicious pull of it had lessened, he just didn't have the energy to move, a delicious lassitude creeping up on him.

He felt like he'd left something unfinished but he couldn't seem to remember what it was. At the end there was a cool hand on his head and a voice in his ear telling him to sleep.

So he did.

Chapter Fourteen

Kara woke up feeling trapped. Again. A heavy arm snaked around her and over her stomach, a hand pressing between her breasts. A possessive kind of hold.

She lay there for a moment, her eyes closed, enjoying the sensation. It felt good to be held like that. As if she wasn't allowed to get away or escape. Not that she wanted to. In fact there was nothing much she wanted to do but lie here in Vin's arms.

After a moment, the body lying curved around hers moved, hot bare skin shifting against her back. A muscular thigh eased between her own, pressing gently against her sex. She shivered, desire igniting in her blood.

She hadn't been able to resist crawling into bed with Vin. He'd gone to sleep so quickly, the vodka and the orgasm doing their work almost too well. She hadn't minded.

"I don't want the slave tonight. I want you."

She knew he wanted her. Shit, she'd always known that. But it hadn't been until he'd said those words that she'd truly believed his desire wasn't just because she fulfilled his need for control. That it was her, Kara, that he wanted. Not only the slave girl.

And it hadn't been until that moment that she understood *she* wanted to be more than that for him too. She knew he didn't feel about her the way she felt about him but that didn't mean she had to hold back. He wanted her. He wanted Kara in all her fucked-up glory.

So that's what she'd given him.

At first she'd been hesitant, used to the master-slave dynamic during sex, but that hesitancy had soon gone by the wayside. She hadn't touched him for so long and he was so beautiful. All tanned skin and sculpted muscle. Not an ounce of fat on him. The legacy of his hard, physical job.

It had been intoxicating. The way she'd made him shake, made him moan, made him cry her name. For once she'd had the control, the power and the confidence, and she'd loved every second of it.

She hadn't even cared that he'd gone to sleep, only getting in beside him and wrapping her arms around him. Warming herself against his heat. Feeling so good that finally she'd been able to give him something. A measure of the peace he'd once given her.

The hand between her breasts shifted, sliding down and under her T-shirt, his palm sliding over her bare skin. She let out a small, ragged breath as he cupped one breast, his thumb gently tracing around her nipple. It hardened beneath his touch.

"Hey," he murmured in her ear, his voice soft and roughened with sleep. "I'm sorry. I was selfish last night."

"You'd had four shots of vodka and an orgasm. I would have been amazed if you'd stayed awake more than two seconds."

He shifted again, the heat of his erection against her hip. His thigh pressed a little harder and she found herself pushing down onto it, the friction tantalizing her. "Yeah, but still. Given the quality of the orgasm, you deserved more than me going to sleep on you."

You deserved more...

Yeah. She was starting to think she bloody did. "Such as?"

"Such as me returning the favor." His fingers pinched her nipple, sending a bolt of pleasure straight to her sex.

Kara shivered against him. "And here was I thinking we weren't sleeping together again."

"This isn't sleeping."

"You know what I mean."

"I can't change my mind?" A very conscious imitation of her words the day before. His hand shifted beneath her, curling under her arm, sliding under her T-shirt. His other hand cupping her other breast. Doing the same thing, thumb circling her nipple then brushing over it. Pinching gently. The breath escaped her. She could feel herself getting wet. Aching for him.

"I think we need this, baby," he murmured against the back of her neck. "Both of us do. It's better than pain. Better than vodka. And I just don't think I can keep my hands off you when I'm close to you."

He was right. They did need this. The release. The comfort. The connection with another person. Hell, not just another person. It was each other they needed.

She would never find this with another man. She would never love another man. It would only ever be him because there was no other person who understood what she needed like he did.

"Yes," she said, arching against him, gasping as his fingers brushed her now button-hard nipples. "Yes, do it." She lifted her hips, working herself against his thigh. Desperate for more contact, for more friction.

The feel of him naked against her was amazing. Always it was she who was naked, he who was clothed. Now their positions were reversed and it was an insane turn-on.

He kissed her behind her ear, bit her gently at the sensitive point where shoulder met neck. Not as hard as he'd done that time in her bathroom, but enough to add a sharp edge to the pleasure.

"Easy," he murmured as she trembled, his kiss soothing at

the same time as his hands incited.

"Oh...don't...I can't..."

"Hush." His breath slid over her shoulder, pleasure twisting harder inside her as he moved a hand down, stroking over her stomach. Sliding under the waistband of her panties, pushing through the damp curls between her thighs.

"Oh...Vin..."

His clever fingers stroked through the wet folds of her sex. Then he shifted suddenly, tugging down her panties, pulling them off her. Turning her over onto her back, he gently pressed her thighs apart and Kara's breath caught.

She trembled, feeling open and exposed. Laid bare to his gaze. "You meant it, didn't you?" she whispered. "Last night. When you said you wanted me?"

He didn't smile for reassurance. Just gave her that hard, level look that was by now familiar to her. "You really have to ask me that question? After all that stuff I told you last night about how beautiful and sexy you were?"

"You were drunk. And...no one's ever wanted me, Vin. Not one single person."

That piercing gaze remained on hers, searching. "You think I came here last night only for the vodka? Shit, if I'd wanted that I could have gone to the nearest booze shop. No, I came for you, Kara." He said it so firmly and with so much certainty there was no denying it. "And now I want you to lie there and let me give you what you gave me last night."

She couldn't speak, a dense, heavy emotion sitting in her throat.

"It's okay, baby," he said, his voice softening, becoming even rougher. "It'll be good, I promise."

Of course it would be. It always was with him.

He shifted lower between her thighs, spreading her open.

Then his head bent and his mouth covered her.

She let out a strangled cry.

His tongue flicked over her clit lightly before pushing inside her. Tasting her. She lifted her hips but his hands gripped her hard, holding her down onto the bed as he began to explore her, taking his time like she was a landscape he wanted to map and had to do so slowly and carefully in case he missed something.

She closed her eyes as the pleasure wound tighter and tighter. And it felt like she was leaving herself behind. Not just shedding her skin but erupting out of it. Becoming something else.

Something without the self-doubt and the anguish. The guilt and the worthlessness. Something better. More truly herself than she'd ever been.

She reached down, threaded her fingers in the softness of his hair, tangled them tight. Gasped his name, giving herself up to him totally.

He murmured against her skin, encouraging words, erotic words. Words that added to the fire. "Fuck, you taste good. Like honey." He slid his hands behind her knees, lifting them up and over his shoulders, teasing her clit with short, hard licks while he slid his fingers inside her. "God, I could eat you forever, baby, and never get tired of it."

"Oh, Jesus...Vin..." Her hands twisted in the sheets, the pleasure building to levels she couldn't contain. Couldn't keep inside. But then she didn't want to. She wanted to break out of the cocoon she'd been in. Break out of her whole goddamned life.

"Yeah, that's right," he murmured in a dark, hungry voice. "Give it to me, baby girl. Give it all to me."

Kara put her head back and cried out in ecstasy as Vin drove her over the edge, feeling herself fly free. Weightless. And when she came back down to earth, she knew that nothing would ever be the same again. She was different. Changed.

She lay there still shivering with the aftershocks as he turned her on her side, sliding up behind her, one arm pushing underneath her to wrap around her waist, holding her against him. His other hand gently coaxed her knee up, hooking it behind his. Then he shifted his knee out, easing her leg wide, positioning himself. And slid into her, deep and slow.

Kara groaned, still far too sensitive for the hard length of him. But his arms circled her, holding her tight until her breathing had slowed and she could manage. Then he reached for her chin, turned her head, leaned forward and took her mouth in a shattering kiss. She could taste herself on him, a small electric thrill of arousal shocking her.

Vin began to move, slowly, carefully, and she didn't think she could do it again, the last orgasm had been so intense. But somehow she was there once more, in the middle of a current, surrounded by his body, by his heat, by the taste and feel of him.

For the first time in her life, she felt totally protected. Totally safe.

For the first time in her life she felt she was home.

She twined around him like a vine, kissing, moving restlessly, the sensation building and building until he took them both over again, until they were shaking and panting and breathless.

And when it was over, Vin pulled her in close, keeping a tight hold of her as if he couldn't let her go.

Neither of them said anything for long moments.

"Why didn't you stay in the car yesterday?" he said at last.

"I told you, I wanted to help. Was that so bad?"

"It is when your pregnant partner is close to your violent, schizophrenic mother in the middle of a psychotic episode."

"I'm sorry. I didn't know."

She felt his head turn, his breathing warm on the back of her neck. "I did tell you stay in the car for a reason."

"When have I ever done what you told me? Apart from the slave stuff, naturally."

His arm tightened around her. "You should have."

"I know. But...you have to deal with so much stuff on your own, Vin. And it's not fair."

"It's not about fairness."

"Yeah, yeah, life's not fair, right? I just think...you shouldn't have to do it all by yourself. You're helping me with the baby. Why shouldn't I help you with your mum?"

Silence behind her. Just the sound of his breathing.

Then he said bleakly, "You can't help. She's not ever going to get better."

Kara put her hands over his where they rested on her stomach. "No. Maybe I can't help her. But I can help you."

"Why?" His voice was a whisper. "Why would you want to help me?"

"Because I know what's it like to feel you're alone."

He said nothing and she wondered if she'd perhaps overstepped the mark or gone too far somehow. But it was too late to take it back and besides, she didn't want to. Things had changed.

"She tied herself to the towel rail. Do you know why?" he said at last.

"No. Why?"

"Because she has a demon in her head that tells her to kill. And she's terrified she'll obey so she ties herself up so she can't. That's also why you couldn't find a knife in her apartment. I took them all away. She can't have them, not even an ordinary butter knife."

Kara went very still, afraid even to breathe in case he stopped talking.

"She was okay when Dad left," Vin went on. "At least for the first year. But then her episodes got progressively worse. She drank and wouldn't take her meds, which didn't help. And then, when I was seventeen, I caught her outside Ellie's room with a knife in her hand. The demon told her to kill her daughter so that's what she was going to do."

"Oh my God," Kara whispered, the breath freezing in her chest.

"I knew I couldn't leave her alone with Ellie after that," Vin said, his voice going flat. "I had to lock away the kitchen knives in a safe too, just to be sure."

He had to deal with that. At fifteen. God, that was too young to be responsible for his own parent. Too young to be a parent to his own little sister. And she should know—she too had been made to take responsibility far too young.

He'd always seemed such a control-freak. Now she knew why.

She blinked fiercely, her eyes prickling with tears. "You never got help?"

"Help?" A bitter laugh. "What help? Social services? The medical profession?"

"What about your dad? Did you ever try and get in touch—"

"Fuck no. He ditched all responsibility the moment he walked out that door. And there was only one other person who cared enough to protect Ellie and save Lillian from herself and that person was me. I had no help and I didn't need it."

God, no wonder he was hard. No wonder he took everything so damn seriously. He'd had to shoulder such a tremendous burden. "Ellie doesn't know, does she? I mean about how sick your mother is?"

"No. She doesn't. And she never will."

Kara couldn't argue with that. Knowing your own mother wanted to kill you—even if she was sick—would be a pretty terrible thing.

"I won't tell her," she said thickly. "I promise."

Vin said nothing. Just held her. But she could feel the weight of his anger and frustration and grief pushing against her like a tide.

She couldn't let this stand. She couldn't let him do this alone.

Pushing at his arms, Kara wriggled out of his grip.

"Hey," Vin protested, "where are you going?"

She didn't answer, slipping from the bed and going over to the chest of drawers near the door.

"Kara?"

Ignoring him, she knelt and pulled open the bottom drawer. The collar was there where she'd left it, wrapped in an old T-shirt. She got it out, unwrapped it, then stood and went over to her dresser, taking the little key from an old metal tin she used as a jewelry box.

Finally she turned to face him.

He was sitting up, staring at her in puzzlement, the white sheets a perfect foil to his tanned skin.

Kara crossed to the bed then sat on the edge of it, her back to him. "Help me do this up," she said as she slid the cool metal of the collar around her neck.

Behind her she could almost feel his surprise. There was a moment of hesitation then his fingers brushing her skin and the snap of the padlock shutting.

Mine. Yes. *He* was hers.

She turned, met his dark blue gaze. "Any time you need vodka. Or me. I'm here for you. Understand?" Then she held out the key. "This is yours."

His eyes widened, a look of shock crossing his face. "Kara—"

"I will never be anyone else's slave, Vin. Only yours. So take it. And then take me."

He was immobile so long she thought he'd refuse, but she didn't let herself be afraid. Neither did she look away. She'd accepted she needed him, now he had to accept he needed her. And he would. Because like he was the only one who could give her what she needed, she was the only one who could do the same for him.

He didn't say word, just took the key, long fingers closing around it, accepting her gift to him. Then he took her mouth in a kiss that tasted of grief and longing and possession and desire all rolled into one.

Then, pushing her back on the bed, he took her.

"You better not do anything to hurt her." There was a fierce note in Ellie's voice. "She may look tough but she's not. Not really."

Vin stood in the doorway to his nearly-completed house, watching as Kara gingerly made her way through the newly installed French doors that led out to a huge wooden deck. From the deck he could see down through the thick bush, over the roofs of other houses, right down to Piha Beach at the bottom of the hill. The ocean was blue and wide, and on quiet days he could hear the surf. He'd always liked it out here. On the days when he had some very rare spare time, he'd often come out with a board, catch some waves. Or just sit on the beach and imagine the things he would do when Ellie grew up. When he didn't have so many responsibilities.

He leaned against the doorframe, still holding the phone.

Jackie Ashenden

"No, of course I won't."

"But what exactly are you two doing then? I mean, you're really marrying her?"

"Are you questioning my intentions, Ell?"

"Well, if you put it like that, yes. I am. She's kind and caring and my best friend, and she deserves everything, Vin. And if you're not going to give her that, then you need to know I will hunt you down and kill you."

"Hey, this is me you're talking to, don't forget. She's having my kid. She'll be looked after."

"That's not what I meant and you know it."

She deserves everything...

Unease clenched in his gut as he watched Kara wander over to the edge of the deck, looking out at the view. She wore a simple loose summer dress today, blue cotton that reached just to mid-thigh, and Docs patterned with Union Jacks. The purple was still in a long streak through her hair like amethyst through a seam of gold and he was starting to kind of like it, though he hadn't admitted that to her yet.

His gaze dropped to the piece of jewelry she wore around her neck—the collar he'd given her. His collar. With the key he kept on his key ring in the pocket of his jeans.

Shit, he probably shouldn't have accepted it—he'd never meant his ownership of her to be quite so real. But she'd taken that choice from him when she'd offered that key back to him. Offering herself. And as screwed up as it was, he couldn't refuse her. Because he wanted her. Wanted what she had to give. Wanted her wearing that collar of his. Wanted the key in his pocket, the symbol of her trust in him.

His chest felt tight. Fuck, she looked so beautiful. Hell, she *was* beautiful. Kind and caring, like Ellie said. Kara had a big heart. A heart well hidden under snark and sarcasm and weird clothes.

A vulnerable heart.

He shifted against the doorframe, realizing he'd been silent a long time. "So what did you mean then?"

"She'll give you everything, Vin, that's just what she's like. Don't leave her with nothing in return."

"I won't. We're going to the registry office to make it legal next week. After the twelve-week scan."

"But you're not in love with her, are you?"

The tightness in his chest gripped harder, prompting a completely inexplicable surge of anger. "This isn't about love, Ellie. It's about responsibility. It's about doing what's right for my kid."

"And what about what's right for Kara?"

"She's not in this for love either. She told me so."

You sure about that?

He scowled at the ground, trying to ignore the thought as Ellie said, "She hides stuff, Vin. Don't forget. She'll give you everything and you'll never know."

"Yeah, well thanks for the update, but I've been living with her for three weeks now and I think I know her pretty well."

After the first week of sleeping with her every night, it was Kara who'd suggested he move his stuff into her apartment. It was such a better arrangement than crashing in his office that he hadn't thought twice about agreeing. It meant he could keep an eye out for her much more easily too.

But there were other bonuses. Such as having someone to come home to. Having someone smile when you walked in the door and open their arms to you. Or even just having someone ask you about your day and be interested in the answer.

He'd never had that before. Never had someone be there for him like Kara was.

Oh, it hadn't all been plain sailing. She was stubborn as

hell and they'd had a flaming argument over his application to architecture school. He'd insisted on putting it off for another year and she'd told him to stop being so stupid. Then she'd gone and rung up the university and told them to put through the application.

Bloody woman.

"Sure you do," Ellie said sarcastically. "I don't know much about her past and I'm, like, her best friend."

Out on the deck, Kara turned, stepping back through the doors and wending her way through the building detritus back toward to him.

She hadn't told Ellie about her past, huh? Well, she'd told him.

Kara smiled as she came closer, her face lighting up. "Who are you talking to?" She raised her eyebrows. "Your secret lover?"

"Sure. I'm talking to my secret lover while you're standing right in front of me. It's Ellie."

Kara lit up even more. "What? Gimme!" She whipped the phone out of his hand before he could move. "Hey, babe! I guess big bro here is giving you all the goss, right?"

Vin watched as she turned away, still talking animatedly to his sister.

A small thread of an emotion he didn't recognize wound through him. As if he could stand here all day, watching her talk on the phone to Ellie. Watching her lovely face brighten as she chatted to her friend. Hearing her laugh. She looked relaxed, at ease. So much more than a few months ago when he'd first picked her up from that abortive one-night stand.

Was it the baby that had made her so happy?

Because yeah, that's what she looked like. She looked happy.

The thread of feeling inside him deepened. Shifted. And he wasn't sure he wanted to know what it was this time.

Vin turned away, busying himself with checking on the plaster that had been put on now that the walls had been lined.

"Did I tell you, I've got a fulltime manager now?"

He turned to find Kara behind him, her conversation now clearly over. She handed him back his phone, grinning. "For the café, I mean. She started last week and she's awesome. Tom's pretty happy."

"That's good news."

"Yeah, I know. Plus she's quite keen on buying me out so I may take her up on the offer." She looked around the half built structure. "And as for the house... It's pretty amazing, Vin."

"You think you could live here then?"

"Oh my God, yes. The view is incredible."

Something released inside him. A breath he hadn't known he was holding. "It's a bit of a drive to the city."

Kara lifted a shoulder. "I don't care. It's worth it just to be close to the sea." She glanced away, up to the high, vaulted ceilings, the windows going almost to the top to take full advantage of all the natural light. "You designed this yourself?"

"Yeah. Pretty much."

"It's so cool." Her gaze came back to his. "And see, this is why you have to get your architecture degree. Your business is going to go *off* once you're able to design for people. Especially if this house is an example of what you can do."

Her praise only seemed to add another dimension to his strange discomfort. He stepped over to a wall, examined the layer of plaster critically. Wasn't as smooth as he would have liked, this bit. "It took a while to get right. The solar panels take up a lot of roof space. Plus you want to be careful about your window placement so you get as much sun in the house as possible without making it too hot."

"I can imagine." She gave him an amused look then shook her head.

"What?"

"You and your eco stuff."

"Hey, don't knock it. It's where the money's at." He frowned at a rough bit of plaster. "And it's important for the industry too. Someone has to start doing this kind of shit. Set an example so people can see it's a genuine option and not a fad."

A silence fell and he could feel her watching him. He glanced away from his study of the plaster, meeting her brown eyes. "What is it now?"

"You feel quite strongly about it, don't you?"

"Yes. I do. Why, did you think it was just about the money?"

"I suppose I did." She lifted a brow. "Going to thank me for ringing the architecture school and getting them to take your application out of the bin?"

"Kara—"

"You're welcome, Mr. Fox."

He pushed his hands in his pockets. Perhaps he should have argued with her more about that. But the architecture thing...it had been such a dream for so long. A dream he'd thought he'd have to put off yet again.

"What about you?" he asked gruffly. "You must have some kind of dream."

Kara blew out a breath, her bangs fluttering. "Yeah, well, I did. I do. Just...you know. Have a family. Have a normal type life. And that's enough for me to cope with at the moment." She bent, picked up a wood off-cut from the floor, examined it. "I think it's going to take me a while to work out what I want from life. I've spent a long time coasting, not really hoping for anything, or even trying for anything, just in case it didn't work out. In a year or so, once the baby's born and I figure out how my life's going to be, then maybe I'll think about what else I want to do."

He stared at her. "You want to know what I think? I think that's bullshit."

She dropped the bit of wood, not looking at him. "It's not bullshit."

"Yeah, it is. You can't tell me you're a woman who doesn't know what she wants."

Slowly she met his gaze and he could see something burning in the depths of her eyes. "There's nothing wrong with wanting a family."

"No, of course there isn't. But there's more to you than marriage and babies, Kara."

She rolled her eyes. "Well, thank God I have the patriarchy to tell me what I want."

Oh no, he wasn't going to take that from her. Not now. "You're just afraid to go out and take it."

A fraught silence fell.

Kara looked away from him, a hand going to the collar around her neck, touching it as if for reassurance. And suddenly he wanted to know exactly what her dreams were. What she wanted from life. She'd given him her body but sometimes... Sometimes he got the feeling she was holding something back. And he wanted whatever that was. He wanted it all.

"Tell me." The words came out in the same voice he used when they indulged in master-slave play, but he didn't bother to apologize for it. He wanted to bloody know.

Her dark eyes flicked to his, her fingers still touching the collar. "You really want to know? I want to draw. I want to be a manga artist. I want to be published and sell my own work."

Well, that made total sense. He'd seen the drawings around her apartment and they were amazing. "You totally should, in that case. We can—"

"And I want to be loved. I want to be loved for who I am." There was no denying the look in her eyes. It speared him straight through the chest.

Fuck. Ellie was right. "Kara," he began.

"You don't think I deserve it?"

Somehow this conversation had gotten away from him and he didn't know how or why. "Of course you deserve it," he said, trying to regain some control.

"So why are you marrying me then? When you don't love me?"

Oh bloody hell. "Jesus, where is this coming from? I thought we had this discussion? The baby—"

"Yeah, yeah, the baby. But what about me? What about what I want? What if I fall in love with someone? And what if he loved me and wanted me to marry him?"

A burst of jealous anger went through him. Which was weird because why should he care if she fell in love with some other guy? His jaw felt tense, his hands curled into fists in his pockets. "But you'd be my wife."

"That wasn't what I asked."

"You told me you were mine. You gave me that fucking key."

Her chin lifted, her gaze never leaving his. "But you said I deserved love."

"Oh, you deserve it all right. You just won't get it from me." Because how could he give her love? Love required you to open yourself to someone. Open yourself completely. Made you vulnerable. And he could never be that, not with anyone. It had taken everything he had just to talk about Lillian, share his fears for Ellie with her. And he'd only done that because he owed her, both for her understanding and the comfort she'd given him.

But you felt better afterwards, didn't you?

He ignored that particular thought.

Kara stared at him. "So what will I get from you then."

"A husband. A home. You wanted normal. That's what I can give you."

"What if I want more than that?"

Vin slowly walked over to her, anger burning hotter inside him. He knew logically he had no right to deny her what she wanted. But his logic had never worked that well when it came to Kara Sinclair. His brain told him she was his and she'd stay his.

He looked down into her dark eyes. "You're mine, baby. And that's final."

She didn't back away. Met him head to head. "So you're essentially telling me that even though you won't love me, you won't let me find someone else who will."

He didn't even bother to deny it this time. "Damn fucking straight." No, it didn't make any sense why he should feel so strongly about it, but he wasn't going to spend all day figuring it out or justifying himself.

Anger glowed in her brown eyes. "I thought you said I deserved love, you bloody Neanderthal."

"I'm going to give you fucking everything, Kara. Everything I'm able to give."

"But you're not able to give love?"

She stood so close to him, all warm softness and the sweet smell of a flower garden. And suddenly his anger spilled over into something else, into desire so intense he almost couldn't breathe. He wanted her right now. No, he couldn't give her love, yet he couldn't give her up either. In fact he wanted to make her even more his than she was already. Put some kind of mark on her. Claim her.

Yeah, she was right. He was a Neanderthal. Or some kind of animal wanting to mark his territory. So primitive and so wrong and yet he couldn't stop the urge to do it.

He reached for her, tugging her hard against him. Her hands came up, pressing against his chest. Holding herself away. Her cheeks had got pink, the look in her eyes darkening in the way they always did when she was aroused.

"What are you doing?" she demanded huskily.

Vin rested his hand at the base of her throat, his fingers curving around her neck beneath her collar. A dominant hold to remind her of what she'd been to him—his slave. "You wanted to be mine, baby. Remember that."

He felt her throat move under his palm, the flush in her cheeks deepening. "And what do I get in return?"

"You get this house. Me in your bed. Support and help in whatever you want to do."

Her mouth tightened. "That's not enough."

"It'll have to be. I can't give you anything more."

"Can't or won't?"

But he was sick of this conversation. It didn't lead anywhere pleasant. "Put your head back," he ordered instead, his voice sounding like he had a mouthful of gravel.

Her eyes had darkened into black. "No."

"Do it, slave." He didn't call her that anymore, but somehow it felt vital she obey him now.

Only she didn't. Instead she reached up and pulled his mouth down on hers in an aggressive, hungry kiss that knocked the breath from his body. There was anger in it and demand, her fingers winding tightly in his hair, holding him to her. And, Christ, he wanted her. Now. Here. Up against this wall. Claiming her so hard she'd forget all this shit about falling in love with someone else.

He kissed her back, just as hungry, just as aggressively, keeping his hand on her throat. But she wouldn't be contained. She rose up on her toes, gripping him even tighter than he was gripping her, kissing him even harder. Then she bit his lower lip.

She'd never done that to him before. Never been the aggressor. Never fought him. In their master-slave play she'd done exactly what she was told and when. And sometimes she disobeyed him but he never punished her with force, only with pleasure.

This was different. This was a direct challenge. And as pain fired his nerve-endings, the dominant part of him, the part he still hadn't fully come to terms with yet, roared into life.

He shoved her hard against the wall, trying to grab her wrists to hold them above her head, but she'd wound herself around him and he knew he wasn't going to be able to pull her away without hurting her. Her legs were around his waist, her arms around his neck, fingers twisted deep in his hair, her mouth on his, passionate and wild. And furious. So furious. He could feel her anger battering against him like hurricane winds.

In some dim part of his brain he knew why she was angry and that sex wasn't going to help. But somehow her anger found answering anger in him and suddenly he was just as furious. Just as wild. He reached up under her dress, hooking his fingers into the waistband of the lacy knickers she wore and ripping them away.

Kara only bit him again and this time there was blood mixed in with the fury.

Jesus, this was crazy. Their whole relationship was crazy.

So screwed up and wrong. And yet that didn't stop him from clawing his jeans open and reaching for the hot, wet heat between her thighs. Thrusting so hard inside her she cried out, her mouth leaving his, her head going back against the wall, her body arching in his arms.

He pinned her to the wall with his body, bracing himself with hands slapped to the plaster on either side of her head.

She was panting, gasping for breath, golden skin flushed with anger and arousal.

Vin thrust hard, deep, a rhythm that drew gasps from her with each movement. But she didn't soften, didn't lean back and take it. She arched up, her hips moving in time with his, riding him. Her furious dark gaze met his, held it.

"Coward," she said in a thick, harsh voice. "You fucking coward."

And through the pleasure and the anger battling for dominance inside him, he felt inexplicable pain strike home.

She's right. You are a coward.

But he didn't want to face that, didn't want to think about it, not when her body was wrapped around his, her pussy gripping his cock like it never wanted to let him go. So he lowered his mouth to hers, stopping her from talking, hungry and desperate and wanting the ache in his heart just to fucking stop hurting.

Her mouth was hot, tasting of anger and pain, and as their movements became faster and faster, pleasure overriding everything, at the last minute she pulled back.

And just as the orgasm exploded in his head, turning him inside out, she whispered, "I love you."

Chapter Fifteen

Kara was shaking with anger as she stormed back into her apartment, slamming the door behind her. She could still hear the roar of the Corvette as Vin pulled away from his house mere seconds after pulling away from her. Leaving her panting and trembling from the sex they'd just had. He hadn't said a word, just gone and left her standing there. She'd had to call a taxi to get back into town, but that wasn't what had made her angry. Neither was it the fact that that he'd left seconds after she'd told him she loved him.

What she was absolutely fucking furious about was the fact that he'd dragged her dreams from her, made her acknowledge them for the first time in her life, and then told her she couldn't have them. Well, not the manga artist one, the one about being loved.

The coward. The fucking Neanderthal bastard prick coward.

Kara flung her bag onto the floor of the lounge then began to pace up and down the length of the small room, fury burning like a petrol-soaked fire in her veins.

So was this the way it would be? Him giving her everything she'd always wanted and yet withholding the one thing she wanted most? And expecting her to be happy with it? After telling her she needed to aim higher? That she needed to want more?

She stopped beside the coffee table, struggling with the rage that stuck in her throat.

A lot of mail had been stacked into a neat pile on the table, waiting for either Vin or her to get to it. And beneath a garish scatter of junk mail, a long white envelope rested.

A familiar white envelope with *Return to Sender* written in block capitals and red pen across the top of it. An old pain caught at Kara, a sharp jab like standing on a piece of glass.

It was the letter she'd posted to her mother, telling her about the baby. Sent back. Unopened.

She stared at it. Great. So her mother wouldn't know about her own grandchild because she'd done her usual thing and not opened the bloody letter. Rejected yet again. Why did she keep sending these things out? Why did she keep hoping for more?

She'd even once sent one addressed to Rose and Liam but that had been sent back too. She hadn't tried it again—rejection from her mother was one thing but rejection from her siblings, whom she'd taken care of for so long, had been too much to bear.

Kara bent and picked up the envelope, holding it. And found herself staring at her reflection in the battered old mirror she'd hung on the wall opposite.

A young woman looked back. A woman with piercings and purple dye streaking her hair. A woman with a collar around her neck and a padlock that said *mine*. A woman who wore weird clothes and got off on being ordered around by a man who called her his slave.

A woman as far from normal as it was possible to get.

A woman who had been happy.

And it struck her then, like a wrecking ball straight to her stomach, that yes, the past three weeks living with Vin, she *had* been happy.

Tears filled her eyes but this time she didn't blink them back. She held her mother's letter and stared at herself in the mirror. Saw herself, really *saw*.

Piercings and dye. Contacts and razor scars. Collars and Leia costumes. Fucked up, screwed up, so not normal. But this was Kara. This woman was who she was. A woman who'd been through pain and guilt and anguish and come out the other end strong. A survivor.

A woman who deserved more than a *Return to Sender* letter in the mail.

A woman who finally realized what she wanted. And then had the strength to ask for it.

A woman who demanded love.

Kara looked down at the envelope in her hands, adrenaline surging like a tide through her.

"Fuck you, Mum," she said hoarsely. Then she ripped the envelope in half and in half again, ripping and ripping until the letter was nothing but a handful of little white squares.

Then she threw the bits of into the air, a weird kind of release singing through her as she watched the remains of the letter settle on the furniture and the floor like snow.

There would be no more letters. Not from her. Not anymore. She didn't need her mother's acceptance. She accepted herself and that was enough. More than enough.

The front door of the apartment slammed and she looked up to see Vin coming to stand in the doorway. The expression on his face was hard, his posture tight with tension.

"I'm sorry," he said flatly. "I didn't mean to leave you like that." His gaze flickered around the room, clearly noticing the scattered white remains of her mother's letter. "What happened?"

Calm descended on her. "I wrote a letter for my mother. I wanted to tell her about the baby. I mean, it's her grandchild so I thought she should know. But it came back unopened. The usual *Return to Sender* job."

He did another scan of the room. "You tore it up?"

"Yeah. I don't need her approval anymore."

Slowly, his gaze came to hers. "You never did."

"No. And I don't need yours either."

Something changed in his face, a lightning flicker of emotion. "Kara—"

"Where the hell did you go?" she demanded. "You screwed me up against a wall and basically buggered off."

Vin shifted on his feet, ran a hand through his dark hair. "I'm sorry. I wanted..." He stopped then said, "There's something I wanted to give you. Call it an early wedding present if you want."

"What?"

Vin eased away from the doorframe and came into the room, pulling something from the back pocket of his jeans as he did so. A long wallet full of paper. He crossed over to the coffee table and put it down, flipping it open as he did so.

It looked like an itinerary. There were flights on it, a hotel. And information on one of Tokyo's largest anime conventions.

She stared at it. Her name was in the flight information. "What's this?"

"Flights to Tokyo. A hotel booking. And..." He hesitated. "A meeting with your favorite manga artist. She's going to be at that convention."

"What the hell? This is for me?"

"Yeah. Like I said, an early wedding present. A honeymoon if you like. Except that I can't come with you, not with Lillian being the way she is at the moment. And there's some business stuff I have to take care of. But there's no reason you can't go without me."

Kara looked down at it then back at him. Yet again, Vin had done something for her. Something that six weeks ago she wouldn't have been able to accept because she wouldn't have let herself have something so amazing.

Well, she wasn't going to let herself now either. Because it wasn't what she wanted.

If she was going to finally accept the person she was, weird shit and all, then she also needed to accept what she wanted. And not just accept but ask for it.

She'd never asked for anything for herself in all her life.

Maybe it was about fucking time she did.

"I tell you I love you and you give me tickets to Tokyo?"

The perfect lines of his features hardened. "I've been planning this a while, with Ellie. But now seemed like a good time to give it to you."

"Why? As an apology? A consolation prize?"

"I said I was sorry. And I wanted to make it right between us."

"Because nothing says I care like air tickets?"

Lines of tension bracketed his mouth. "Jesus, Kara. I don't know what the hell else you expected me to say."

"Oh, I don't know, how about you love me and you can't live without me?" She folded her arms. "Certainly I expected more than you fucking off in your Corvette like a kid having a tantrum."

"I didn't want you to fall in love with me. I didn't ask for it."

"Who the hell cares what you did or didn't want? That's what happened and I'm not making any apologies for it." Something had changed inside her, a strength she never knew she had flowing through her. She met his dark blue gaze, unflinching.

"I've got nothing to give you in return. You know that, Kara. I told you."

"Nice excuse, Vin. Got anymore where those came from?"

Vin cursed, shoving a hand through his dark hair. "It's not an excuse. And it doesn't mean I don't care about you, okay?"

Kara lifted her chin. "That's not good enough. Not anymore."

The line of his jaw hardened even further. "I can't give you love, Kara."

"*Won't* give me love, you mean."

"Can't. Won't. Does it matter? Love was never supposed to be a part of this."

No, it wasn't. But it should have been. "Why?"

"What do you mean why?"

She took a few steps toward him, looking up into his eyes. "You love Ellie. Why can't you love me?"

"Ellie's my goddamned sister!"

"And I'm going to be your goddamned wife. So what's going on, Vincent? Am I too weird for you? Is that what the problem is? Am I too screwed up? Too much baggage for you to deal with?" She got closer, right up close. "Kara the cutter too much for you to handle?"

Anger flared across his face. "No, fuck, that's not it!"

"Then what?" She was shaking but it wasn't with fear, it was with rage. "Because I love you, Vin Fox," saying it out loud again because she was going to own this damn emotion whether he wanted her to or not. "And I want to marry you and have your child, and become the best damn manga artist in the world. But if you haven't got the guts to love me in return then the least you can do is giving me a fucking explanation as to why not!"

Steel blue flared in his eyes. "I don't have to give you anything."

"So that's the answer you're going to give our child? When he or she asks why Daddy doesn't ever tell Mummy he loves her?"

A dangerous tension filled the air around him. "Our relationship has nothing to do with our kid."

"Bullshit it hasn't! I want the child to grow up seeing their parents in love. Seeing what an adult relationship can be. And I want them to grow up wanting that for themselves. To not settle for less." Her voice cracked. "Not settle like I've been doing my whole damn life!"

Vin held her gaze for a long moment, the tension pulling agonizingly tight. Then he turned abruptly, moving away from her toward the window in a sharp, restless movement. "I can't do this, Kara." The words sounded dragged out of him. "I don't want to do this. I can't love someone else. I'm so fucking tired of caring. Of worrying. Of being afraid I'll make a mistake and screw up and fail. Of hurting someone. All the love I had, I gave to Ellie. I don't have anything left for anyone else."

She could hear the exhaustion in his voice. She knew how tired he was. And of course she was just adding to the responsibilities he had. Six weeks ago that would have consumed her with self-loathing. But not today.

"That's crap, Vin. Love isn't a finite resource. You can't use it all up. That's the world's stupidest excuse and you know it. You're just letting fear make your choices for you."

Slowly he turned and the look on his face was as bone weary as she'd ever seen it. "You know what? I don't give a shit who's making my choices for me. The only thing I'm sure of is that I'm not giving anyone else a piece of me ever again."

"And what about the baby? Does our child not deserve a piece of you? Or is it only me you don't want to give it to?"

A flash of what looked like pain flickered in his eyes. Then it was gone. "This isn't about the baby. This is about you and me."

Pain settled around her heart. Pain for him and for herself.

For the decision she'd already made. But she was used to pain, she could handle it. She was stronger than she'd ever thought possible.

Kara squared her shoulders. Lifted her chin. "If you think love isn't about the baby, that it's only about you and me, then I'm afraid we can't be a family."

His expression became fierce with denial. "No."

"A family without love isn't a family, Vincent. And I know, I've lived it. I don't want that for my child and I don't want that for me."

He moved, coming toward her, six foot four of broad, angry male. But she didn't back away or back down. Just continued to stare at him, challenging him.

And he stopped, eyes glittering. "You can't take the child away from me. I won't let you."

"That's not what I'm saying. I wouldn't, you know I wouldn't." She swallowed. "But I'm not marrying you, Vincent."

"You have to fucking marry me!"

"No, I don't. And I won't. I'm not marrying someone who doesn't love me, baby or not."

He stared at her, anger burning in his eyes, his hands clenched into fists at his sides. "I thought this was what you wanted?"

"No, it's not. It's settling. It's *good enough.* And I don't want *good enough* ever again. I want more. Shit, I *demand* more."

He took another step toward her. "And what about what I want? Doesn't that matter?"

She looked at him. At his hard, beautiful face. "Of course it does. Which means this is the best solution. Because you don't want this either. You're only doing it because it's right. Because taking responsibility is what you do."

"We're a family, Kara."

"No, Vin. No, we're not."

"Why not?" he demanded. "What the fuck changed?"

"I did." She felt calm. Sure of herself. More sure than she'd been of anything in her entire life. "I finally accepted who I am. This is me, Vin. Take it or leave it."

For a long moment, he just stared at her. Then abruptly he pushed past her to the doorway, where he paused. "We're getting married in three days. I'll be there. And if you want a family for our child then you should be there too."

Then he went out, the apartment door slamming behind him.

Kara finished the last of her packing then sat on the edge of her bed, looking at the ticket to Tokyo in her hands. Changing the dates had used up the last of her meager savings since the cost of a last-minute ticket change was horrendous.

Jesus, it really was an awful thing to jilt your groom. But there was no other choice. She wasn't going to marry him and settle for whatever he felt like he wanted to give her. Loving him but getting nothing in return.

He'd taught her she should aim higher, figure out what she wanted and go after it. So she was. She was aiming for the fucking sky. And if he didn't want to be a part of that then that was his loss.

It would hurt. It would hurt badly. But she was strong. She would manage.

Leaving without telling him where she was going, without even telling him she wouldn't be turning up to the registry office, was pretty low. But Vin wasn't a man who gave up easily once he'd decided on something. If she told him she wasn't going to turn up, he'd probably come and find her. And they'd go through the whole thing again because for some reason he just wouldn't let her go.

Oh, he couldn't make her marry him if she didn't want to but it was easier this way. Easier on them both. He wouldn't know she'd gone until after she was safely on her way to Tokyo.

Outside in the street, she heard the horn from the taxi she'd ordered.

Kara slipped off the bed and picked up her bag. Bent and gripped the handle of her suitcase. She glanced once at the pillow on Vin's side of the bed, where he usually slept but hadn't for the past couple of nights, staying away from her. Her note still sat there. A paltry goodbye but she couldn't leave him without some explanation at least.

The taxi horn sounded again.

Time to go.

Vin waited on the steps outside the registry office. It was in the middle of downtown Auckland, the streets full of people out on their lunch break. He kept peering into crowds, hoping to see Kara walking toward him. But he hadn't managed to spot her yet.

He tried to ignore the ache of anxiety in his gut.

He'd left her to make her own decision about whether to turn up or not. Had given her a few days of total space to come round to the idea. But he had no doubt she would.

She didn't mean those things she'd said that day in her apartment, of course she didn't. Love. What the hell did she even mean by that? Christ, he was giving her a house, a father for her baby, all his support. A family. All the things she'd told him she wanted. Love didn't give anything extra, didn't add anything. Love just took from you and left you with nothing.

Why the hell would she want that?

I love you, Vin Fox.

He pushed the words violently from his head. What she felt for him was irrelevant. Completely. It meant nothing to him.

He looked down at the bouquet of white orchids he held in his hand, checking to make sure they were all in order. They were. He'd bought them for her because every bride should have a bouquet and because they were rare and delicate and just a little bit weird. Like she was.

A flash of color in the crowds going by, a streak of purple hair, brought his attention from the flowers and he stared after the woman it belonged to, his heart beating fast. But it wasn't Kara.

The ache inside him intensified. Shifted.

For the past three days he'd been crashing at the office because he'd needed the space. Because he didn't know what to say to her. How to make things right between them again.

He didn't love her. He didn't want to. He was just so goddamn tired of love and its demands. Of how it made you give away bits of yourself until you didn't have anything left.

You coward.

Yeah, well, coward or not, once you'd given those pieces of yourself away, you wouldn't ever get them back. The person you gave them to would take those pieces with them when they left you and then you'd be broken. Never to be put back together again.

He'd already given so much of himself to people. To his father. To his mother. To Hunter. To Ellie. There was nothing left to give Kara.

Does our child not deserve a piece of you?

The pain inside became sharp, raw. Fuck, no. He couldn't think about the baby yet. He couldn't. What with all this stuff with Kara, it felt too much. Too big.

He forced the thought away as the clock on the university building up the hill near Albert Park began to chime, the sound blanketing the city.

Shit. She was now officially late.

Vin stalked into the building and asked the officials to wait another five minutes.

Then he went back outside again, the orchids still gripped in his fist. It would be okay. Brides were supposed to be late, weren't they?

He walked up and down the stairs, unable to keep still.

Where the fuck was she?

Unease and anxiety began to morph into anger, which was so much easier to handle than the underlying bitter disappointment that began to creep through him. Disappointment laced with an anguish he didn't want to acknowledge.

It shouldn't hurt that she wasn't here. He should be feeling relieved. Because she was right, he didn't want to marry her anyway. No, he didn't. She was too much drama, too much work.

It was just for the baby's sake and if she didn't want to then that was fine. Christ, it was better all round, right?

Someone came out of the building, asked him where Kara was. She was now ten minutes late. He wanted to tell them that she'd be here, of course she'd be here. But in his heart he knew she wouldn't.

She'd aimed higher. She'd wanted more than what he could give her.

Vin cancelled the ceremony then stood outside on the stairs, still clutching the bouquet.

The jilted fucking groom. What a joke.

Furious, he stalked over to a nearby rubbish bin and chucked the flowers into it. So she didn't want to get married, what did he care? At least he wouldn't be tied to a woman he didn't love. At least he wouldn't have to deal with her shit from now on. And as for their kid, well, they'd organize custody. It wouldn't be a big deal.

For a second he stood there on the sidewalk, not knowing what the hell to do with himself, the ache of anxiety mixing uncomfortably with the anger in his gut.

First, he was going to have to make sure she was okay.

Digging into his pocket, he hauled out his phone and sent off a terse *where the fuck are you?* text to her. There was no response.

The anxiety tightened. Jesus, where was she? Had something happened to her? He flicked off a text to Ellie in case she knew and was surprised when, a minute later, a text from her came back. *She's on her way to Tokyo, asshole. She left this morning. Didn't I warn you not to hurt her?*

Tokyo. Kara had left him and gone to Tokyo instead.

The ache twisted into pain. A pain with no relief.

Vin gritted his teeth, put his phone away, then went to a bar and got pissed.

Much later that night, drunk and still unaccountably furious, he found himself outside Kara's apartment building without any real idea of how he got there.

He really didn't want to go inside but he found himself heading up the stairs and through the door anyway. And as soon as he got there he knew he'd made a mistake.

The whole place smelled of her and he couldn't stop from checking all the rooms, his subconscious telling him she was there, that she was near.

But she wasn't.

Standing blankly in the empty, dark bedroom, he felt her absence so acutely it was as if someone had cut a Kara shaped-hole in his chest.

His attention fell on a piece of paper on one of the pillows on the bed. The side he usually slept on. It had his name on it.

A fucking *Dear John* letter.

The fury, still simmering away inside him, flared bright and before he could even think straight, he'd bent, picked up the letter and ripped into a million white scraps of paper, scattering the bits all around the bloody bedroom. Just like she'd done with the letter her mother had sent her.

Which should have made him feel better. But it didn't.

He turned around, wanting get the hell out of there but his phone buzzed so he pulled it out and there on the screen was a text. *I'm sorry it had to be this way, Vin. I told you I wouldn't do it and I meant it. I changed my flight. I'm in Tokyo.*

Yeah, and wasn't that a goddamned relief? He'd escaped the whole marriage deal. And good job. Now he wouldn't be tied down, weighed down by yet more responsibilities for yet another person.

It was a relief, that's what it was.

Vin deleted the message. Then, because deleting wasn't enough, he flung the phone at the wall where it made a satisfying crunching sound before landing on the floor.

But the violent movement didn't help. He felt like a building with rotten foundations, slowly listing to one side, crumbling in on itself. And he had no clue as to why.

So Kara had gone. It wouldn't be the first time someone had left him and it wouldn't be the last. What was the big fucking deal? Why did he feel so...hollow?

It was the alcohol. The anger. That's all it was. Tomorrow, he'd feel better. Of course he would.

Vin lay down on the bed on his back. Closed his eyes. Suddenly all he wanted to do was sleep. So he did.

When he next opened them, the room was bathed in sunlight and he didn't feel better. He felt worse. His head ached and his mouth was dry, his stomach unsettled. The mother of all hangovers pounding behind his eyes.

But what was worse, infinitely worse, was being surrounded by a familiar scent. Of flowers and sex. Warm arms and gentle hands. Worse was forgetting what had happened and reaching blindly for the soft, female body he knew was right beside him. Only to find nothing.

And then remember.

She had gone. She had left him.

Loss filled him. He rolled over toward where she should be and wasn't, his fingers brushing soft, silky fabric. A short nightgown she'd left behind. He closed his hand around it, bringing it close, turning his face into it like a child smelling his mother's clothes for comfort.

He was pathetic. He was a mess.

You got shitfaced and pissed for a reason.

Just like he was holding her nightgown, inhaling her scent for a reason.

Hating himself, Vin flung the nightgown away and hauled himself out of the bed, feeling like shit. He went over to his phone where it lay on the floor and picked it up. Stupid bastard that he was, he'd now have to get it fixed.

He went back out into the lounge, intending to keep heading to the front door but at the sight of the dirty dishes that were scattered around, he stopped and surveyed the untidy room. Christ, she'd really left in a damn hurry.

Gathering the dishes up, he went into the kitchen to put them in the dishwasher.

The kitchen was kind of a mess too, so he cleaned that up as well. Once that was done, he decided he'd better call the café to check on the new manager she'd hired, make sure everything was running smoothly. It was. After that it seemed only logical to put a stop on her mail so it wouldn't overflow her post box then call her doctor to check on when her next appointment was. He'd have to cancel it if it was while she was in Tokyo. How long would that be? Why hadn't she considered all this?

Once he'd finished speaking with the clinic, he opened the fridge to see if she'd got rid of any perishables. She hadn't. Almost automatically he began clearing out the leftover milk and various other items, putting them on the floor to either take with him when he left or to chuck in the trash. As he did so, he glanced down at his watch, checking on the time. He'd meant to go see his mother in the hospital today and he really didn't want to be late.

Shit. He'd been there too long. If he didn't get a move on, he'd miss visiting hours.

You've just spent half an hour tidying up her apartment and now you're cleaning out her fridge. What the hell are you doing?

He blinked, the thought hitting him like a bullet. Good fucking point. What *was* he doing tidying her fridge? She'd jilted him. Left him standing on the steps outside the registry office like a dickhead. And yet here he was, neatening up her apartment, checking on her appointments and cleaning out her kitchen. Looking after her just as he always did.

You know why.

Vin stilled, his heart starting to race.

You love her. Be a fucking man and admit it.

The truth of it was too strong to deny this time. Yes, he did love her. That's why he'd gotten so angry with her when she didn't turn up at the registry office. Why he'd gone and gotten drunk. Why he was here now, cleaning her apartment.

He loved her and she'd gone. She'd left him. Just like his father had left him. Just like everyone fucking left him.

Bullshit. She didn't leave you. She never left you. You were the one who walked away.

Something caught hard under his breastbone. A pain that took his breath away. A realization that tipped over him like ice cold river water on a hot day.

He sat down heavily on the floor, staring unseeing at the fridge.

Jesus, he *had* walked away. She'd told him what she wanted but he'd been the one who'd refused to give it to her and shut her out.

Guess you're just like your old man after all, buddy.

Vin put his hands on his knees, bent his head. "Shit," he whispered.

All his life he'd looked after people, took care of them, made sure they were okay. Accepted the responsibilities that came to him. Because stepping up to the plate made him a better man. A better man than his father.

But he wasn't a better man. Turned out he was just like him. A selfish, self-righteous prick who abandoned the people he loved because he couldn't take it. And it didn't make any difference that he hadn't walked away physically. He had emotionally. He'd shut out the people who mattered in his life because he was too damn scared. Scared of not being good enough. Scared of them leaving him.

Pain tightened, twisted inside his chest.

He'd been blind. Kara had gone and he had nobody to blame but himself.

Vin didn't know how long it was that he sat in Kara's kitchen but eventually the beeping of the fridge door shook him out of his depression. Christ, he couldn't just sit there. He had his mother to see to and he was late enough as it was. There would be time to figure out the rest of it later.

He left the apartment, went back to his office for fresh clothes and a shower, then he made his way to the hospital and the psychiatric ward.

She was sitting in one of the patient lounges, reading a book, and as he approached she looked up and frowned. And he knew this was going to be bad because there was nothing but lucidity in her eyes. Christ, he hated the lucidity. Because it always made him so aware of what he'd lost.

"Vin? You look awful. What's happened, sweetheart?"

He sat then because those rotten foundations were going to collapse and he was going to break and if that happened he had no idea what he would do. "I'm fine." He had to say it, had to make it true.

"Sure you are." She put her book down, leaned over and patted his hand where it rested on his thigh. "Tell your mum."

"Ellie's gone," he made himself say. "She left for Tokyo."

A shadow crossed Lillian's still lovely face. "Good. I think...that's good."

It was good of course. They both knew that. "I'm going to miss her," he said.

"You'll have Hunter to keep you company though, won't you?"

"He's gone too. He went with her." And at Lillian's puzzled look, he added, "They're together now."

His mother sat back on the couch. "So it's just you and me."

But it wasn't really just him and her. It was only him.

Because he lost her with every episode.

You didn't lose her either, dickhead. Like Kara, she's always been there. You're the one who's been too resentful to see her properly.

He swallowed, another hard and painful truth settling inside him.

Jesus, he'd done this to everyone, hadn't he? Had let his anger at his father color his whole life. Turning the people he loved into burdens he had to shoulder. Crosses he had to bear. But they weren't.

If he truly wanted to be a better man than his father, he needed to let go of his anger.

He needed to take on those responsibilities without resentment. Without frustration. Without anger. He needed to take them on not to make him feel better about himself but because he wanted to. Because he cared.

The shadow in her eyes didn't lift. "I don't think I've been much good to you, have I? I haven't been much of a mother at all."

Vin looked at her. For the first time in years, he truly looked at her. Without anger. Without resentment. Copper hair and blue eyes. Lines of hardship and pain around her mouth. And a familiar weariness that was so much like his own it hurt.

"It's okay," he said softly. "You did just fine.... Mum." The word sounded strange in his mouth because it had been so very long since he said it. But it felt good to say. Like he was reclaiming something.

"Mum," she repeated then smiled, her expression lightening. "I haven't heard that in a while."

"Because I haven't said it in a while." He leaned forward, putting his hand over hers. "And here's something else I haven't said in a while. I love you. I hope you know that."

The shadow vanished completely. "Oh sweetheart. I love you too. You've always been there for me. Every single time."

Well he hadn't, not really. But he would be from now on. Not because he had to or because he had something to prove, but because he wanted to. Because he loved her.

Just like he loved Kara. Who hadn't left him. Who'd always been there for him. Who'd given him everything he hadn't realized he'd even wanted. Not just sex but understanding. Kindness. Someone to lean on. A place to rest. A place to be safe. A haven.

He'd made a mistake. A big one. He'd nearly pushed away the best thing that had ever happened to him because he was angry and scared and not willing to deal with his own shit. But now he was. Now he could. Now he could make this right and he would.

This time it would be for her. Truly for her.

Something of his thoughts have shown on his face because his mother asked suddenly, "You okay?"

Vin squeezed her hand gently. He couldn't go after Kara like Hunter had with Ellie, but he had another plan. A better plan. She was away for two weeks. He'd have to make them count.

"Yeah, Mum. Actually this time, I think I am."

The flight back to New Zealand was long and by the time she landed back in Auckland, Kara was jetlagged, her eyes gritty from lack of sleep and her legs aching from lack of movement, a vaguely nauseous feeling in the pit of her stomach.

She'd missed Vin while she'd been away. So much it hurt. The ache settling down into her like rust into metal, eating away at her from the inside out. But no matter how badly it hurt, she didn't regret walking away from him. He'd helped her build up her pride in herself again and she wasn't going to let him shatter it.

Even so, every day in Tokyo she'd had to bite down on her urge to ask Ellie whether he'd rung. Whether he'd sent his sister a text or an email, because he hadn't rung or texted Kara. And only once did she break.

Ellie had shaken her head then said, "But remember, Vin's default setting isn't only to protect. It's also to rely on no one but himself. And that's because he simply didn't have anyone else. After Dad took off, he was the only one left."

Kara knew that feeling. Knew it so well. "So what are you saying?" she'd asked.

"I'm saying he's not a guy who's exactly in touch with his feelings all the time. Especially the softer ones." Ellie had hesitated, brushing her copper colored bangs away from her eyes. "Vin needs someone. Looking out for me, taking care of Mum, growing his business...he's been so busy there hasn't been much time for friends or relationships for him. And everyone, no matter how strong they are, needs a person they can be weak with. Someone they can be vulnerable with."

Kara had felt her throat tighten. "I just don't know... I just don't think Vin can let himself be vulnerable with anyone."

"Give him a chance, Kar," Ellie had said. "In many ways, you're stronger than he is and he needs someone strong."

She tried to put the conversation from her mind because simply getting through the immigration nightmare due to a huge planeload of people arriving just before her was bad enough. Then her suitcase took forever to get onto the baggage carousel. Just about every single person from her flight had got theirs by the time hers came out and then she couldn't find a trolley to put it on.

An hour later Kara finally got through customs and pushed her trolley out into the arrivals hall feeling like crap.

Then she caught a glimpse of a tall, familiar figure amongst the crowds of people waiting for new arrivals. And she came to a dead stop.

Vin stood there like a rock amid a sea of shifting sand. He had his hands thrust in the pockets of his jeans, his blue-gray eyes fixed on her as if she was the only person in the whole airport worth looking at.

She felt the impact of his gaze like a shock applied to a stopped heart, setting it beating again. Making her blood pump hard through her body, calling her back to life.

What the hell was he doing here?

She wanted to run to him, fling herself into his arms, let his strength and his heat fill up the ache inside her, scour away the rust. The urge was so strong she had to grip tight to the trolley to stop herself from doing so.

Vin's gaze didn't waver, neither did he move. He just stood there, staring at her, the look in his eyes hungry, like a sailor desperate for the sight of land.

It had only been two weeks since she'd seen him but it felt like far longer. A lifetime. Forever.

She began to move toward him because there simply wasn't anywhere else to go. Anywhere else she wanted to go. He was magnetic north to her compass needle. She'd always be drawn to him wherever she was.

He remained still as she approached, something unfamiliar in his expression. In his whole posture. But she couldn't pinpoint what it was so all she said was, "What are you doing here?"

"Picking you up."

She'd been expecting to get a taxi or an airport shuttle, too tired to manage the logistics of a bus with a big case. But both were expensive and she didn't have much in the way of New Zealand cash on her. Vin's offer was welcome. Yet it changed nothing.

"Why?" she asked bluntly. "I thought I was clear about things when I left."

Still he didn't move. "Yeah, you were clear. And I guess I should be grateful for the text."

Kara flushed. "Okay, so I'm sorry about that. It was...wrong. But did you get my note?"

"No," he said, just as blunt. "I ripped it up."

Oh shit. He must have been really pissed in that case. "I'm sorry," she repeated, not knowing what else to say. "I had to go."

"I know."

"And seeing you would have made things worse. I couldn't..." She stopped as what he'd said slowly sunk into her jet-lagged brain. "What you do mean, 'you know'?"

"I mean I know you had to go." He paused, his gaze roving over her. "And I was angry about that, which is why I ripped up your note. But...I'm not angry anymore."

She gripped the handle of the trolley, staring at him, searching his face. Yes, that's why his expression was so different. The fierce, angry spark that so often glinted in his blue eyes was gone, as was the rigid tension that usually characterized his posture.

He looked relaxed, calm. And very determined.

"Vin?" she asked slowly. "Did something happen?"

"You could say that. But I'm not going to talk about it now. You look dead on your feet."

"Yeah, well." She suddenly felt more tired than she'd ever felt in her entire life. "I am."

A small silence fell between them.

"I need to show you something, Kara."

"Show me something? Show me what?"

"I can't explain. You need to see it."

This was harder than she expected. Seeing him again, having him here to pick her up. The look on his face so different she hardly recognized it. It made her ache "Why? Vin, I'm really tired and—"

"Please." He didn't say anything else. Just that one word. And she knew she wasn't going to refuse.

The breath went out of her. What could it hurt? "All right. But once I've seen whatever it is, I want to go home."

He nodded then finally took his hands out of his pockets. "The Corvette's outside. I'll deal with the luggage."

She let him take over because she was too tired to argue. Shit, he could take her case, it wasn't like she wanted to deal with them.

Vin pushed her trolley outside and unlocked the car for her so she could get in. And as she did so, the pressure in her chest got worse because the smell of the leather upholstery reminded her of him. Of the times she'd been in this car with him.

"You never did tell me why a Corvette," she said as he got in and started the car. "It's kind of pretentious."

"I wanted one," Vin said shortly. "So when I had enough money I bought one. It's the first thing I ever had that I wanted for myself." There was a pause then he glanced at her, a brief searing look. "The second was you."

Kara caught her breath. "Look, I don't know what you're expecting but—"

"Don't speak. Don't say anything until you've seen what I've got to show you."

Maybe she should have argued but today she couldn't be

bothered. Tired and jetlagged, oppressed by the tension between them, by her the sheer weight of her own need for him, she shut up and turned to look out the window instead.

But it was difficult to relax when he was right there, right next to her. And she was so aware of him on just about every level. The muscular length of his thigh encased in blue denim. The sun highlighting the copper strands in his dark hair. The familiar, spicy Vin-scent she remembered. And the tension she could feel coiling around him, the evidence clear in the way he held the steering wheel, his knuckles white. In his powerful shoulders. In the hard line of his beautiful mouth.

Whatever it was he had to show her, it was clearly freaking him out.

She didn't know whether that was a good thing or not, so she tried not to think about it.

Soon it became obvious they weren't going to her apartment. Vin didn't take the motorway exit that led into the CBD, carrying on driving out to the northwest of the city. She bit down on the questions, saying nothing as they drove on, the silence growing larger and heavier the farther from the city they got.

By the time they hit the twisty, windy roads that led out to the beaches west of the city, she recognized where they were headed. To Piha. Where his house was.

But still she kept quiet, not saying a word as eventually they pulled into the narrow, gravel driveway that led to his house.

Until he stopped the car outside it.

Wooden steps led up to the front door, a few plants in pots clustered around the entrance.

She blinked. Those hadn't been there before, had they?

Vin kept silent as he got out of the car, coming round to open her door and as she slid out of the car, he remained silent, walking quickly up the steps to unlock the front door.

"Vin," she said hesitantly.

"Come inside." He pushed the front door open for her.

Slowly she did so, unable to quite believe it when she got inside.

The place was no longer the half-lined structure she'd been in once before. It was finished.

The walls had been painted plain white, the wooden floorboards polished. The hallway was full of light, the sun streaming through windows high on the walls, conveying a feeling of peace, of openness and warmth.

Pictures had been hung at intervals down the hallway. Pictures she recognized because they were hers.

"Vin..." she said again, not really understanding what was going on.

He'd gone back to the car for her case and now dumped it in the hallway by the door. Then he said, "Come down here." He didn't wait for her, walking on down the hallway to what she remembered was the main living area.

She followed him, her heart beating fast for seemingly no apparent reason. And then when she came through the doorway, she stopped.

More fresh white walls and polished wood floors. Lots of windows facing the amazing view of the sea. Lots of sun and light. A bookcase full of books, little knickknacks on the shelf, more pictures on the walls, a long leather couch with a familiar throw on it.

In fact, most of the things in the room were familiar because again, they were all hers. There were a few other items that weren't, the couch for one, and the bookcase. A sleek console table that held an expensive stereo. An armchair by a window that had a quirky, retro look to it that even though definitely wasn't hers was certainly something she'd buy if she had the money.

"Why are my things here?" she said, her voice sounding hoarse in the silence of the room.

But Vin didn't answer. Silently he came up to her and took her hand, sending a shockwave of heat through her. Then he led her back down the hallway and up a short set of stairs, and into another, smaller room with a sloping roof, skylights bathing the whole place in light. Through the windows, amongst the green leaves of the trees outside, she caught a glimpse of the sea.

There was a large desk against one wall, an artist's desk with pens and inks all neatly arranged on it. The wall opposite was covered completely with artwork. Hers.

The colors were vibrant against the simple white of the décor, like artwork in an art gallery or something.

Kara couldn't speak. This was a room for drawing, for inspiration, for creating art. An artist's studio. The kind of room she'd dreamed of having once a long time ago.

His fingers tightened around hers and he tugged her out of the room and farther on down the short hallway, into another room. This one had a rug on the floor, muffling their steps. There was an armchair in one corner near the windows, a high wing-backed one she'd found in a second-hand store and always planned to restore one day. A crib stood near one wall, all smooth, shining oiled wood. It looked handmade. And on the walls...

The sound of her indrawn breath was loud in the room. She had no idea how he'd done it but somehow he'd gotten a wall decal made of Dark Shadow, Ellie's heroine that she'd been drawing. She was in mid-air, her arm raised, and her hair—the last bit Kara had done—was blue. And on the other wall, Iron Wolf, her supposed nemesis, looking like he was preparing to meet her in battle. Or to help her...

Kara's eyes were full of tears. This was their baby's room. With her art on the wall.

In fact everywhere, throughout the whole of Vin's house, she was there. As if he'd built it for her alone.

She turned to face him.

He'd drawn away slightly, his hands in fists, the tension in him so obvious.

"I don't understand," she blurted out. "This whole place is full of my things. Why?"

"Because it's for you," he said, his voice even rougher than normal. "All of it is for you and the baby."

"Me? I don't—"

"When I was seven, my dad asked me to draw a picture of a house. The kind of house our family would live in." The tension around him seemed to coil even tighter. "So I did. And I kept that drawing. I swore to myself I'd build that house one day. For my family."

She blinked. "I'm not sure—"

"Kara. Let me speak."

She shut up.

Vin turned, went over to the crib, ran a gentle hand over the wood as if checking it for splinters. "But then Mum got sick. And Dad left. And our family wasn't a family anymore." He touched one of the metal fittings that held up the sides of the crib. "Then one day I decided, fuck him, I'd build that house anyway. But it would be for me. Just me." His hand fell away and he turned back to her, the look in his eyes pinning her to the spot. "And then I met you. And things changed and I realized this house *would* be for my family after all. For our child." He became very still, staring at her. "For you. Most especially you. This is your home, Kara. The apartment is still there if you want it, and I left some of the furniture behind in case you want to go back there, but this house and everything in it was made for you. It's yours."

She could feel tears prickling, her throat so tight she could barely breathe. "Mine?"

"I transferred the title into your name."

"What?" That didn't make any sense. "Why? Why would do you do that?"

His throat moved, his hands dropping to his sides then shoving into his pockets as if he didn't know what to do with them. "I've been taking care of people for a long time. When Dad left someone had to do it and I stepped up because I thought taking responsibility made me better than him. But it didn't." He hesitated as if trying to find the words. "I wasn't doing it because I wanted to. I was doing it to make me feel better about myself." Vin stopped again, taking an audible breath. "Dad didn't tell me he was leaving. He said he was visiting friends down south and would be back in a couple of days. But he didn't come back. And I was so angry with him. I...I've been angry ever since."

"Oh..." His figure wavered, tears filling her eyes.

"I have to let that anger go, Kara. If I want to be a good father. If I want to be a better man. If I don't want to be a selfish prick like he was." His throat moved as he swallowed. "So that's why this house is yours. Why I won't be in it. Because you're strong and independent. And I don't want you to have to be reliant on anyone. Even me."

That knocked the breath from her. "Vin—"

"No, there's just one more thing I need to say. And...I don't know how... I'm not good at..." He stopped again, let out a breath. Then he took a step forward, then another, until he was standing so close to her they were almost touching. His gaze never left hers and she felt the pressure inside her come to screaming point. Then abruptly he dropped to his knees in front of her and wrapped his arms around her waist, pressed his forehead against her stomach. "I just fucking love you, Kara. And all I want is for you to be happy."

The words were muffled and thick but she heard them. Oh God, she heard them.

She stood there in shock, Vin's warm arms around her like they were holding her up. Or maybe she was holding him up because he was shaking with tension.

She looked down, copper gleaming amongst the nearly black of his hair, the tanned skin of his arms around her waist, the black cotton of his T-shirt pulled tight over his shoulders.

This powerful, strong man, who was on his knees in front of her. Whose grip on her was so tight, it was like he was afraid she'd disappear if he let her go.

Who'd bared himself so completely to her in a way she never thought he would.

The ability to speak had long gone so she didn't even try. Instead she let her fingers sift through the silky strands of his hair, soothing. Gentle. Letting him know she'd heard him. Letting him know he wasn't alone.

Because he wasn't. Neither of them were. They'd both been alone for far too long.

He'd never known true fear until this moment. At her feet, telling her the truth that had been in his heart so long it was amazing he'd managed to lie to himself for as long as he had.

He'd never given himself like this to another person in all his life, and he felt like his heart would explode out of his chest with want, with yearning. With fear.

He wanted her so desperately. But he wouldn't force her into anything she didn't want to do for his own selfish reasons.

He was done with that. Right now, this was truly her choice.

And then her touch, the movement of her fingers in his hair. And he began to shake with relief. With the sheer intensity of the emotion that swept through him. It was so powerful, so immense. So vast. He'd never understood that till now.

He couldn't move for long moments, just kneeling at her feet, the warmth of her body like the first rays of spring sun in a dark arctic winter.

When she'd come out of customs at the airport, it had taken everything he had not to go to her and hold her. Because she looked so tired, dark circles under her eyes behind the lenses of her glasses, her honey-gold skin pale. Her hair was dyed pastel pink, and the oversized T-shirt and faded skinny jeans she wore made her look small and fragile. He'd never seen anything so beautiful in all his life.

But he hadn't wanted to touch her or talk about it until she'd seen the house. Until he had a chance to explain.

Fancy, romantic phrases had never been his specialty. So he hoped she'd understand what he'd been trying to do with the house. To show her how much she meant to him. How much their baby meant to him. How sorry he was for hurting her.

How much he loved her.

After a moment, he loosed his arms from around her and rose to his feet. Her eyes were dark, liquid.

"I guess that means you're staying, right?" He couldn't quite keep the roughness from his voice.

"Yes, I'm staying."

"Then I'll leave you to—"

"On one condition." Her expression full of everything he didn't even know he'd been wanting. "You have to stay too."

Vin stilled. "I meant it, Kara. This house and everything in it is yours. You don't have to have anything to do with me if you don't want to."

"But I do want to." A small tear leaked out of the corner of her eye. "Nothing's changed for me, Vin Fox. I'm still just as much in love with you as I was when I left."

He wasn't sure if he should breathe, in case the moment shattered. "You really want me to stay?"

"Yes."

"Because if I do...I don't think I could ever bring myself to leave."

"Idiot," Kara said. "I don't want you to leave. I *never* wanted you to leave."

He should be gentle, he really should. But he didn't know if he could.

Vin took off her glasses and put them down on the dresser near the crib. Then he slid an arm around her waist, bringing her hard against him, cupping the back of her head with the other. Without the heavy black frames her face looked naked, vulnerable. Just like he felt.

"You'll stay here with me, Kara? You'll never leave me?"

She didn't look away from him. Stared right at him, into his soul. "No. I'll never leave you, Vin."

And all his longing overflowed. He bent, covering her mouth with his own, desperate and hungry for her. The taste of her skin. The feel of her body. The sound of her voice. Everything.

"Oh Christ, I missed you, baby," he whispered as he kissed her throat, her jaw, her neck. "I missed you so much."

He couldn't wait anymore. Tightening his arms around her, he lifted her, carrying her into the bedroom down the hallway. Then he set her down on the white bed and began to undress her. His hands were shaking. Jesus, he was a mess. But that was okay because hers were shaking too and the expression on her face was as raw and desperate as his.

It felt like forever till they were finally naked but then he had her on her back on the white sheets and he was between her thighs, and finally, finally, he was inside her, the wet heat of her welcoming him at last.

Such relief. Like coming home.

He buried his face in her neck, inhaling the sweet scent of her, shaking, hearing her gasp. Feeling her legs wrap around his waist, holding him to her.

How had he managed without her? How had he thought he could?

He wrapped her in his arms, holding her close like a secret. The desperation had eased now he was here, where he belonged. In the house he'd built for her.

"I'm sorry," he murmured against her skin. "I'm so sorry I hurt you."

"It's okay." Her hands stroked down his back, soothing. "Just love me, Vin. Give me everything you have."

So he did. He gave her everything.

And when she gave it back, he felt, for the first time in his life, whole.

The warm pressure of something on her stomach woke her. She opened her eyes, unsure for a second where she was because the room was unfamiliar. Opposite her was a window that gave a perfect view out over the sea. It was open, fresh salty air filtering through the other scents of fresh paint and polish.

And she remembered.

Kara turned her head and there he was, beside her. He had one hand on her naked belly, stroking gently. Already it was slightly curved. Soon she'd be showing.

Sensing she was awake, his eyes met hers. There was no gray in them, the blue deep and brilliant. Then he smiled and she wanted to cry.

Stupid man.

"What changed your mind?" she asked into the silence.

His hand continued to stroke gently. "I was cleaning out your kitchen—"

"My kitchen? What the hell were you doing in my kitchen?"

"Keep quiet and I'll tell you. So, yes, I was cleaning out your kitchen, after spending the night cuddling your nightgown."

She laughed. "Oh my God, you did not."

"I did. I ripped up your note then fell asleep drunk on your bed with your nightgown. Then I woke up with a mother of a hangover and started doing the cleaning."

"Sounds about right."

"And as I was doing it, I suddenly started wondering why the fuck I cared enough to clean out your damn fridge." He paused. "That's when I realized what a dickhead I'd been. That I loved you."

She lifted a hand to the powerful curve of his shoulder, unable to stop touching him. "You *were* kind of a dickhead."

"I know, believe me, I know. Anyway, afterwards I went to see Mum and she was lucid. She was my mother again. The mother I lost. But of course... I never really lost her. She was always there. I was the one who was lost, so caught up in resentment and anger at Dad, I couldn't see what was in front of me." His stroking fingers halted but he didn't remove his hand. "I shut a lot of people out of my life because I was angry. Because anger was easier. I shut out Mum. And Ellie." He paused. "And I shut out you."

She put a hand over his. "You know why I left, don't you?"

"Yeah. And I meant what I said at the airport. You were

right to go. You were right to want more."

"I didn't want to hurt you."

"But I needed it, Kara. I needed to feel it. Because if you hadn't left me, I don't know if I'd ever have had the guts to change. You made me see how angry I've been. How I've let resentment color my whole life. And I just didn't see it until you'd gone."

Her fingers tightened on his. "And you made me realize how strong I was. Stronger than I'd ever thought possible."

"You *are* strong, baby. You're going to be the best mother." He leaned down, kissed her stomach. "And I'm going to do my best to be a decent dad."

Kara threaded her fingers through his hair, tugging him gently up. "Are you sure you want to do this still?"

"Yes." The answer was unhesitating. "I don't want to be angry any more. I don't want to be resentful. That's not any kind of attitude I want to show my kid. And I figure the one sure way I can be a better man than my dad is to be a better father." He looked at her. "I want this, Kara. I want it not for me but because my kid deserves it." There was such intensity in his eyes. All that ferocious protectiveness that was so much a part of who he was.

She bit her lip. "Great. Thanks for making me cry."

He moved, brushing his mouth against hers. "I'll take that as a success since neither sex nor sharp objects were involved."

She gave a breathless laugh, blinking. "It's just weird to cry because you're happy."

But a tear must have escaped anyway because gently, his fingers stroking the side of her face, his thumb smoothed across her cheek. He didn't speak for a long moment, just stared at her. Then he said, "Kara, will you marry me?"

Her heart felt like it would burst apart. "Is that a formal

marriage proposal?"

"Yeah. Am I going to get a formal answer?"

"Can I think about it?"

The look in his eyes was serious now, her Vincent Fox. "No."

Kara swallowed past the lump in her throat. "Demanding bastard. Give me those words again and I'll give you an answer."

The corner of his mouth curled. "This won't be an easy marriage, will it?"

"You really want easy?"

His smile deepened. "Of course not. I love a challenge."

"The words, Vin."

He slid his fingers into her hair, tangling, tightening at her nape. "I want a honeymoon too. With the slave costume."

"You're upping the stakes. It's going to mean not just saying the words but following up with some serious action."

Vin laughed and the sound was warmer than the summer sun filling the room. "Like that'll be a problem. What are the words again?"

She loved it when he teased her. It was a side he never normally showed. "You know."

His fingers tightened even further, tugging her head back so her mouth was close. "You'll have to give me an example."

"I love you, Vincent Fox."

"Oh," he murmured. "Those words." He kissed her, softly, gently. "I love you, Vincent Fox."

"Idiot." Kara hit him on the shoulder and he laughed again, slowly easing his body over her, the weight of him pressing her deliciously into the sheets. One arm slid under her, his palm running up her spine, gathering her close. His smile faded, his expression becoming serious, but the warmth didn't leave his eyes. "I love you, Kara Sinclair. I love your smart mouth and your weird dress sense. I love the way you never back down. The way you always argue. The way you give everything you've got to people you care about. Shit, I think I even love the colors you put in your hair."

Ah, those words. She'd never get sick of hearing them.

"My answer, baby. You're going to marry me, aren't you?"

She nibbled on her lip, making him sweat a little. "Hmmm. I'll think about it."

Vin bent his head, bit the side of her neck. Kara gave a gasping laugh. "Okay, okay. Yes, I'll marry you."

"And you'll live here with me?"

"Yes."

"We'll be a family. You and me and our kid?"

"We will, Vin."

"And speaking of family, I think you should try contacting your brother and sister again."

Her breath caught, an old, reflexive fear tightening in her chest. "I don't know if they even still remember me."

"They'll remember you, Kara."

Typical Vin. So certain. But Rose and Liam *were* part of her family. And it was time to claim them back. "I guess I've always been afraid to try and make contact with them. I can't imagine Mum would have told them anything good about me. But...you're right. It's time."

"Damn straight."

A small silence fell as he settled against her, holding her tightly. Then he said, "I don't have an engagement ring for you. But..." His gaze met hers. "I still have a key."

She didn't miss the reference, thinking of the little circle of precious metal she'd carted all the way to Tokyo and back again because she didn't know what to do with it. Because she didn't want to part with it. Vin's collar.

Kara smiled up at him. "Give me a minute."

"You have two seconds."

She laughed, slipped out of his arms and went downstairs, opening up her suitcase. The collar was at the bottom, rolled up in a T-shirt. She took it out and went back upstairs to where he waited for her.

He didn't smile when he saw what she held in her hands, but a spark in his eyes glowed suddenly hot. "You kept it."

"Of course I did." She held up the little padlock that went with it. "And I have this too."

"Come here."

She went over to the bed. God, she missed hearing that note in his voice. The command. The authority. It made her want to get down on her knees for him.

"Put it on," he said.

So she sat on the bed and put the collar around her own neck, turning her back to him. His fingers brushed her nape as he swept aside her hair, and then came the soft click as he snapped the padlock closed.

And it felt so right. A part of her.

His arms slid around her, pulling her back against him. "You're mine forever now."

She reached up above her head and back, her fingers trailing in his hair. "I'm okay with that. As long as you're mine too."

"You know I am." He kissed the back of her neck, just below the catch on her collar, the soft skin where the padlock rested. "It's going to be good, baby. It's going to be so good."

And it was.

About the Author

Jackie has been writing fiction since she was eleven years old. Mild mannered fantasy/SF/pseudo-literary writer by day, obsessive romance writer by night, she used to balance her writing with the more serious job of librarianship until a chance meeting with another romance writer prompted her to throw off the shackles of her day job and devote herself to the true love of her heart—writing romance. She particularly likes to write dark, emotional stories with alpha heroes who've just got the world to their liking only to have it blown wide apart by their kick-ass heroines.

She lives in Auckland, New Zealand with her husband, the inimitable Dr. Jax, two kids, two cats and some guppies (possibly dead guppies by the time you read this). When she's not torturing alpha males and their stroppy heroines, she can be found drinking chocolate martinis, reading anything she can lay her hands on, posting random crap on her blog, or being forced to go mountain biking with her husband.

You can find Jackie at www.jackieashenden.com or follow her on Twitter @JackieAshenden.

It's all about the story...

Romance

HORROR

www.samhainpublishing.com

CPSIA information can be obtained
at www.ICGtesting.com
Printed in the USA
BVOW03s1848010217

475089BV00002B/112/P